"Do you and Mommy like each other again?"

Cody couldn't have asked the question at a worse time, Michael thought. *Sweet heaven, what can either of us say?*

Jennie spoke first...slowly searching for the right words. "Your dad and I will always care about each other mostly because we share you."

At that exact moment Michael knew what he had to tell his son.

"The together part of our lives is over, son. Your mom and I tried to be married once and we couldn't be. That's how it has to be."

Michael and Jennie looked at each other. Was this really it? Was everything that had built up between them these past days—every hope, every possibility—shattering? Did all those tender feelings that had come to the fore each time they'd been together mean nothing?

Or was it possible their eight-year-old son saw something they were too stubborn to admit?

Dear Reader,

Four more fabulous WOMEN WHO DARE are heading your way!

In May, you'll thrill to the time-travel tale Lynn Erickson spins in
Paradox. When loan executive Emily Jacoby is catapulted back in time
during a train wreck, she is thoroughly unnerved by the fate that awaits
her. In 1893, Colorado is a harsh and rugged land. Women's rights
have yet to be invented, and Will Dutcher, Emily's reluctant host, is
making her question her desire to return to her own time.

In June, you'll be reminded that courage can strike at any age. Our
heroine in Peg Sutherland's *Late Bloomer* discovers unplumbed depths
at the age of forty. After a lifetime of living for others, she realizes that
she wants something for herself—college, a career, a *life.* But when a
mysterious stranger drifts into town, she discovers to her shock that she
also wants *him!*

Sharon Brondos introduces us to spunky Allison Glass in our July
WOMEN WHO DARE title, *The Marriage Ticket.* Allison stands up for
what she believes in. And she believes in playing fair. Unfortunately,
some of her community's leaders don't have the same scruples, and
going head-to-head with them lands her in serious trouble.

You'll never forget Leah Temple, the heroine of August's *Another
Woman,* by Margot Dalton. This riveting tale of a wife with her
husband's murder on her mind will hold you spellbound...and
surprised! Don't miss it!

Some of your favorite Superromance authors have also contributed to
our spring and summer lineup. Look for books by Pamela Bauer, Debbi
Bedford, Dawn Stewardson, Jane Silverwood, Sally Garrett, Bobby
Hutchinson and Judith Arnold...to name just a few! Some wonderful
Superromance reading awaits you!

Marsha Zinberg
Senior Editor

P.S. Don't forget that you can write to your favorite author

    c/o Harlequin Reader Service
    P.O. Box 1297
    Buffalo, New York 14240
    U.S.A.

Debbi Bedford

After the Promise

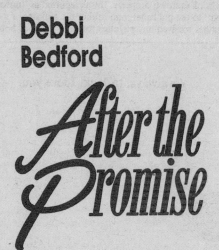

Harlequin Books

TORONTO • NEW YORK • LONDON
AMSTERDAM • PARIS • SYDNEY • HAMBURG
STOCKHOLM • ATHENS • TOKYO • MILAN
MADRID • WARSAW • BUDAPEST • AUCKLAND

As always, to Jack. I love you.

Published May 1993

ISBN 0-373-70546-8

AFTER THE PROMISE

Long ago,
    real life
        brought
            fairy tales
                and castles.
Sitting on the edge of my
        bed
        I'd bounce
        and be a princess on a
        pony.

Now
    I know it's the daily things,
        the love
            life
            brings,
    football by the fire,
    cookie dough in a bowl,
    our son running home from
        school,
        his hair like the
        yellow meadow
        in September.

Now
    our daughter bounces on the bed.
    We watch her playing
            princess on a
            pony.
Someday, too,
        she will see
            the fairy tale's in
                you
                  and me,
                    a reflection of
                    strict reality,
                and our
                  own
                    blessed
                    measure
                  of
                    victory.
                      —dpb

Special acknowledgment
to Laurie Bunting Weesner,
who gave me such lovely insight
at Children's Medical Center in Dallas.
Thank you, Laurie, for your part in this story.
Thanks also to Jessica King.
May all the victories be yours,
little one.

CHAPTER ONE

"DR. STRATTON." The head nurse flagged Michael down as he strode past the station. "Your sitter phoned. She needs you to call home right away."

Michael reached for the phone she set on the counter for him and punched in his number. When the baby-sitter answered, he wasted no time greeting her. "What's wrong, Heather?"

"Cody has a fever of 104 degrees. I think he's really sick. What should I do?"

Michael frowned. Cody hadn't even had a cold for months. He supposed it was time for this. He must have been exposed to something at school. There were all kinds of flu bugs going around that might cause a fever that high. He would have to phone Jennie and find out if she knew of any. "I'm sure he'll be okay until I get home. There's a bottle of children's acetaminophen on the third shelf of the medicine cabinet. Give him four tablets. If his fever doesn't start dropping within the hour, call me back." He handed the phone to the nurse.

"Dr. Stratton. Your patient in 208 is totally dilated," an O.B. nurse informed him as she passed. "The baby's head is at plus one."

"I'm on my way." He washed up and donned his scrubs. When he hurried into room 208, Chris Miller was just beginning to push, her knees bent out at skewed angles while she strained. "I can't do this!" she cried out when the contraction ended. "I really can't do this."

"You *can* do it." Michael covered one of her hands with his own and smiled at her warmly. The human touch. It worked every time. "I know you can. Let's have a baby here. And let's do it now." He moved to the foot of the birthing bed, pulled up the stool and sat down. "You've almost made it, Chris. I can see the head."

"Can you?" she asked breathlessly, raising her head slightly as tears of exertion streamed down her cheeks.

"It's right here. I see dark hair, lots of it. Another push and we'll have it. Come on. Now!"

Michael had seen hundreds of women through labor and delivery. But he still couldn't do it without feeling a little twinge of pride and sadness, thinking of his own son's birth eight years ago. Jennie had been so brave. And Cody had been such a gift to both of them. There had been a time when they both thought that loving their son might be enough to save their marriage. But it hadn't happened that way.

"I feel the contraction coming. It's coming. Here it is. Oo-oo-oh..."

"Don't make any sounds. Focus all your energy on pushing," he instructed her calmly. "Keep your knees wide...hold on to them and pull them out..."

"Very good," the nurse said, encouraging her. "Just perfect. Keep going, Chris."

"Here we go," Michael shouted, enjoying his role as cheerleader. "Right now." He performed a quick episiotomy and Chris pushed once more. The baby's head emerged. A shoulder came next and then the rest of him slipped out, a fine, healthy little boy, already bleating for his mother.

The nurse's assistant wrapped Chris in warm blankets as he handed her her baby. After he had showed the father how to cut the cord and allowed the proud new parents to count fingers and toes, Michael examined the infant himself. "Congratulations!" He shook the father's hand. "You have a handsome son here." He tucked his charts beneath his arm. Then he touched Chris's arm again. "You did a fine job."

He swung briskly out of the room and headed for the elevator making his way to the fourth floor and his next patient. He always looked forward to his visits with Bill Josephs. "Well, Bill," he said, leaning back against the wall and pretending to study his elderly friend carefully from a distance. "You look good to me."

"I am *looking* good," the old man bellowed at him. "I am *feeling* good. When're you gonna send me home, Doc?"

"Well—" Michael appeared to consider as he winked at Bill's wife, adjusting his bedside manner to fit comfortable country folks and friends "—how about tomorrow?"

"Yes!" Bill lifted one fist in victory just like a teenager. "Dr. Michael, it's about time you let me out of this confounded place."

"I'll only let you out if you promise to follow my orders," Michael admonished him as he moved closer and sat down beside the bed. He scribbled out a prescription and handed the little yellow paper to Bill's wife, Marge. "You take that medication three times a day. You don't miss a pill."

"What's gonna happen if I miss a pill, Doc?" the old man chortled. "Will I get pregnant?"

Michael had known the Josephs since he had graduated from medical school. Bill's jokes didn't faze him at all anymore. "You lie down and rest every afternoon," he continued. "The minute the farm news report is over and you've eaten lunch, I want you flat on your back for thirty minutes."

"I'll make him do it," Marge promised.

"No smoking. And when you're drinking coffee with your buddies down at the Ferris Dairy Queen, make sure it's decaffeinated."

"You gonna make me drink unleaded coffee for the rest of my life?" Bill asked him, doing his best to look outraged.

"Yeah." Michael slapped the man's chart shut. "I am. I'll see you in my office in two weeks."

"We'll be there," Marge promised again. "I know how to boss this old coot around."

Michael hugged her. He didn't hug many of his patients, but the Josephs were practically family. "Take good care of him and you're going to have him around for a long time. That is, if you want him."

"Of course I want him. Thanks, Doctor," she said, giggling like a schoolgirl. "That's just what I need."

He waved them goodbye and went upstairs to sign Bill's release papers. As he scribbled, a voice over the loudspeaker paged him. He hurried to the nearest hospital phone. "Your baby-sitter," the switchboard operator told him. "She says it's an emergency."

"I gave Cody the medicine like you told me, Dr. Stratton," Heather wailed when the operator patched him through. "His fever won't go down. And he isn't crying anymore. He's just lying there like a big blob in the bed."

"Is he asleep, Heather?"

"I don't know."

Michael frowned and raked a hand through his thick hair. He glanced at his watch. Cody's fever should have come down by now. Michael calculated. He could be home in twenty minutes.

"I'm coming, Heather. Give him a sponge bath. Can you do it? If it frightens you, maybe your mother can come to the house and help you." Michael felt an unexplainable fear grip him like a vise. Surely all Cody had was the flu. But what if it was something else, something much worse?

I'm a doctor, he reminded himself. *I've just delivered a baby and prolonged a heart-attack victim's life. Cody won't have any problems I can't deal with.*

Even though it was past 8:00 p.m., it took several minutes for Michael to find a break in the Dallas traffic so he could enter Central Expressway. He didn't have to change lanes or pass cars to exceed the speed limit. He sped toward Plano with everyone else, cruising along at over seventy. When he wheeled his car into the driveway, he recognized Heather's mother's car there, too. Inside, he found them both holding Cody in the bathtub, squeezing washcloths of water down his little chest and arms.

"Cody, kiddo, what's wrong?" He stroked his son's hair while his fear escalated. The boy's face was ashen. "Can you tell me if anything hurts?"

"My eyes," Cody whimpered. "And my neck and my head."

Michael bent down beside the tub and gathered his son into his arms. His shirtsleeves soaked up bath water but he didn't care. Cody tried to smile but he was too weak to move his mouth. His eyes lolled back into his head.

Michael succumbed to his panic. He was no longer a capable physician; he was a frightened father, too afraid to know what to do. "We've got to call an ambulance," he told them. "Dial 911 for me. Then give me the receiver." He wasn't going to let Cody out of his arms.

Heather dialed the emergency number and then leaned the phone receiver against Michael's shoulder so he could grip it with his chin. He ordered an ambulance in clipped tones.

"Dr. Stratton, I'm so sorry," Heather cried when she took the phone from him again. "I don't know what I did wrong!"

"You've done a fine job, Heather." He forced himself to reassure the girl. Her round face mirrored the fear he felt himself. "You got me home to him. And I wasn't so easy to convince, was I?" He gave her a sad little smile as he moved around the room with the little boy in his arms, hoping that the air moving against Cody's wet skin would cool him. He felt hot enough to go into convulsions.

Think, he commanded himself. *You've got to examine this child as if he wasn't your own.*

Carefully he propped Cody up on the toilet seat lid and studied his face. Cody said his eyes hurt. And his neck. Or his throat. In eight-year-old language, it could mean either one. "Say 'ah,' Cody. Dad needs to see inside your throat."

"Ah-h-h," Cody obliged listlessly. Michael could hardly see anything without his light. What he *could* see looked slightly red but not inflamed. Gently, he bent Cody's neck forward, testing whether he could touch the child's chin to his chest.

"Ow-w!" Cody cried out.

"We've got to do a spinal tap and culture," he told the paramedics as soon as they arrived. "Radio ahead and have someone from the lab standing by." They were looking askance at him. "I'm a general practitioner," he told them impatiently. "Where are we going?"

"Plano General is closest."

"Fine," he said shortly. "Just get us there."

They sped through the traffic but it felt like a snail's pace to Michael. It seemed an eternity before they arrived at Plano General. After that, things got even worse. He watched helplessly as the paramedics wheeled Cody in on the gurney. An ER nurse tried to direct him. "The waiting room is in here, Mr.—"

"It's Dr. Stratton," he said. "I want to stay with him."

"I'm sorry, Dr. Stratton," she said firmly. "You'll have to wait here. You don't have jurisdiction at his hospital."

He didn't answer her. He couldn't. She was right and he knew it. He walked into the waiting room and turned his back to her. *This is the worst thing, the hardest thing, I've ever had to do in my life,* he thought. But then he saw the pay phone hanging on the wall and he knew he was wrong. *This* was going to be the hardest thing he had done in his life. He had to telephone Jennie.

JENNIE STRATTON flipped her long mane of blond hair back over her shoulder. "So what have we got on Johnson?" She sat atop the stool, her elbow resting on the lighted drawing table, sketching pen in hand, looking down at all of them with a wry grin on her face.

"We've got the fiasco with his neighbor's poodles at his campaign picnic," somebody volunteered. "We've got his granddaughter arrested for shoplifting earrings from K mart. And we've got the fact that he told the press it was none of their business when Taylor asked him if he'd ever been treated for alcoholism."

"Has he been treated for alcoholism?" Jennie asked, toying with the idea.

"No. But he still didn't think it was any of our business to ask the question."

This was a dirt-digging session, just like every other, just like every Tuesday night in the press room at the *Dallas Times-Sentinel.* Jennie Stratton was the paper's most infamous political cartoonist. This week the paper would poke fun at three of Texas's most colorful gubernatorial candidates. Jennie plopped both elbows on the drawing table and examined her sketches. "What else?"

"He's sleeping with his ex-wife."

"Good grief." Jennie tossed the pen into the air. "Not that again! They all do that."

"Of course they do," Arthur Sanderson, her editor, laughed from behind them all. "It's a trap all divorced people fall into."

"All *crazy* divorced people," Jennie clarified. "Not the smart ones." She sighed. "Don't we have anything political on this guy?"

"Oh yeah," somebody said. "He voted against the abortion bill in the house's last legislative session."

"Important but overdone," Jennie said, finally beginning to jot down notes. "We'll go with the campaign picnic and the poodles."

From somewhere in the distance, a phone began ringing. When the answering machine that picked up on the main switchboard didn't get it, Jennie knew it was someone calling in on the private line. She grabbed it quickly so it wouldn't interrupt the meeting. "*Times-Sentinel*. Stratton here."

"Jennie. It's Michael."

Cody must have forgotten something. He always did. It was so hard for him, living in two houses, two homes, with divorced parents. "What is it? I know it can't be his Kangaroo shoes. I made sure I put them in his suitcase. They're underneath his underwear."

"I'm at the hospital," he told her. "I think maybe you should come."

The shock hit her immediately. She forgot the editorial staff seated around her. "Michael, what's wrong?"

"Cody's sick. Very sick, Jen. They're running tests. They don't know anything yet. And I could be wrong. I've been wrong before."

"What do you think it is?"

"I suspect spinal meningitis."

"Michael, no!"

"They did a spinal tap on him. They're growing cultures from the fluid now. They're analyzing blood samples. At least then we'll know what we're fighting."

"Has he been feeling badly before today? Has he been complaining about anything you could have treated?"

Her words put him on the defensive. "There was no indication of any problem until a few hours ago. I would have caught it. I would have seen something, I promise you."

"But he was at your house when it happened."

"He could have been at yours."

"I'm on my way," she said. "Where are you?"

"Plano General."

"Is there anything you need? Or anything I can bring from Cody's room to make him feel better? Maybe Mason?"

"I don't need anything," he told her. "Bring Mason. Maybe if he has Mason . . ."

"I will." She hung up the phone and turned to her colleagues. "My son is sick. I have to leave."

Then she was out the door and driving like a race car driver toward her house. She ran inside and grabbed a handful of things out of his room. Then, for one moment, she stood quietly, trying to get a grip on reality.

When her son had left yesterday morning, he'd been fine.

Cody had two fully furnished rooms, one at each of their houses, so he didn't have to lug things back and forth when he changed homes every week. He had a set of clothes at each house and a group of his favorite stuffed animals and Legos and almost identical desks where he could do his homework.

Even so, he sometimes forgot important things at one house or the other, his vocabulary workbook or his math problems or his favorite pair of Kangaroos, and Jennie would drive over and pick them up, or Michael would do likewise. It made Jennie angry sometimes, even while she scolded Cody for being forgetful, thinking of an eight-year-old child living his life being shuffled between two places, between two people who loved him but not each other.

BY THE TIME SHE ARRIVED at the hospital and found Michael, the doctors in ER had diagnosed Cody. "I was right," Michael told her softly and took her hand. "It's pneumococcal meningitis."

She stood clutching Mason, the big corduroy brown bunny with a turquoise jacket and neon pink buttons Cody always slept with at her house, hanging on to

him as if she were holding on to a lifeline, for herself
and for her son.

"Jen. I'm sorry." Michael reached out to her and
hugged her to him. She looked so small and desolate
and so much like Cody, with her long blond hair and
bangs and her huge, dark frightened eyes. "They're
pouring antibiotics into him. In an IV. It's all they can
do."

She was clutching at him, too, with Mason the
bunny between them, her sheer desperation a sad echo
of all the things he was begging himself not to feel.
"There has to be something else they can do," she
said.

Michael shook his head.

"Can I see him?"

"In a little while. He's in intensive care. They'll only
let us in for ten-minute visits every two hours."

"I want him to know Mason's here."

"I want him to know you're here," Michael said.

"Tell me about spinal meningitis."

"It's an infection that inflames the fluid around the
spinal column," he began, using a mixture of lay and
doctor's terms, doing his best to soften the blow. He
spoke to Jennie the same way he would inform the
mother of any patient who came to him. But Jennie
had been his wife once.

They had been young together. They had thought
that nothing could stifle the spontaneity and the joy of
their romance. But they had been wrong. So very
wrong.

He could list a page full of reasons their marriage
had broken up. His hours as an intern at Parkland

Hospital. The backbreaking student loans he owed after completing med school. Jennie's constant trips to Austin, the state capitol, to search for material for her work. Her low journalist's pay and their arguments about money.

Together, they'd decided to end their marriage four years ago. Neither of them could live a life based on blame. And now, the only thing they shared was Cody.

"Oh, Michael." Tears poured down her face. It had been a long time since he had seen her cry. He didn't think she had cried at all during the divorce. At least, he hadn't seen her do so. He cleared his throat before he said, gruffly, "I know. It's going to be rough, Jen."

"The aftereffects. What are they?"

His voice sounded to him like it was coming out of someone else's throat. "Possible mental retardation. Possible blindness. Possible neurologic damage. We have to wait to see him through it and then count the losses. And, if we're lucky, the losses won't include his life."

The nurse appeared in the doorway. "Are you Cody's mother?"

"Yes."

"You can see him. He's been asking for you."

That was how they spent the next few hours, each of them taking turns visiting Cody for ten minutes every time a nurse would let them in. It was 3:00 a.m. when Michael went in and Cody clutched at his arm. "I'm here, son," Michael whispered over and over again. "I'll always be here for you. Remember that."

"I know," the little boy whispered. He looked so pale and so small in the starched white bed. Michael felt as if his heart would break, just watching his son, and his eyes, so wide, so innocent, trusting him. Michael's helplessness engulfed him, swallowed him, drowned him. He could do nothing except wait while the deadly bacteria assaulted his son. "Jen," he said when he returned to the waiting room. "It's been fifteen years since I've prayed. Will you help me?"

"I will," she said. "I'll help you." They sat together on the plastic sofa, so close, each of them so alone, as she whispered her prayer. "Please, God, I know I don't have the right to ask for anything... but please..."

She trailed off, unable to say more, the tears sparkling like jewels in her eyes.

He reached out to her and touched her arm. "You're exhausted," he told her softly. "You should sleep."

"I can't sleep." She raised her head. Then she shifted on the edge of the chair, one delicate hand planted on each knee, looking at him. Even though they kept up the facade of friendship for Cody's sake, he knew she was always uncomfortable with him.

"You should try." Two couches stood back to back in the room. They could each stretch out on one and try to rest. But Michael knew Jennie, knew how keyed-up and frantic she was. "I think you should lie down, Jennie," he commanded in the same voice he always used to make Cody behave. "Put your head in my lap. You're going to need your strength for tomorrow."

"I couldn't sleep." But, really, she looked too exhausted to fight him. She laid her head where he told her and shut her eyes, the warmth of Michael's body burning through to her.

At that moment it didn't matter to Michael that they had once caused each other pain...didn't matter that they had loved a lifetime ago and that now it was over. What mattered was that she was woven into the fabric of his life tonight...Jennie...the mother of his son, the son who might not live through the next hours.

During the divorce, they had done everything they knew to make it easier for Cody. But there was nothing they could do to ease what he was facing now.

CHAPTER TWO

By SEVEN the next morning, Cody's condition had stabilized enough that he could be moved by ambulance to Children's Medical Center in Dallas. Jennie and Michael followed the vehicle through the already heavy, early-morning Dallas traffic. Jennie drove her Audi, weaving it in and out among the cars to keep up. She glanced sideways at Michael when she heard him yawn. He'd taken his glasses off and was rubbing his eyes with his fingers.

"Your turn comes next," she told him quietly. She hesitated, just briefly. "Thanks for the rest, Michael. I needed it."

"Well—" he said, laughing it off briefly "—one of us needed to be lucid today. I figured it might as well be you." The smile faded. "We may have to make decisions...."

She stared grimly out through the windshield. "I know that."

The ambulance pulled up at Children's. Michael and Jennie followed Cody into the building. A nurse led them to another waiting room. As the morning wore on, Cody's high temperature held and eventually, despite all that the interns did, the little boy slipped into a coma. The next time Michael visited him, he could see Cody's hands and legs turning dark from lack of circulation.

He stormed down the hallway to the nurses' station, hoping he was out of Jennie's earshot. He realized he was being a nuisance. But he knew too much. He wanted them to do everything they could for his son. "Get me one of the interns," he demanded. Children's Medical Center of Dallas was a teaching hospital. It seemed as if hundreds of interns had examined Cody, in groups and individually, every hour.

"My son's circulation is stopping," he told the first one who came to him. "You've got to do something for him."

"We're already on it," the young woman reassured him. "We have a new drug we want to try. It will open every blood vessel in Cody's body and allow circulation to start again."

Michael knew of it. The drug was used primarily for older arthritis patients. "It could be too strong for him."

"That's why we're waiting until the treatment is absolutely necessary. We wanted to talk to you and your wife first."

"Not my wife," Michael corrected her. "My ex-wife. We're divorced."

"Does she have custody of the child?" the intern asked. "We'll need her consent."

"We both do. We have joint custody."

"Then we'll need both of you to sign the papers. You can explain to her that this may be the only chance we have to save Cody's legs," the woman told him bluntly. "We can always stop treatments if it doesn't work."

"I'll tell her," Michael said.

He went back to Jennie and, taking her hand, explained about the drug. When he finished, he was almost surprised by her answer. "I think we should let them try it, Michael. I think we owe it to Cody to try everything the medical profession has to offer him."

"The medical profession hasn't been able to offer him anything so far that has helped him," he said. *And neither have I,* he thought derisively. *Neither have I.*

"That doesn't mean we have to stop trying."

He looked at her then, his eyes full of anguish, surprised she placed faith in medicine when he didn't think he could anymore. Then, drawing on her strength, he nodded. "Okay. We'll try it."

Michael and Jennie stood together, watching, while the doctor administered the first treatment. After that, they had nothing to do but wait. Michael sank back onto the sofa and buried his head in his hands. Jennie sat beside him, just near enough that he knew she was with him, supporting him. When he finally looked up at her, his eyes glistened, full of tears. All of his authority, his mastery, had been swept away. "Everything the medical profession has to offer? My God, that's my own son lying there. And I can't do *anything.*"

She reached out to him and touched his arm, her fingers offering solace when nothing else could. "I know how much you love him."

"I do," he said. "Jennie, I really do." He squeezed his eyes shut as the tears finally wet his lashes. She draped an arm around him and held him as she'd always held and comforted Cody.

JENNIE GAZED DOWN at the dark hair on Michael's forearm. She stroked his arm, felt the sinew of muscle beneath her touch. He was so familiar to her, a man she had once loved.

She knew all too well that marriage didn't always turn out the way it was supposed to. Love didn't overcome every obstacle the way it did in paperback novels. Somewhere along the line, the real world rushed in and took precedence over romance. After a while, romance burned out. Burned out just the same way she and Michael had burned out. Everything . . . gone. *Except,* she reminded herself, *for Cody.*

Michael leaned against her and breathed deeply. "You sleepy?" she asked.

"No," he said. "I'm too tired to be sleepy."

She smiled. It was Michael's favorite line. How many times had she heard him say that after returning home from his internship at the hospital? She felt him relaxing against her.

"You are." Gently she began to stroke the whorls of feather-soft hair on his arms.

"Mmm," he murmured, his voice low and rumbling in his chest. "That feels good."

"I'm glad."

"I'm sleepy," he confessed.

"I know that...I know that..." She was still moving her hand along his arm. "I know that..."

As she said it, he was already losing consciousness.

Jennie heard Michael's steady breathing and knew that, at least for the moment, his body was resting. She sat perfectly still, not wanting to wake him. It had been four years since she'd seen him like this, so vulnerable and exhausted. His body lined up against her own felt familiar and good.

A memory long locked away seeped back into her mind like a perfect vision. How happy she'd been when he walked over to the huge live-oak tree where she was sitting so long ago and asked to see her drawings! She had been watching him for months. He walked by her tree every day with a group of med students going to lab. She remembered glancing up and meeting his sea green eyes. He was tall, with a boyish grin and a headful of thick blond curls under his baseball cap...broad shoulders...long legs. In fact, she decided he was very nice-looking. But what he said next made her think he was cocky, too.

"I know this is nosy but my friends and I have placed a little wager and we would like to know what you are doing over here under this tree every day."

What a line, she'd thought. But she grinned up at him because she already liked him.

"My buddies think you study every day. And I've wagered five bucks that you're drawing something. Now, if you'd just let me borrow your picture so I can prove it to them."

She handed him her sketch pad. "Here it is."

He held it with two hands and looked at it. "Hey! This is the stuff I see in the university paper. This is yours?"

"Yeah, it is."

"That's great," he said, obviously impressed. "I mean, you're almost famous."

"Almost," she said, laughing. "Not quite. People don't mob me for autographs yet."

"You're the one who drew all those cartoons last year about the college president taking college funds and going to Mazatlán?"

"That was me."

"You got him into a lot of trouble." His face was well-proportioned and kind-looking, with an air of distraction about his features, his square chiseled chin, his full, sulky mouth.

"I'm good at getting people into trouble," she said.

"I'll bet you are." His eyes were bright with admiration. "Say," he suggested in his soft North Texas drawl, "since I'm fixing to win five bucks off of you, why don't you let me take you to a movie or something with it?"

"You really expect me to fall for this?" she asked him, laughing.

"Well—" he shrugged and then gazed down at her endearingly, like a disappointed little boy "—I thought it was worth a try."

She let him borrow next Monday's cartoon so he could show it to his waiting classmates. She heard them groaning and then she watched as they all walked away except for him. He brought her sketch back and waggled the five-dollar bill in front of her face. "What do you say?"

She couldn't help herself. She just started to laugh. "Okay. I say 'yes.'"

But that had been a long time ago.

She looked down at him now, down at the huge hand lying on her knee. This hand had helped heal many patients. She knew that. It was the very same hand that had taught her so much about making love. But making love and loving were two very different things. She knew that, too.

How many times had she longed for Michael to stay beside her all night long when, instead, he'd answered his beeper and been gone for what seemed like days? How many times had she ached for him to say, "You're the most important part of my life, Jennie, no matter what other choices I have to make"?

But he hadn't told her that. What's more, she hadn't asked him to. During the six years of their marriage, when he'd been so busy building his practice and his relationship with his patients, she'd been deathly afraid of what he might answer.

IT WAS THREE the next morning when the interns on duty at Children's Medical Center walked into the waiting room and told Michael and Jennie their son was going to make it. His fever was inching down and, without the help of drugs this time, the blood was easing back into his arms and legs.

At four that morning, the nurse on duty led them both into the ICU and, with special permission from the doctors, they visited Cody together for the first time. As Jennie stooped on one side of the bed and Michael stood behind her, she talked to her son the way she had talked to him when he was an infant and she had held him and offered him the world in her arms. Cody remained asleep. They were both afraid he might still be comatose from the fever. But she said anything that came to mind... crazy things... about Mason and what the stuffed bunny had eaten for breakfast... about the swings in the park he used to play on when he was little... about the snow fort he and his daddy had built five years ago when they'd taken a winter vacation to Steamboat in Colorado.

At her words, Michael's throat constricted with emotion. Jennie's quiet, desperate stories reminded him so clearly of the family they'd been once, and of the life they'd given Cody. True, the vacation to Steamboat had been made in part to salvage their marriage, a last-ditch effort to bring the romance back again when neither of them could understand where it had gone. Actually, he remembered the trip as a disaster. But as he listened to Jennie describe the jewel blue day when he and Cody had tunneled into the snow, he remembered other things he hadn't thought of for years: laughter, cold wetness dribbling down his back after Jennie and Cody attacked him with snowballs, Jennie's face glowing golden in the firelight.

"Michael," Jennie whispered to him as she reached behind her and grabbed his hand. "Michael. He's waking up."

Cody's eyelids began to open slowly.

"Son," Michael whispered. "Cody. We're here."

Jennie reached for Cody and stroked his fine, blond hair away from his face. "Yeah, little guy," she whispered. "We're here."

Cody did his best to focus on them. "Hey, Dad..." he said weakly. Then, when he saw them beside his bed together, his voice grew stronger. "Mom? What are you doing?"

"Just talking to you."

"What's going on?" Cody asked. He furrowed his brows and tried to raise his head, but couldn't. "Where am I?"

"At the hospital, honey," Jennie explained softly. "You've been very sick."

"Did Dad bring me here?" the little boy asked. "Did he take care of me?"

"The ambulance brought you here," Michael told him. "You have other doctors, doctors who knew what to do better than I did..."

Cody gazed up at his father with a worshipful expression. "Nobody knows what to do better than you do, Dad."

The tears sprang into Michael's eyes like a vicious enemy. There was no overcoming them. "Thanks, son."

"Why are you crying?"

"Because I love you," Michael answered honestly. Then he turned away from both of them. "I'm going out for a minute, Jen. I'll tell someone he's come around."

Jennie nodded but her eyes never left Cody. "I brought Mason so he can hang around with you," she said lightly after Michael left. "He's sitting right over there."

"Where?" Cody tried to prop himself up to see. He couldn't do it.

As she watched Cody's futile efforts, a sharp fear began to needle at her. "I'll get him." She jumped up.

"Don't try to move, Cody. Here." She set the bunny beside his head where he could see it. She began to stroke his hair again as if nothing out of the ordinary had happened.

"I feel really weird, Mom," he told her. "I wanted to make myself sit up but I can't do it."

Her palm hesitated, then continued to smooth his hair back off of his forehead. "Really?"

"Yeah," he said innocently. "How come that's happening? Do you know?"

"I'm not sure."

"It's probably just because I'm sick, huh?"

"Probably," she hedged.

An intern came into the room just then. Michael entered right behind him. "Hello, Cody," the intern said happily. That was the last thing Jennie heard. She raced out the door and doubled up against the wall, feeling the anger, the fear, the helplessness as intensely as if it were pounding physical pain.

No...no...no... her mind screamed at her. *No... Not my little boy! Not my healthy, perfect little boy...*

"Jennie? What is it? What's wrong?"

Michael stood beside her in the hallway. She hadn't even heard him come out of the room. There were only two beings she could blame for her pain just then. Almighty God. And Dr. Michael Stratton.

Michael was the one standing before her. Michael was the one made of flesh and blood. Michael was the one she had grown used to blaming during the years they'd been married.

"Why couldn't you have done something?" she shrieked at him.

He took one step away from her. One step. "I did everything I could, Jennie. You know that."

"I don't know any such thing. I don't know any such thing."

She was crying and he knew she wasn't coherent. But, even so, it didn't make it easier for him. "Don't do this."

"This would never have happened if he'd been at home this week."

"He was at home. He was at home with me."

"Damn it, Michael," she shouted. "He wasn't *with* you. You were at the hospital. You're always at the hospital. Why couldn't you have been with him? Why couldn't you have seen it coming?"

Michael clenched his fists, his voice steady. "Where would you have been, Jennie? If this had happened while he was at your house, what would you have been doing? You would have been at the newspaper office. You would have been drawing and having meetings and making plans to blow somebody else's political career sky-high in Austin." There. He'd said it. She ruined people sometimes by what she did. He'd questioned her motives the entire time they'd been married. He'd told her that, finally, when they were battling for custody of Cody in the Dallas County courtroom. "You wouldn't have seen it coming. You would have been just as helpless as I was."

"I don't know that, Michael," she said coldly. "All I know is that you fought like hell for joint custody and this week you've proven negligent. You could have done something if you'd been home." *But could he really have done something?* she asked herself. Blaming him was irrational. It was impossible, with all the emotions warring within her, to be rational now.

"Why? Why are you so all-fire ready to accuse me because of my medical career?" Here it was again, the same ugly can of worms. *You could have saved our marriage if you'd been home.* "Do you think I'm magic because I'm a doctor? Do you think I could have done any more than you could have just because I have a medical degree and a license to practice?"

"Yes!" she shouted. "Damn it, Michael, yes!" It was true. She'd always felt Cody was safer when he was with Michael.

"Jennie. Don't hold me responsible for this," he said quietly as she turned to walk away. "Please."

Jennie did not turn to look back at him standing there, helpless. She couldn't.

CHAPTER THREE

THERE WAS NO ONE except the sleeping child in ICU when Andrea Kendall entered the room. She read his name on the chart. Cody Stratton. Age: Eight.

She hummed as she flipped through the pages of medical information there and began to take notes. The interns had called her in on the case early this morning. Mr. Cody Stratton was about to begin the fight of his life.

"Hi," came a bewildered small voice from the bed. "Who are you?"

Andrea could see his eyes peeking out from the bedcovers. "I'm Andrea. Call me Andy."

"Are you a nurse?"

"No. I'm your new physical therapist. I stopped by to take a look at your charts and to meet you. I also want to be your new friend."

Cody smiled at that, apparently satisfied, even pleased with the idea. "Good," he said. "This is Mason."

"Has he been sitting here with you ever since you got sick?"

"Yeah. My mom brought him up. He stays at her house usually."

Andrea surveyed the charts once more. She wondered how much Cody knew about his condition. "Has your mother been here this morning?"

"No. I think my dad was here all night. I kept waking up and seeing him over there in the chair. I don't know where he is now."

"Did he talk to you last night after you woke up, Cody? Do you know how sick you were?"

"Yeah," the little boy said. "My dad told me."

She probed further. "What else did he tell you?"

He looked her straight in the eyes. "That I won't be able to use my legs for a while and probably not my arms, either."

She sat down beside him and laid one hand on his leg. His little face was grave. "That's right. That's why the doctors want me to work with you, Cody. I've got exercises that will get our arms working again. I've got others that will keep your leg muscles toned."

"Can Mason do them, too?"

"He can," Andrea said, grinning. At that moment she was thankful beyond measure for children's resilience. "I'll bet he'll be good at it."

There came a knock at the door.

"Come in," Andrea called.

The woman who entered was tall and beautiful, her blond hair piled in a fashionable twist atop her head. She nodded to Andy with a smile. "Hello, Cody." She knelt beside the bed. "How's my kid this morning?"

"I'm good." He said it matter-of-factly. The two women in the room knew it was the farthest thing from the truth. But that was okay. It was what Cody thought that mattered.

"How's Mason?"

"He's good, too." Cody glanced at Andrea. "And so's my new friend. That's Andy. My new..."

"Physical therapist," Andrea helped him out, winking at him.

"Hi," Jennie said. "I'm Cody's mom. Jennie Stratton."

Andrea stepped forward to take Jennie's hand. "I'm glad you're here. I need to start working with Cody this morning and I wanted you to be in on it so I can teach you what to do when you get him home. You and your husband will have to do this, too."

"I don't have a husband," Jennie said sharply. "Cody's father and I are divorced."

"Who does he live with?" Andrea asked. "The parent he lives with will be the parent to administer his therapy."

"He lives with both of us. We have joint custody."

"Eventually, then, your ex-husband—"

"Michael," Jennie said. "Dr. Michael Stratton."

"He's Cody's father?"

"Yes." Jennie perched on the edge of the blue plastic chair, leaning forward like a little bird poised for flight. "He is."

"Dad was here all night," Cody told Jennie. "He slept in that chair." He eyed his mother. "How come you didn't stay, too?"

Jennie hesitated. "I had to go home for a while. I'd been at this hospital for a long time. Last night I began to feel very, very angry because you were so sick."

"But Dad stayed. Wasn't he mad, too?"

"I knew your father would be with you," she answered gently. "So I knew it was okay if I left." That much was true. Despite the things she'd said to Michael last night, she had trusted him enough to storm away and leave him alone, protecting Cody.

"We need to get started." Andrea motioned to Jennie. "Come over to the side of the bed and watch." The therapist straightened the bedding around the little boy and then she took Cody's hand and began to massage his palms, stimulating and relaxing the muscles that worked his fingers. As she gently rubbed, Cody's fingers began to spread apart. Then she took his hand, pushed it flat and straight against her own, so the little boy would bend his elbow. "See," she said, grinning at the bunny. "That's all there is to it, Mason. You can do it, too. This is what we call intensive stretching therapy. What do you think, Cody?"

"I like it. Maybe," the little boy told her dubiously.

"I'll never be able to do that," Jennie commented.

"You will. Just wait." Andrea continued to manipulate Cody's muscles. "It'll get to be second nature to you. Every time you talk to Cody or do something with him, you just do this a few times. See . . . watch this. Now, let's see you try."

"What if I hurt him?"

"You won't."

Jennie looked as doubtful as her son about the exercises but she gamely rolled up her sleeves. With a deep breath she turned to look at Cody. "You're sure about this?"

"I'm sure about it," Andrea said.

"I'm sure about it," Cody said.

Andrea held on to Jennie's hand, helping her feel the way it should move against Cody's muscles. "There you go. Look at *that!*"

"*Great,* Mom!" Cody cheered from the pillow.

She kept working at it.

"There you go," Andrea told her. "Perfect. *Perfect.* You're a natural at this."

"Really?"

"Yes," Andrea said, encouraging her.

"Yeah, Mom," Cody added as he lay there with his hand in hers. "Really."

MICHAEL STOOD in the shower, his back against the tile, as hot water ran down his skin. Every muscle in his body ached from sleeping in that hospital chair. He stuck his head under the steaming water and held his breath. The pain in his muscles began to ease. The pain in his heart did not.

Jennie's words from the night before continued to echo in his head. Just as they'd done all night long.

"Why couldn't you have done something?"

Why couldn't I have done something?

And it turned into a futile prayer. *Dear God, Why couldn't I have done something?*

He stayed in the shower until the hot water ran out on him. Shivering but soothed at least physically, he stepped out onto the rug and toweled himself dry.

He had already telephoned his receptionist and instructed her to cancel his appointments for the rest of the week. One of his colleagues had agreed to take care of any emergencies. Michael had nothing left to do except dress and go back to the hospital again.

He wondered if Jennie were already there. He'd only left this morning to shower and change clothes because he'd been certain Jennie would soon be back to sit with Cody.

He still knew her, knew how she thought, knew how she struck out in frustration when she was tired and how she acquired new perceptions in the light of morning. Most of all, he knew how much she loved her son. She'd left last night because she'd needed to get away from her own emotions. But, even so, he couldn't forget the damning questions she had asked him.

Why couldn't you have done something? Why couldn't you have been with him? Why couldn't you have seen it coming?

He stood in the center of his Spanish-tiled dressing room and stared into the mirror without seeing. Where had his life gone? What had happened to everything that he'd once held dear?

He focused on a snapshot of Cody he had taped up above the light where he shaved. A 35 mm of Cody in his Little League uniform. There were other pictures, too. A Polaroid of Michael's mother and father holding hands at the Honolulu airport while a young Hawaiian girl slipped a lei over his father's head. Another 35 mm of Cody in the bathtub, a pointed beard of bubbles hanging off his chin.

He had taken that one at Christmas. He couldn't remember the year. Maybe 1987. The only thing he knew for certain was that Jennie had been there, standing beside Cody just out of the eye of the camera. They'd been playing Santa Claus, trying to make Cody understand, though he was only two years old, what incredible miracles would happen on Christmas Day.

"You look just like him," Jennie had told Cody as she scooped up another mound of bubbles and let them dribble down the baby's chin. "He's got a long, white beard and he's going to come on Christmas Eve and bring you everything you've ever dreamed of."

Everything you've ever dreamed of.

It happens, Michael reminded himself. *Some people get what they dream of.*

As Michael stood there measuring the fractions of his life, it honestly surprised him how he'd been able to edit Jennie out. Five years ago, he had thought cutting her out of his life would be impossible. But he was living on his own now, conscious that all that was left for him was an occasional dinner date with a lady friend if he ever found the time, this row of glossy photos and four days a week with his son.

He wondered why he was suddenly remembering Jennie now as she had been when he first met her under the live-oak tree on the university campus. She had been one of the prettiest girls he'd ever seen, with hair that looked like Bernini's gold, and flint gray eyes so full of spunk that he could have sworn they were striking sparks at him. Beautiful. Young, with the world standing before her...the future waiting... waiting for both of them.

He yanked a comb through his hair harder than he had intended. He'd already been away from Cody too long. He pulled on a pair of jeans and buttoned his shirt. He looked in the mirror and sighed. A sigh that wound down to the very depths of his soul.

Time to go back to the hospital. Time to face Jennie again and to face what had happened to their son. He didn't know if he could do it. Because, when he faced Jennie and Cody, he knew he was also going to have to face himself.

As JENNIE WATCHED ANDY now, she could tell Cody was exhausted. "Now this," the therapist told him. "Push your hand against my hand. See if you can do it just enough so I can feel the pressure."

"Can't you stop now? He's getting so tired."

"Let me show you this·and then we'll quit. This exercise will make his muscle tone come back. But you must perform it with him at least thirty times each day. Like this..."

Cody groaned at last. "I don't want to do anymore. It hurts."

"Don't hurt him," Jennie said. "Please don't hurt him."

Andy stopped and stroked back his hair just the way she had seen his mother do it. "It's going to hurt sometimes, little guy. And sometimes it might not hurt but it's going to be uncomfortable. I'm sorry. But it's the only thing that's going to make you better." She sat down beside him on the bed. "I've got lots of exciting things planned for you, Cody. In a month or two, you'll be ready to go into a therapy swim program. Water therapy's great. My brother's been working with kids just like you and they have a great time."

Just then, it all sounded too overwhelming for Cody. "I don't know if I want to get better," he said as big tears began to roll down his little cheeks.

"You do," Andy told Cody, her voice full of confidence. "You'll be more sure of that as the days go by."

"Hey, kiddo," asked a jovial voice from the doorway, "what's wrong? What are the tears about?"

Jennie looked up to see Michael standing in the doorway. She didn't think she'd ever been so glad to see somebody. After everything she had said to him, he was here again, ready to stand beside Cody. She didn't have the time or the desire to examine too closely the relief she felt.

"We're learning about therapy," Jennie told him. Michael's breath caught a little when he saw how, for the first time, the smile she'd given him went clear to her eyes. "Cody's been doing fine. But he's exhausted now. I'm worried about him."

"He's discouraged. And you're discouraged." *Just like I'm discouraged.*

He read her perfectly. She was surprised he could. But maybe she shouldn't be after the hours they had spent together in the waiting room holding each other up. "I am. Silly, right?"

"No," he said. "Not silly. Just human." He'd counsel any of his patients this way. But because he was telling Jennie it meant more.

"Dad." Cody addressed him from the bed. "This is Andy. My new friend. My—" He glanced up at her,

trying to remember the right word. This time he did.
"—physical therapist."

Now Michael saw the cheerful-looking woman
waiting quietly on the far side of Cody's bed. "Nice
to meet you."

"Likewise, Doctor. I'm Andy Kendall." Then,
without more preamble, "Jennie will teach you what
she's learned. I'll work with you, too, of course. You'll
need to know these exercises since you have joint custody of your son." She made a note on Cody's chart
and then she was out the door. "I have an outpatient
appointment. See you tomorrow, Cody."

Cody didn't answer. He was already asleep.

"She worked him hard. That ought to be good for
him, though." Michael turned to Jennie. "What did
she tell you?"

"Enough to scare me," she whispered. "But then,
I was already scared. I would never have said the
things to you I said last night if I wasn't scared."

"I know that," he told her. "It's okay, Jennie. I
know how much you love him. I also know how you
get when you're tired."

She gave him a sad little smile. "I wish you didn't
know me so well."

He needed to touch her. He reached out with one
finger and stroked her chin.

She raised her head at his gesture, meeting his eyes.
For one long, poignant moment, neither of them
spoke. Neither of them moved. Neither of them even
breathed. They just waited—for what, neither of them
knew—matching gaze to gaze. Finally Michael

dropped his hand to his side, feeling awkward. "It would have been harder to go through this alone."

"No," she said. "Nothing would have made it any harder than it already was."

He gazed down at her clear, open face for a moment. "Maybe you're right."

"I am."

"You look like you didn't sleep again last night."

"I didn't," she answered. "I paced Cody's room at the house all night."

Michael smiled. "You should have been here with us, Jennie. Me and Cody, we did fine together. I guess it was because I was here with him. I really *did* get some rest last night."

"I'll take my turn tonight," she volunteered. "I could use some sleep."

"No," he said, half teasing her. And he was surprised at how good it felt, just pretending to be light-hearted. "Then I'll be at home pacing the floor and *I* won't get any sleep."

"Well," she said innocently. "Maybe we should stay up here together."

"Maybe. Maybe that's the best idea of all."

Jennie sighed, her weary mind already moving on to other things. "You should hear all the exercises Andy wants me to do with him. There must be about a hundred of them. And I have to do all of them twenty or thirty times a day."

He just looked at her, thinking how vulnerable and tired she looked. And how beautiful. It had been a long time since he had looked at her and thought of her that way. "It sounds impossible to do all that every day."

"I almost think it is." She knelt beside their sleeping child, gazing at the face that could be either impish or angelic. "I almost think it is. But we can't let it be impossible, can we, Michael? We have to do it for him. Not matter what it takes."

CHAPTER FOUR

THE THERAPY SWIM SESSION was almost over. Megan, the youngest girl on the team, shivered in her bright red bathing suit as rivulets of water ran down her legs and her crossed arms. Her teeth chattered like castanets.

Mark Kendall handed her a towel. "Here you go, kid." He helped her drape it over her head and around her little body. "What's with the goose bumps?"

"The water's c-c-cold...." She pulled the towel so tightly around her that he could see her small, bony shoulder blades jutting through the terry cloth.

"We'll take care of that." He grabbed another towel and started to dab at droplets of water glistening on her arms. "You did great today, Megs."

"You think so?"

"I think so."

Megan grinned.

"Tomorrow we'll get you to swim a little farther."

She wrinkled her nose at him. "I got tired today."

"You can do it, though. I know you can. When you do, you'll be really proud of yourself. Just wait and see."

"You think so?" she asked.

"I think so."

"I'll swim farther tomorrow—" Megan bargained "—if you'll let me get a Coke today."

He laughed at her. "You sound like Wimpy. 'I will gladly pay you Tuesday for a hamburger today.'"

She looked blank. "Who's Wimpy?"

"You know. Wimpy. On Popeye."

Megan still looked lost.

"Oh, great." He slapped his forehead with the heel of his hand. "This girl doesn't know about Popeye!"

She clambered up to plop onto his lap. *Along with everything else,* he thought as he winked at her, *I feel old.* "Popeye is a cartoon. Where this guy eats spinach and he gets strong and he beats up this bad guy named Brutus."

"It doesn't sound like a very nice story," she said primly. "Beating up people."

"Oh, it's okay." Mark was quick to defend his hero. "He gets the girl, too. A real cute one named Olive Oyl. All because he eats a lot of spinach."

"If I eat lots of spinach, will I get strong?" Megan asked him. "Will I be able to use my arms better so I can swim really fast?"

Mark hugged her. "Nope. It's a nice thought, little one. But it's all pretend stuff. The only way your arms are going to get stronger is by doing what we're doing. Lots and lots of hard work." Mark glanced up and waved at his sister, who'd just stepped inside the door. Andy waved back.

"Do I get a Coke now?" Megan asked.

"Nope," Mark told her. "That's your mom's department, not mine. Here she is, too."

A sleek Buick pulled up outside the doorway. Mark saw Megan's mother lean across the front seat to open the door for her daughter. He stepped up beside Andy and held the double glass doors open for Megan. "See you next Tuesday," he shouted as the little girl climbed inside the car.

"'Bye, Mark!" Megan hollered back, her little arm fluttering at him outside the window.

He turned inside. Andy was shaking her head. "I can't believe Megan's growing so fast," she commented.

"I know. It's incredible, isn't it?" Mark began to gather his supplies. "I wish you could have seen her swim." He picked up dented kickboards, several mismatched pairs of water wings and a ball, then pitched them into a plastic laundry basket. "Her arms are getting so much stronger. It's good to see that the water therapy is working the way it's supposed to."

"I'm glad you're having success." She bent down and picked up one wayward ball. "I stopped by to tell you I'm going to have a new team member for you soon. I have a new patient. His name's Cody. When he gets stronger, I think you can do him a world of good."

Andrea and Mark were as close as twins could be. Their father, George Kendall, had been disabled in the Vietnam conflict...back long before it had been a war. Together, Mark and Andy had watched him cope with life from a wheelchair. He'd taught them everything they needed to know about courage, about pushing ahead to tiny victories each day. He was the main reason they'd both grown up to become physical therapists.

"You want to go for a hamburger?" Mark grabbed the bundle of folded towels and tucked it under one arm.

Andy shrugged. "Sure." She didn't have anywhere else to go during her lunch hour. "You pick the place. I'll drive."

"You drive and I'll buy." He picked one of his favorite restaurants.

When they arrived, the hostess seated them at a little table for two covered with a red checkered tablecloth. "Onion rings," Mark said, grinning. "It's been ages since I've had onion rings."

"Me, too."

Mark lowered the menu and eyed her. "So...now that I've got you here, how are you *really* doing?"

She screwed up her mouth at him. "Is that what this is? You bring me out for lunch and then interrogate me?"

"I'm not interrogating you. I just want to know."

"I'm fine. Really." She switched to a safer subject. "You'll like the little boy I just started working with at Children's. He's a resilient one. I can tell he's probably going to surprise everybody."

"His name's Cody? How old is he?"

"Eight."

"You think he'll get very far?"

"He will. The doctors aren't certain yet, but I am."

Mark toasted her with a paper cup full of Dr. Pepper. "My sister. The person who won't let herself ever expect anything but the happy ending."

"It's the exact way Dad was—" she said quickly, her face softening at the memory. "He always looked and found the good side of things."

"You're right. You're exactly like Dad."

Their conversation lulled. Someone flipped a TV on over in the corner and Texas sports scores blared into the restaurant.

"The city council voted down funding for the swim team again," Mark commented offhandedly.

"Oh, Mark, I'm sorry." She leveled her dark eyes on his. What a tremendous blow to him. He'd been working on a proposal for funding for months.

"We'll keep going, I'm sure. The YMCA's said we can use this pool for at least another year. We need to build a therapy pool that isn't so deep, though. I can get by without new water wings for the kids. The kickboards are disintegrating but those will have to be a second priority, too. I'm going to try to keep the bathing suit fund ready in case I get more kids who can't afford a bathing suit."

"I wish I could do something to help," Andy said, her words heartfelt. The swim team meant everything to Mark. "Maybe I could take up a collection at the hospital. Or maybe someone would like to donate bathing suits. . . ."

Their conversation lulled again.

A waitress brought their burgers and Mark's order of onion rings.

The TV blared out: "In Major Indoor Soccer League action last night, the Dallas Sidekicks lost to the Colorado Comets. Even though striker Marshall

Townsend tried several times and left forward Chuck Kirkland..."

Someone switched it off.

Great, Mark thought. *Just great. Talk about perfect timing.*

Andrea stared at the dark screen, acting as if she hadn't heard the soccer score. But Mark knew she had.

"So," he said, knowing he had to mention Buddy now. "Do you ever hear from him, Andy?"

"No." She turned away from the television to stare down at her hamburger. "He doesn't call."

"The man's a fool."

"No, he isn't. Buddy has his own problems to work through."

"Ahh... and even now you defend him."

She still stared at her hamburger. "Yes. I guess I do."

"Does he really deserve that, Andy?"

"I was pretty hard on him, Mark." She met her brother's gaze at last. "It's tough reasoning with a therapy patient when you're emotionally involved. A lot of it was my fault."

"What did you say to him?" Mark asked.

Andy sat back in her chair and let her mind wander. What did I say to Buddy? What *didn't* I say to Buddy?

DURING THE PAST YEAR, she'd gotten used to the thought that she'd always be a part of Buddy Draper's life. They'd met at a New Year's Eve party, laughing and throwing confetti and cheering as the clock struck midnight.

"You've got stuff in your hair," he'd said, his eyes sparkling with mischief as he picked a silver swirl of paper off the top of her head. Everyone around them was kissing and singing "Auld Lang Syne." It was the first time she'd ever laid eyes on him. Yet, still, he seemed vaguely familiar.

"Everybody has stuff in their hair," she'd said, trying unsuccessfully to come up with something witty to say. "It's midnight on New Year's Eve."

"It's 1992," he said, his eyes locked on hers. "Another eight years and we'll be at 2000."

She extended her hand gracefully. "Happy 1992, Mr...."

"...Draper. Buddy Draper."

A slight pause. She'd figured out later he'd been waiting for her to recognize his name. But she hadn't. "I'm Andrea. Andrea Kendall. My friends call me Andy."

"Nice to meet you, Andy."

"Hello." They'd shaken hands. Then they exchanged pleasantries for another half hour before she'd gathered her belongings and had taken her keys out of her purse.

"I'll take you home," he suggested.

"No," she said, playing coy. "I just met you. That would never do." Even so, she was pleased that he'd offered.

The next morning, early, he phoned her and asked if she wanted to attend the Cotton Bowl parade with him.

"This is crazy," she said, sitting straight up in bed and holding the receiver with both hands.

"It isn't crazy. The parade starts up Commerce Street in an hour. We can certainly be there."

"It'll be hard to find a place to stand coming that late."

"I bet you'll be surprised," he told her. "We'll find a place."

"Okay," she said, still clutching the receiver, with a fluttering in her stomach that made her feel as if she were thirteen years old. "We'll go for it."

An hour later she gasped as they climbed the steps to the grandstand and Buddy pulled out a metal chair for her beside the mayor of Dallas.

"Why are *we* up here?" she whispered to him after she'd been introduced to half the public officials in Dallas.

He crossed his arms and stretched out his feet. "We're here because this is where I always sit."

It wasn't until the J. J. Pearce High School Marching Band tromped by playing the theme to *Robocop*, halfway through the parade, that he offhandedly mentioned he played soccer.

"That's what you do for a living?"

"Yeah," he said, chuckling. "At least it was last time I looked. But maybe I'd better check again. I might be an insurance salesman now."

That's when it all started piecing together in her mind and making sense, the name, the vaguely familiar, handsome face, the seats of honor they occupied. "You play for the Sidekicks," she said in a whisper. "You're Buddy Draper."

He didn't look at her. He just took her hand. "I thought I told you that last night."

After the day of the parade, Andy's priorities had shifted. She loved her patients and urged them forward. But, now, with Buddy in her life, her patients weren't the compelling force that drove her soul any longer. Buddy took over a new, special corner of her heart. The two of them spent quiet time alone together every weekend. He gave her tickets to every Dallas Sidekicks' home game. She sat with the other players' girlfriends or wives and cheered him on.

She wasn't certain she loved him until one afternoon in March when the Sidekicks played for the Indoor National League Cup. The Tacoma Stars defeated them in Tacoma. She drove to Dallas/Fort Worth International to meet the plane and, when she went to the Continental gate, there was a crowd of people waiting to greet the team when they came in.

Just before the plane landed, a security guard came up behind her and took her by the arm. "You Andy Kendall? We're bringing the plane into a hangar away from the terminal. Those players are exhausted and Harv Siskell doesn't want them to have to face this crowd right now. We've got all the wives boarding a shuttle. Liza Townsend saw you standing here and thought I should inform you."

"Thank you," she said quietly, quickly following him. The shuttle bounced across the tarmac and they disembarked inside the cavernous hangar, huddling in a group as the huge jet pulled inside, too.

Liza Townsend's husband, Marshall, was a striker on the team like Buddy. She held their little boy in her arms while he squirmed. He was ready for bed, dressed in a fuzzy blue blanket sleeper. And, as the steps went up and the players started to climb down, Marshall Townsend was one of the first off the plane. Liza set the little boy on the floor and he ran to his father, squealing with delight, arms outstretched.

No defeat would be that bad if you had a child to greet you, Andy thought. So here was the real portion of life for these players. It had nothing to do with what happened on the soccer field. It had everything to do with reunions and families and belonging to each other. As Andy saw Buddy starting down the metal stairs, looking disheveled and exhausted, all she wanted was to mean as much to him, too.

She met him at the bottom of the steps and he wrapped his arms around her.

"Hi," she said.

"You're shaking," he said.

"I'm glad to see you."

His eyes drank her in. "Me, too." Then he kissed her. A long, deep, soulful kiss.

"Interesting spot to meet an incoming flight," she commented, teasing him.

"Was there a crowd in the terminal?"

"Yes. A big one."

"I would never have made it if I couldn't just hold you right off."

"I wouldn't have, either." She gazed up at him. "Buddy. I . . ." But she stopped, shy. This wasn't the place or the time to tell him how she wanted to belong to him. Still, the longing welled up so strongly inside of her, she felt as if she might shatter.

"What?"

"Nothing."

"No. Tell me. What?"

"I missed you, is all."

"Good." He sighed. "I wanted you to miss me. That's the only way I survived the end of that game, knowing I was going to get on a plane and fly back here to you."

"It was a good game, Buddy. You didn't embarrass yourselves."

"We didn't win, either."

"In my eyes, you won."

"You're prejudiced."

"Isn't everybody?"

"No. Just you."

She laughed, a light tinkling sound that seemed to waft up and hang in the air above them. She pulled her keys out of her purse. "Here. I'm the chauffeur for the evening."

"Good," he said, grinning, but his eyes showed how exhausted he was. "I'm too tired to even drive." He was too tired to make love that night, too. They lay on the floor listening to Mendelssohn, Andy's chin propped on her palm, while Buddy talked about the game. He fell asleep on the floor and, before she left, she covered him with an afghan he usually kept spread across an armchair. She kissed him once on the forehead then gazed down at his sleeping face, figuring that the next time she saw him she'd tell him how much she loved him.

It was the last time she saw him before the accident.

She drove home and went to bed in her lonely one-bedroom apartment. The next afternoon, when she finished with her patients in the gym and went to check her messages, the call from Harv Siskell had come in. She'd driven like a maniac all the way to the hospital. When she got there, they told her he was in intensive care and no one could see him except immediate family. Four days and four sleepless nights later, he moved to a private room and she finally got to see him.

"I wrecked my car," he told her as she stooped beside his bed.

"I know that."

"I wrecked my legs, too."

"So I hear."

"Oh, Andy," he whispered to her. "What am I going to do? I've got to play soccer again. It's the only thing I want."

"You'll play again," she promised, taking it to heart. "I know just what to do."

For months he went to physical therapy as an outpatient at Parkland Hospital. For months Andy pushed him even further. They worked in the gym at Children's for what seemed like an eternity. As Andy expected, it paid off. Buddy walked again. He ran again. Just not as fast as he'd run before. And he couldn't run as far. When the Sidekicks assessed him for the next season, he wasn't nearly as certain of himself anymore.

"Well," he said as he sat down on Andy's sofa one evening. "I made a decision today."

"About what?" She came around the arm and handed him her favorite healthy concoction, a drink blended from cantaloupes and bananas.

"I told Harv Siskell that I'm going to retire."

She'd stopped in mid-sip of her own drink and eyed him as if she were eying a stranger. "Buddy. No. You can't."

"I have to, Andy. It's the only choice I could make."

"It isn't." Then fiercely. "It isn't at all."

She couldn't believe it. As she watched him sitting not quite so complacently now beside her, all she could think of were his desperate words from not so very long before.

What am I going to do? I've got to play soccer again. It's the only thing I want.

"I can't make myself do it," he said, peering into his glass and shaking his head. "It just won't work."

"You're short-changing yourself," she said softly, hoping the low volume of her voice would cover all the frustration she was feeling, but it didn't. "You're short-changing both of us."

He stood up and glared at her. "Why do you say that? What do you know about what I'm feeling? You don't want me this way, is that it? You don't want me if I'm not a soccer player." She knew what he was thinking, but it made no difference. This had happened to him all too often before; women agreed to go out with him because he was a celebrity. And now he was obviously thinking she was no different from the others.

She rose to square off with him. "You've got it wrong, Buddy. I'm against this because of how much you wanted it, because of how hard you worked to come back. Because of how hard *we* worked..."

"Tell me something." His eyes were cold. "Did we spend all those evenings in that gym for *me* or for *you?*"

"For you, Buddy," she said desperately. "Because of what you wanted."

"Then why can't you accept what I want now?"

"Because I don't think it's what you really want. You were happy, weren't you, Buddy? You were happy being the celebrity soccer player as long as the goals and the fame came easy for you. But now that you won't be the star player anymore, now that you won't make so many goals, now that you're going to have to work for it, you *give up*. I think you've decided to take the easy way..."

She faded out. She didn't know what else she could say to him. It was impossible for her to watch him surrendering and not be angry about it. So maybe he wouldn't be the best-loved player on the team anymore. But at least he'd be doing what he wanted to *do*. After all the work she'd done with children who might not ever be able to walk, she couldn't believe he was standing before her now, a whole man, telling her he was backing away. "Anything I ever did for you—" she told him now in a quavering voice "—was because I loved you."

There. She'd said it, after so many months. But she'd said it much, much too late for both of them.

"You're a coward, Buddy. I don't think I want to see you again."

"Andy," he said, his voice pleading now as he draped his jacket over his arm. "Don't judge me by this. Unless you've played the game, you don't realize when you're running out of options."

"I *have* played the game," she said, tears streaming down her face as he stepped past her toward the door. "It just isn't in me to let somebody give up."

And so, they'd given up on each other. That had been almost six months ago. Andy hadn't seen or heard from Buddy since. Her life was empty again except for her brother, Mark, and the caseload of children that kept her busy at Children's Medical Center.

"ANDY." Mark prodded her now from across the table. "Your mind is wandering. I asked you what you said to Buddy that last night."

She smiled sadly. Now she was relieved to be pulled out of her reverie. "I told him he was a coward."

"Really?" Mark looked distressed. Andy knew he was wondering what he could say to dissipate the pain he saw in her eyes. He was her brother, after all. "That's reasoning, all right. Telling the great Buddy Draper of the Dallas Sidekicks that he's a coward. The man was one of the greatest players in the game."

"Thanks," she said wryly. "And I'm the craziest sister you've got."

Andy ate her hamburger after that, then pulled the keys out of her jacket pocket. "Can I drop you somewhere? I need to get back to Children's. I've got another outpatient this afternoon."

Forty-five minutes later Mark, the swim team and the rest of their lunchtime discussion were all but forgotten as Andy turned her total attention to Kara Johnson. "All right!" she said. "Let's see turtle legs kicking... kicking..." She clapped her hands for the little girl who lay beside her on the green plastic pallet. "Good girl. That's what I like to see." She turned to the two parents sitting beside her, watching. "I can tell you've been working with her at home."

"We have been," the proud father told her. "Every day. All the time."

Andy motioned for the candy striper to bring her a towel from the cabinet on the wall. "Let's see if she can do something new." She kissed the top of the little girl's head. "Challenge time, kiddo." Andrea rolled the towel up and placed it beneath the eighteen-month-old's stomach. She showed Kara how to place her arms to balance herself. Then she dug around in the toy bin.

"Let's see what we can find that's interesting in here."

Andy pulled out a tin funnel, its rim lined with holes and metal rings and six different sizes of measuring spoons.

Kara squealed and reached for them as they jangled.

The little girl flopped over against the towel and rolled off it.

"Oops." The therapist caught Kara and laid her on the rolled towel again. "Let's try it again."

Kara reached over and over again for the jangling spoons. And over and over again, she toppled off the mount Andy had made for her.

"She's right where she needs to be." Andy reassured the child's parents as she reached out to catch the little girl. "Eventually this will come easy for her. She's a fast learner."

"Do I need to do this at home with her, too?" the mother asked.

"Of course." Andy laughed, teasing them. "Do you even need to ask that? Whenever she sits up, just push her over slightly. Her center of balance will be off. When she starts to fall over, help her catch herself with her hand. We'll try this again next time you come in. When's your next appointment with Kara's doctor?"

"Two weeks from Friday," they said together.

Andy stared out the window for a moment, her fingers cupping her chin, trying to remember her schedule. "I'd like to see her before then."

She caught the worry on Kara's mother's face.

"Is that a problem?"

"I don't think we'll have enough for bus fare that soon," Kara's father admitted.

"That's fine. I'll make an appointment for the same day she'll see the doctor. You can bring her for therapy when you're already here."

"That would be better. Maybe next month we can bring her in more often."

"Okay." She motioned to the candy striper to bring her schedule book. "We'll see her again two weeks from Friday."

It was the most painful thing Andy could think of, a child who needed therapy but who couldn't get it as often as needed. She understood her brother's financial frustrations so well. In many ways, they were her own.

Children's Medical Center charged its patients based on their ability to pay. But what about the children like Kara whose parents couldn't afford the bus fare to bring her in? It was for that very reason that Mark had established his bathing suit fund. For some of Mark's water therapy patients, a new bathing suit was as unattainable as a new house.

The other kids didn't know how lucky they were. Kids like Cody Stratton whose parents would be able and willing to give him anything...everything...to make him well again.

Others, like Buddy Draper, could buy the moon and it still wouldn't be enough.

Andy frowned. Now where had that thought come from?

Buddy is out of my life, she lectured herself. *He is not my patient anymore. He never really was. What happens to him now is none of my business.*

I did my best with him. And for him. My very best.

But, somehow, as she jotted several notes about Kara and prepared herself for her next therapy patient, Andy couldn't quite convince herself of that.

CHAPTER FIVE

BUDDY DRAPER STRETCHED his loafer-clad feet atop his desk and leaned back to watch the Dallas Sidekicks game video for the third time. He groaned as he watched striker Marshall Townsend struggle to catch up with the ball. He shook his head as he noted the point where the man gave up and began falling back.

I never would have played it that way, he thought. *I never would have given up.*

For some odd reason, Andy Kendall's words came back to him at that instant.

You were happy, weren't you, Buddy? You were happy being the celebrity soccer player as long as the goals and the fame came easy for you. But now that you won't be the star player anymore...now that you won't make so many goals...now that you're going to have to work for it, you give up.

He had asked her the same questions he was asking himself. *Isn't it better, Andy, to leave them remembering how I used to play? Isn't it better for me to stay who I used to be without making a fool of myself?*

You are a coward, Buddy Draper, she'd told him. *You are a coward and I never want to see you again.*

He spoke aloud to the television set. "Never...never...fall in love with a physical therapist," he told the machine. "You'll get into trouble every time."

And so, Buddy faced his dilemma. He'd lost Andy Kendall months ago. And he couldn't help feeling that he had lost himself, too. Especially every time he sat on his sofa, ensconced in his corporate papers and corporate pressures, remembering what it had felt like to run across the indoor field in pursuit of a ball rolling so fast it was only a blur sometimes, while his fans roared.

But it wouldn't be the same, he reminded himself over and over again. It wouldn't ever be the same.

The phone call he'd received this morning had taken him by surprise. He had been away from the field for so long now that he thought most people had probably forgotten he ever played.

"Buddy," Harv Siskell had boomed at him over the line. "I'm sending a courier over with game tapes. I want you to look at them and tell me what's wrong with my game. I want to know why we didn't win last night." Harv had been coaching Buddy since he'd been a sophomore at Southern Methodist.

"Why does it matter what I think?" Buddy asked him brusquely.

"Because I need a new assistant coach!" Harv bellowed at him. "I want to know what's wrong with my game. Then I'll tell you what's right about your input."

"Suppose I'm not interested in viewing your tapes?"

"Too late, Bud. They're already on their way. And, Bud..."

"Yes?"

"Don't worry about tipping the courier. He's my nephew. He was drooling buckets just to ring your front doorbell and have a look at you."

"Thanks, Harv." His tone said, "Thanks for nothing."

"Call me as soon as you've made notes."

"Maybe. Maybe I won't."

Even with the advance notice, Buddy jumped at the knocking on his door six minutes later.

"Gee, Mr. Draper...Buddy..." the boy said, stumbling in his excitement. "It's great to meet me...I mean, meet you!" He held the package out to Buddy. "My uncle sent these over. He told me I could bring them so I could meet you."

Buddy took the package and handed the little boy a dollar bill. "Thanks, son."

The kid never even noticed the tip. He just kept staring at Buddy. "I'm in the fourth grade at Prairie Creek Elementary School in Richardson. We play soccer every Saturday. I've been playing since I was five years old. I practice all the time so I can play just like you."

"That's what it takes," Buddy said, standing there holding the door open and waiting for the boy to leave, for no good reason deciding he was in a hurry now to tear open the packet and watch the game. "It takes hard work and practice...for all your life..."

"That's what my uncle says, too. He got us all tickets to the last three Sidekicks games. He can get them for us anytime we want them."

"That's nice," Buddy said.

The boy just stared up at him, his brown eyes huge and glowing. He looked so excited that Buddy thought he could see his freckles dancing.

"That's really nice," he repeated, touched.

"Oh, gee, Mr. Draper...Buddy...would you mind...? I mean, if you've got time...I really wanted..."

"Yes, son?"

"Would...would...you give me your autograph?"

Buddy grinned. It had been ages since anybody had asked him for his autograph. "Sure thing, kid."

"I forgot to bring a pen and paper. I was too excited. Can I borrow your pen? Can I borrow a piece of paper? I thought about you signing my soccer ball but it gets kicked around so much that I knew it would rub off. You don't mind, do you?"

Buddy invited the boy in. His eager guest followed him to his desk. He pulled his ink pen out of its holder and fished around for a piece of stationery. "Here," he said when he found it. "Now. What's your name, son?"

"Billy," he said. "Billy Siskell."

Buddy hated to admit it but he felt better than he'd felt in a long time. He looked at the little boy again. "B-I-L-L-Y? I want to be sure I spell it right."

"That's right," Billy told him.

"Here it is."

"To Billy Siskell," he wrote, "an excellent courier and soccer player. Keep on Kickin'. Buddy Draper. The Dallas Sidekicks."

It wasn't until he'd scribbled the last part of it that he realized he couldn't officially write "The Dallas Sidekicks" beneath his name anymore. But then, maybe he could. He would always be who he had been.

He handed Billy Siskell the paper.

"Thank you, Mr. Draper. Thank you so much." The boy reached over and pumped his hand, trying very hard to be a man. "Thank you."

"You're welcome, Billy."

Then Buddy stood, smiling now, genuinely smiling, watching the kid pick his bike up out of the grass and ride away.

IT WAS EXACTLY TEN DAYS after Cody had gotten sick. When Jennie Stratton arrived at her office at the *Dallas Times-Sentinel* that morning, she felt oddly out of place. It startled her that everything could go on as usual, day in and day out, despite what had happened to her son. The AP and UPI wires clacked away in the corner and the phones were ringing off the hook in the newsroom. She felt as if she'd stepped outside herself and were watching things from some vast distance.

Someone spoke to her. "We're so sorry about your little boy."

"Thank you," she said. "It's been very hard."

She made her way up the stairs to Art Sanderson's office. In one hand, she clutched the portfolio containing cartoon sketches she hadn't worked on in days.

Her editor met her at the top of the stairway. "Our sympathies, Jennie. We're sorry about what happened to Cody."

"The flowers were lovely, Art." The staff had sent a huge bouquet of flowers to Cody's room at Children's, big purple carnations and yellow mums, topped off with ribbons tied to a half dozen brightly colored balloons. Cody had loved the balloons.

"You up for a staff meeting?" he asked her. "You need to know what everyone's doing. We had to go ahead and make some decisions about the gubernatorial series."

"That's fine."

"I don't know if you're going to like the decisions we made or not. We made them in a pinch, without you. We did the best we could."

Her gray eyes flashed as she swung her long blond hair back over one shoulder. "You'd better call everyone together and fill me in."

She could tell by the guarded pleasure in Art's eyes that he was impressed that she'd returned to work so soon after Cody had taken ill. That was fine. Let him be. She *was* going beyond the call of duty. But she was doing it for herself, not for anyone else.

I have to do something to keep from hurting. Only it never stops.

Jennie went to her own desk and sifted through her papers. She flipped through several rough sketches to remind herself what she'd been working on. She jotted down several notes to herself and was in the middle of organizing them when a thin young man with unruly brown hair stuck his head in the door. "Jen! Hello! I've been trying to call you for days."

"I haven't been home much, Kirby. I've been at the hospital with Cody."

"I haven't seen you looking this exhausted since you were going through the divorce."

"Thanks, Kirby." She flipped a pen at him. Kirby had been the entertainment editor at the *Times-Sentinel* for years, an aging dancer who had long since retired from the Dallas Metropolitan Ballet and turned to reviewing performances instead. He had proven a loyal friend over the past years. "It's good to see you, too."

"I've been worried about you."

"Everybody's been worried about me." She smiled wryly but she appreciated his concern. Just talking to Kirby helped her get a little of her spunk back.

"Has it been tough spending so much time with Michael?" he asked her.

She sighed. "I haven't had time to think about it," she answered honestly. "This has been a lot more traumatic than anything I've gone through before."

Kirby sat on her desk, his long fingers touching the wood. "You've forgotten, I think. Your divorce from Michael was pretty traumatic. All those days you could hardly work because you were so upset. And what about the night you waited up for him until three in the morning to come home from the hospital? The night you finally confronted him for caring more about his patients than he cared about you?"

"Kirby..."

"He didn't deny that, did he?"

"Some things," Jennie said quietly, "are just too painful to remember."

"What about the day he came storming in here waving your latest cartoon at you and accusing you of ruining Buzz Stephens's career? That man ruined his career all by himself, Jennie. You just drew a cartoon about it."

"Kirby," she said quietly. "Michael and I made a career of accusing each other of things. We're still doing it. I don't want to talk about this right now." For some reason, she felt as if she were betraying a close friend by rehashing all of this today. Michael had just helped her too much during the past days. He didn't deserve this from her now.

She gathered up her things and walked down the hallway with Kirby to the meeting. She perched on the stool at the drawing table, her usual spot, and called them all to order. "Okay," she said, and it struck her as bizarre just then, that this was just where she'd been sitting, these were just the people she'd been talking to, when her world had turned upside down. "Tell me what we're doing. Art says he doesn't know if I'll like it."

"We had to trash the idea about the poodles at the picnic," one of the artists told her. "Art thought that, by the time you could get it drawn, it wouldn't be relevant anymore. He wants us to go with an entire series about—" he hesitated almost imperceptibly, but it made Jennie steel herself for what was coming. Something was up: "—the Texas politicians who are having affairs. Art thinks it'll be a nice satire, something they might even pick up for *Texas Monthly*." The other heads around the table nodded in agreement.

"No." She shook her head. "No...no...no." It was all so incredibly stupid and trivial. She tried to remember when political satire had meant something to her. Certainly it had. But no more. "We can't *do* that. I'll talk to Art about it. Don't do anything yet."

They went on to other things. At the end of the meeting, she sat feeling incapable and out of touch while her entire staff filed by her, chattering. Her meeting with Art later wasn't much better. "We've done too *much* of that," she told him, referring to the "Adulterous politician series," as she'd started to think of it. "I wanted something creative. I wanted something that would make people laugh instead of saying 'Oh, no, not again.'"

"Jennie, you've got to go with me on this one. People will eat this up."

"I hate it," she said matter-of-factly, jumping up off the chair and prowling around like a cat, her hair hanging in a gold sheath down her back. "Art, I hate it."

"I did the best I could without you." Art leaned back in his chair and watched her pace the room. "I'm not going to change it now."

So that's where it ended. She went back to the artists that afternoon and told them to start working where they'd left off. Everyone knew she'd been overruled.

MICHAEL AND JENNIE walked down the hallway. They had just come from a visit to Cody, and had left him fast asleep.

"It was a mistake, going to work today," Jennie told Michael. "I thought it would help me forget for a few hours. I needed to get the artists going again. So we had a meeting where I told them they couldn't do what they'd planned. Then I promptly turned around and told them they could. We accomplished a lot.''

"I'm still not seeing patients. I couldn't have diagnosed a child this week if the president of the United States had brought one in. Russell's covering for me until further notice.''

She looked up at him, surprised he was referring all his patients to someone else. When they had been married, he'd never done that.

Her gray eyes were huge. And her questions were telling, filling him with questions of his own. ''We're good parents, aren't we?'' she asked.

They looked at each other wordlessly. Neither of them could answer that question.

They had reached the lobby of the hospital, but Jennie didn't want to say goodbye to Michael just yet. She needed to be near him, just as she had needed him for the past few days. She needed not to be alone now.

"You want to go get something to eat?'' she asked tentatively. Michael nodded. Together they walked to the hospital cafeteria. They both bought sodas and hamburgers wrapped in greasy paper. Then they sat down at a table and sipped their sodas. For an eternity, neither of them spoke.

"You know what I was thinking about just now?'' he asked abruptly. ''An answer to your question.''

"What question?''

"About whether we're good parents.''

She bit into her hamburger, then wiped mustard off her lips with the tiny napkin. ''What's your answer?''

"Remember when I was serving my internship at Parkland and Cody was teething?"

She thought back, then grinned, covering her mouth with the napkin. "You mean when his bottom ones were coming in?"

He nodded, smiling for perhaps the first time in days. "The first tooth. You brought him into the hospital at three in the morning so I could get a look at it."

"You think that was funny?" She couldn't resist teasing him just a bit. During their married life together, they'd jousted often. "It was better than sitting there on the sofa with him, listening to him cry all night long. Riding in the car always made him feel better. So we rode in the car and came to see you."

"I was so proud of that new tooth."

"Yes," she agreed. "You were so proud. You showed it to every doctor doing night duty at Parkland."

"They were all so impressed, too."

"Oh, I'm sure they were," she said, tilting her head at him and laughing. "I'm sure they'd never seen anything like it before in their lives."

That was back in the days when I thought I could perform miracles, Michael thought. *I really thought I could.* "I thought that tooth was a miracle." Then he chuckled. "You know, they always say doctors make the craziest parents. We're even more amazed by all our kids' feats than other people."

"You certainly were."

Silence came between them again. A companionable silence lasting a long time.

He broke it again.

"We were good parents, Jennie. Maybe crazy sometimes, but good. You were a good mother. You still are."

She plopped her elbows on the table, chin in palms, surveying his features, honestly surprised at how comfortable she felt with him. His face was familiar to her yet it was different, too, with wrinkles at the corners of his eyes where wrinkles hadn't been before, deep lines around his mouth that spoke of his concern for his patients and of his painstaking work.

Their eyes met. She looked sad. "I just wasn't a very understanding wife."

He didn't answer. They both knew she was right. But it didn't really matter because it hadn't been her fault. They had both decided, a long time ago, that it would have been better if they hadn't married one another in the first place. Each of them had been sailing in a separate direction, seeking dreams and a life, each of them unavailable when the other needed support. They'd both been very, very young.

He fingered his paper cup. "Those days don't matter anymore, do they?"

She shook her head. She didn't know what she could say. And then she looked up at him again. "No. They don't matter. Except to remind us that neither one of us was to blame."

"Or that both of us were."

The silence came again.

"Come on," he said finally, laying two quarters on the table for the busboy who was mopping tables with a big soggy rag. "Time to go home."

She pulled on her jacket and heaved her bag over one shoulder and walked beside him, still quiet. At last, just as they arrived in the lobby, she touched his arm to stop him.

"What is it, Jennie?"

"I blamed you for this, Michael. I blamed you for everything that's happened to Cody."

"Yes," he said. "I know that."

She had to say the rest of it. She knew him so well from so long ago. And she could see it in his kind sea green eyes. "And *you* are blaming yourself, too."

He stared straight ahead, out the plate-glass window toward the parking lot. After a few moments he said, "I blame myself."

"It's wrong of us to blame you."

He glanced at her, acknowledging her absolution but knowing it wasn't going to be that easy for him to accept forgiveness. He let her lead him to a row of blue upholstered chrome chairs lining one wall. They sat.

"I had to blame somebody, Michael. It was between you and God Almighty. And you were the one who was there, flesh and blood, standing in the room with me."

"Do you know what I would give," he asked, "if there had been something...anything...I could have done for him?" He stared at the ceiling, at the splotchy drywall there, seeing only his son's little body and the baby-sitter's frightened face when he rushed in from the hospital to them. "I would die myself if I could trade that for what's happening to my son. I want to know how I could have made it different. I want to know why I didn't see it, why I couldn't stop it."

"I'll always have questions, too," she told him softly. "But they won't be questioning your abilities. I have faith in everything you did for him, Michael."

He gripped her hand and looked at her for the first time in long minutes. "Will you, Jennie? Will you have faith in what I have done? In what I didn't do?" He swallowed, looked uncertain. But Jennie already knew what he was feeling. "Oh . . . J-Jennie . . . I'm so sorry . . . s-so . . . sorry."

"Michael." He was such a strong man one moment, more vulnerable than his son the next. Without even thinking, she gathered him into her arms. "Michael." She stroked his thick blond hair the way she would have stroked it every night if only he'd been able to stay beside her, if only he hadn't always been called to duty at the hospital. If only she hadn't been so young when they'd been married. If only she could have understood then what he had to do.

"I'm-m—so—sorry—J-Jennie-e-e . . ."

"Shh." The familiar head tucked up beneath her chin and she held him the way she would hold a child, the way she would hold Cody, as he wept.

CHAPTER SIX

CODY STRATTON KNEW exactly when Andy was going to come in every day. He loved to hide from her and make her laugh. He'd groan when he saw her opening the door and then he'd do his best to burrow down into the covers so she couldn't find him.

"Guess where I am," he'd say, doing his best not to giggle. But she always found him no matter what he tried. Then, after she did, it was always the same, up and down...up and down...up and down...his knees and legs folding up accordion-style against his belly while she worked with him.

"Now. You do this at least three times a day," Andy always told his mother. "You've got to work at this to keep him from getting so stiff. When you work with his hands, Jennie, you want to move your fingers in a circular motion like this, relaxing his fingers apart instead of prying them. When you stretch his neck, you want to move it in a circular motion, too, like this...."

Cody's mom always wrote everything down. There was no way she could remember all this stuff if she didn't. At least, he didn't think so.

"I just realized," she said once to Andy while Cody watched her, "you don't give any review questions.

You just plow into something new every time I see you.''

"When you're working with his elbows, you want to rotate the movement just this way. . . ." Andy kept right on going.

"Hey," Cody said to both of them. "This isn't fair, y'all. All Mom has to do is write down the stuff. But I'm the one who has to *do* all of this stuff."

"You!" His mom bent down close to him and kissed his nose. "You're doing a *great* job! You're doing the hardest work of all and we all know it."

Cody loved the way his mom smelled, like roses and outside. Andy smelled good, too, but his mother was special. He loved the way she told him he was doing his hardest work. And, best of all, he loved it when she cuddled with him now, though he knew he was getting much too old to admit that.

"You're getting your tone back in your arms," Andy told him. "It won't be long before you're *swimming*."

"Yeah." Swimming sounded like the best thing in the world after lying in bed for so long. He listened while she told him all about her brother Mark and what he did with kids in the water. She told him about a little girl named Megan and how working in the water had helped her to be able to use her legs again. All the while Andy kept working on him and moving his arms every which way while his mom took enough notes to fill a book.

He was the first one to see his dad standing in the doorway looking at his mom. "Hi, Dad!" he hollered so loud he made his mom jump. "Dad's here!"

"Hello, kid." Michael walked straight to the bed and gave Cody a huge hug. Cody knew his dad was pretending that he'd just gotten there. He wondered how long his father had been standing at the door watching them.

"You're sweating," his dad said.

"That's because I'm doing therapy."

"And doing a good job of it," Andy said as she laid his leg down and covered it with the blanket. "He's doing great moving his arms. They're loosening up nicely." She touched him lightly on the nose. "Time for a break now, kiddo."

"I get to go to the therapy gym tomorrow," Cody told Michael. "It'll be my first time."

"Son..." And, for a moment, because his dad hesitated, Cody thought that he might not know what to say. "...I think that's great. I wouldn't expect a patient to do as well as you've been doing." He bent over the bed and gave Cody several well-placed tickles right on the ribs as Cody rolled onto his side in a fit of giggles. "Stop doing so good! You're doing too good!"

"I can't *help* it," Cody squealed. "It's just happening."

JENNIE SAT and watched her sleeping child for a moment, watching the flicker of lashes on his slightly flushed cheeks and the rise and fall of his small chest. "Thank heaven," she said after a long silence. "Thank heaven for every breath that little boy takes."

But Michael wasn't looking at Cody just now. He was searching Jennie's face, thinking how beautiful she looked. Their eyes met and held.

"So," he asked at last. "How, exactly, do you go about learning all this?"

"I've got outlines of the therapies we're supposed to do with him when we get him home. Or—" she corrected herself, realizing what she'd said, "—when *I* get him home . . . and *you* get him home. I'll never remember all the things Andy is telling me we've got to learn if I don't take notes."

He swallowed. Hard. It made his Adam's apple bob up once on his neck. He felt off-center. All he wanted to do lately was be around Jennie and do things for Cody. "You want to show me those notes? Are you up for another cafeteria hamburger?"

She almost said "yes." But then she allowed a slow smile to lift the corners of her mouth. "You want the truth? The *real* truth?"

He grinned, too, a warm, full smile that made her heart feel as if it were flopping in somersaults. "Say no more. I don't want to hear the truth, that you'd like to go down to the cafeteria and slaughter every single one of those hamburgers with a shotgun."

"Okay. I won't say it."

"That's it, then." He stood and helped her up. He had half a mind to suggest they eat out somewhere. But, calculating the days since he had last eaten a home-cooked meal, he said instead, "Lunch at my house. Cooked by yours truly."

At the mention of a meal at a real table with real forks and glasses instead of paper cups, Jennie's eyes widened. "I'd give anything."

"Come on," he said. "Let's do it."

He drove her in his car, all the while intensely aware of her sitting beside him, her hands folded neatly in her lap, her eyes cast upward through the sunroof. It seemed like forever since they'd driven along together like this, even longer since the two had cared what was happening in each other's life. For one brief, insane minute, Michael found himself wishing he could reach across the front seat and take Jennie's hand.

But he wouldn't do it. He couldn't do it. Because they'd been married once and it would mean too much. He concentrated on the expressway, both hands gripping the steering wheel. He could think of nothing to say.

Finally they pulled into the driveway at his house. The garage door whirred as it began rolling open for him. He was nervous, fumbling with the house key. She followed him into the house carefully, holding her handbag in front of her. He strode into the kitchen and started rummaging in the refrigerator. "Look what we've got here." Moldy peas. Some macaroni and cheese wrapped in a Baggie. Half an overripe cantaloupe.

Jennie watched him, amusement flickering in her eyes. Finally she burst out laughing. "If you really want to know the truth," she told him candidly, "it *still* looks better than the cafeteria hamburgers."

"Trust me," he said, shooting her a little grin. "I'm going to find something in here that's edible. It'll just take a minute." He poked his head farther into the fridge.

"Don't let anything attack you in there. Some of it looks deadly."

"This is it. Here. I've got it." He pitched out an unopened package of flour tortillas, a tomato, a head of lettuce that was a little wilted but would do, and some salsa. "I'll defrost the chicken in the microwave and we'll have *fajitas*. It won't take long."

"Thank you," she said, laughing. "You've saved my stomach. I would have killed you if you had gotten my hopes up for nothing."

They set to work, side by side. She chopped the lettuce into little strips and diced the tomato while Michael took care of everything else. She didn't look up when she heard him go out onto the patio to start the grill.

Now that he wasn't standing within feet of her, she contemplated how odd it felt to be preparing lunch with Michael in his kitchen. It felt right. And wrong. And funny.

Michael wandered back inside looking for a match to light the grill.

Jennie dissected the tomato perfectly, paying close attention to the little squares she made, trying to pretend she wasn't so incredibly aware of Michael's powerful masculine presence. After almost two weeks spent discussing Cody, she couldn't think of one thing to say.

"I had to get the matches," he said. "Can't start a fire out there if I can't find the matches." For a moment he just stood there, watching her with her head bowed over the tomato and all the wheat-colored hair flowing down her back. Then, as if in a vision, a memory came back.

It had been their first night in their tiny apartment in Highland Park. He'd come to find her standing much as she was standing now, her long sheet of hair gleaming down her back, her head bowed. But when she turned to welcome him home, he could see she'd been crying.

"Where were you?" she had asked, sniffing and trying to act as if she wasn't upset with him for being late.

"I was with a patient. A man who had abdominal surgery last week. He came in tonight with an infection in his incision." He glanced at the clock above the stove. It was the first time he'd checked to see how late it really was. It was already past nine-thirty.

She turned back to the counter as he hung up his coat. And, this time, when he looked at her, the sniffing had turned into sobs and her shoulders were shaking. "I w-wanted d-dinner to be so g-good..."

"Honey." He remembered moving across the kitchen to gather her into his arms. He remembered her laying her head against his shoulder. "Don't be mad at me. I should have called. I will next time."

"I—I'm—not m-mad at y-you...." she'd wailed. "I'm mad—at—that—s-stupid—stuff...." She'd pointed to a big pile of goo in the sink that looked like it had been spaghetti once. Now it was charred on one side and sticking straight up like quills on the other. "I'm—n-never—going to—cook—ever..."

To his credit, it was one of the times of his life he had done the right thing by her. She was only twenty-one and he knew how important it was to her to please him. He hadn't even cracked a smile. "I love you, whether you can cook or not. I love you, Jen...." He'd stood there for what seemed like forever just stroking her hair. Then, after he'd helped her throw the horrible stuff away, they'd ordered out for pizza. They'd eaten it by the fire and they'd toasted their marriage with wine in crystal goblets that reflected the firelight and then he'd made love with her right there on the floor.

What was it about today that made him remember the first few romantic months of their marriage? he wondered. Matches in hand he turned away from her, went back outside and started the grill.

Twenty minutes later they were munching away at the kitchen table.

"It's good," she said. "Better than good."

"I think so, too." He leaned back in his chair, stretching his arms up around the back of his head and crossing them there.

Her eyes met his. "Thanks."

"You're welcome."

She didn't look away. She seemed unable to pull her gaze from his, even if her life depended on it. Watching her brought back thousands of memories, not all of them good. But she looked so appealing, more relaxed than he'd seen her in days, and so lovely.

His eyes stayed on her. He'd been married to this woman for six years. She'd always been pretty. But what he saw now was something more...something mature . . . and full and strong. Maybe, he wondered, he was just recognizing those qualities for the first time because he was seeing how she was devoting herself to Cody.

"So when are you going to use all those notes you took and start teaching me how to do therapy?"

"Anytime you want."

"As soon as we can," he said.

"That's fine with me."

Their eyes still held.

"We should get back," she said finally, jumping up to begin gathering silverware and plates. "Cody'll be awake."

Michael stood quickly to help her. He stacked the glasses, then went to the sink beside her. They stood shoulder to shoulder. He set the glasses down. "Jennie?"

"Yes." She turned toward him.

"Do you know," he whispered to her, "how badly sometimes I need to reach out and hold you?"

He heard her intake of breath, saw the emotion begin to pool in her eyes.

"Sometimes," she said, her voice as gentle and as smooth as her fingers would have been if they'd brushed against his skin. "Sometimes I think I do. Because I need it, too."

Michael knew exactly what he would do now. Her words were all he'd wanted her to say, and more. Her hands were still in the sink, wet from the running water, but he didn't care. He took them, suds and all, into his own and held them there. He pulled her to him then, sliding both hands up the length of her sleeves until he grasped her forearms.

Jennie tilted her head back and studied his face. She reached one arm up as he held her and touched his hair. She gripped the fabric of his shirt as he pulled her fiercely toward him and whispered her name. "Jennie."

It was the first time in years, even when they'd been married, that she had felt so totally protected in his arms. He gripped her to him now as if he would never release her, ever. His breath became labored, arrhythmic. And, beneath the cool cotton of his shirt, she could feel the heat of his skin and the solid pumping of his heart.

He lifted all her long silken hair from her neck with one hand, gathering it and then, fingers spread, letting it spill out as he watched it fall, just absorbing the nearness of her. How glad he was that she hadn't pulled away from him.

He leaned toward her then, in their embrace born of mutual need, and felt a new bond beginning to grow. It was a bond they'd never shared during their marriage.

Michael wished he could entice her to turn her face toward his so he could kiss her. In his mind he pictured himself claiming her lips with his own, kissing her wildly the way he'd kissed her so long ago...when he had felt as if the whole world was waiting for him...waiting for them...together.

But she didn't turn her face up toward his.

She clung to him now with her nose and her eyes buried in his shirt, her warm breath searing his skin through his clothing.

He pulled her even tighter, squeezing her just for a moment, reveling in the feeling of her, pretending he could make it last forever. But he knew he couldn't.

"Come on," he said to her. "I'll take you back."

BUDDY DRAPER SAT in the front office of the Dallas Sidekicks fidgeting like a little kid. He straightened his tie. He stretched his legs. He crossed his ankles. He wished he had worn a polo shirt and casual pants instead of this suit.

He was so far out of touch with the world of the Major Indoor Soccer League that he hadn't even known what to wear when he came to visit Harv Siskell.

Harv Siskell. The man who had come to watch him play soccer at R. L. Turner High School his junior year and who had wooed him on to the team. Harv Siskell, who was too good a friend now to ever give up on him.

Buddy straightened his tie again, feeling more and more uncomfortable.

"Harv is ready for you," the secretary told him.

He practically jumped out of his chair and grabbed the packet of videos with both hands. "Thanks, Margaret."

She winked at him and it was enough to calm him down just a little bit. "It's good to see you back in this office, Buddy."

"Thanks, Margaret."

Harv was standing beside the desk waiting for him. "Buddy. Come in. Have a seat." And then the man did a double take. "Jeez! You look like you got dressed for somebody's funeral."

"I couldn't decide what to wear."

"How about number fourteen?" He gestured toward one of Buddy's old jerseys hanging against the wall amid the many team photos and trophies. In big green numbers it said 14, with DRAPER above. "We retired your number."

Both he and Harv stood looking at the jersey for a minute. "Brings back memories," Buddy said, feigning nonchalance.

"So." Harv took the videos from Buddy's hands. "How's your love life?"

Buddy shot him an astonished look. "What?"

"You seem really uptight. Obviously you aren't in the mood to discuss what's on those tapes yet. Let's talk about women instead. You always *were* good at that."

"Harv," Buddy said, laughing, and finally settling into the chair. "You never change, do you?"

"Nope," he said. "I don't. Now, tell me about her."

"Which 'her'?"

"You know which one. The pretty dark-haired lady you used to bring around to all the games before you forgot how to drive your car and crashed it."

Oh, he knew which one all right. "I don't see her anymore."

Harv sighed. "Sorry, kid. Guess she was just a groupie, huh? Did she only want you when you were a famous Sidekicks soccer player?"

Buddy thought about Harv's question for a long time. That hadn't been Andy's motivation at all. Andy wasn't like any other woman he'd ever known. "I wish," he said to Harv, smiling sadly. "It would have been easier that way."

"What do you mean?"

"Andy's a physical therapist. She works with the kids at Children's Medical Center. When she heard I was going to quit playing soccer, she let me have it. She didn't know that the front office pulled my contract. She thought I gave up because I wouldn't be the best anymore."

"Interesting." Harv nodded knowingly. "Very interesting. And you never bothered to set her straight."

"She'd worked so hard to help me play again, Harv. It meant everything to her because she knew it meant everything to me. I couldn't tell her that all the hard work she put herself through for my sake just wasn't enough. All she could see was *me* giving up. And I'll tell you right now, Andy learned a long time ago not to let people give up."

Harv sighed. "She was a pretty girl."

"She still is."

"Maybe that's what you need to make you happy, Bud." Harv gave him a fatherly pat on the back of the hand, knowing Buddy would recognize his teasing for exactly what it was. Half advice, half trite nonsense. "Find a nice girl. Settle down. Start a family."

"No," Buddy told him. "*You* find a nice girl. I've got what I need." He pointed to the packet of videos on Harv's desk. "I need what you're offering me, Harv. It's been a long time since I've been this excited about anything."

"Really?" The words were music to Harv's ears. "You interested in the job?"

"If I wasn't, I darn sure wouldn't have come all the way down here in this suit and tie."

"I want you to remember one thing while we discuss this," Harv told him, his eyes crinkled up in a smile. "I want you to know what you're getting into before you tell me you'll do it. Coaching from the sidelines is a lot different than being a player. Sometimes it's easier. Sometimes you see things a whole lot clearer. Other times it's hell."

"I'll keep that in mind," Buddy said.

He took out his notepad while Harv turned on the VCR and slipped in a game tape. In no time at all, the two of them were absorbed in watching the runners moving around the field.

CHAPTER SEVEN

MONDAY MORNING, almost two weeks after Cody had taken ill, Jennie returned to work for good. She had a million and one things to do; sketches to complete, staff to manage, and an editor to assuage. But all she could think about as she sat behind her desk with a thousand responsibilities weighing down on her, were three things:

Number one, I wanted Michael to hold me as badly as he wanted to do it.

Number two, for five minutes, standing in that kitchen, I actually forgot to think about Cody.

And, number three.

Most important, this number three.

We had six years to make things work between us and we couldn't do it. What would make it be any different now? If Cody hadn't gotten sick, would I still need Michael?

She absentmindedly shot a rubber band across the room. It hit Art Sanderson on the thigh as he passed by. "I hope that wasn't intended for me."

"I always intend them for you, Art." Quickly, she pulled herself together. She grinned and aimed another one.

At that precise moment, Art stepped into his office and the object of her previous thoughts stepped in, neatly dressed in an open-necked turquoise shirt that complemented his eyes and wavy blond hair. She froze, the rubber band still in hand. "Michael?" She whispered even though she didn't need to. "What are you doing here?"

"I've come to ask you out on a date," he said with breathtaking nonchalance.

"Now?"

"Now is as good a time as any. Six Flags is open all afternoon."

"Six Flags?"

"I want to go somewhere with you, anywhere with you, that we can both relax and have a good time for a few hours. We deserve it."

She stood up and looked at him as if he were absolutely bananas.

"Is that so crazy? Is that so wrong? It's been so long and I...I just..." He walked over to her desk. "I needed to prove something to myself."

"Like what?"

"That when I held you against me on Saturday, what I felt wasn't a figment of my imagination."

She just looked at him.

"Jennie."

"No."

"Please."

"No."

Suddenly he smiled. "It scared you, didn't it?" he said very softly. "It scares you just as much as it scared me."

"Nothing scared me. Absolutely nothing scared me," she said with more conviction than she felt. She wondered why her heart was beating so fast and her face felt so flushed.

He went down on one knee. It was the most ridiculous thing she'd ever seen. "Go with me this afternoon. Please? I'll win you something. I'll get you the biggest, tackiest animal on the midway. I'll ride all your favorite rides twice."

"Michael," she reminded him quietly. "This is my first day back at work. I've got a million things to do."

"Is she giving you a hard time, Michael?" Art asked, coming out of his own office.

"Well," said Michael, "she's apparently loaded down with work."

"Go ahead, Jennie," said Art. "There's nothing here that can't wait one more day. Just go and have a good time."

Art and Michael left her no choice. Michael brought the car around and they went on their way. They walked hand in hand among what seemed like hundreds of kids and teenagers. "What shall it be first?" he asked her as they stood watching the six flags of the different countries that had once claimed Texas for their own. The flags of France, Spain, Mexico, the independent Texas flag, the Confederate flag and the United States flag all snapped and rippled in the breeze.

She thought a minute. "The go-carts. I always liked the go-carts the best. Then the Log Flume and the Runaway Mine Train and the Spinnaker..."

When he stopped laughing at her enthusiasm, he had to ask her. "When's the last time you were here?"

She narrowed her eyebrows and thought back. "I must have been a senior in high school. We came here on a senior trip."

"We never came together, did we?"

"No. Remember? We were always going to bring Cody when he got old enough." But, when Cody had finally been big enough to ride all the rides, they'd been pursuing their divorce.

"I'm glad," he said quietly, "we've found a spot on neutral ground."

"Neutral ground nothing," she said, suddenly smiling mischievously. "I'll take you on at the shooting gallery. Then you'll figure out we're not on neutral ground."

"Okay," he said, letting her take his hand and drag him. "You show me."

They rode rides all afternoon. She beat him three times at the shooting gallery. He teased her incessantly because one of the rides she wanted to ride wasn't there anymore.

"They've torn it down," he kept saying, "to make way for bigger and better things. That should make you feel old."

"Hush, you," she said, waggling a finger at him. "Today's been wonderful. It's made me feel young instead."

"But they've torn down the Flying Jenny!"

"It always was my favorite when I was a little girl," she admitted, honestly saddened.

"Probably—" he laughed "—just because it was named after *you.*"

"Leave me alone."

"I don't want to leave you alone."

They went to the Mexican section and he bought her a huge tissue-paper flower. They sat out on the deck, watching twinkling lights flicker on all over the park, stuffing themselves full of enchiladas and refritos at El Chico's. After the waiter took their plates, he dared her to ride the enormous spinning pink Mexican hat they'd been watching across the way.

"After eating this much?" she asked him, eyes huge. "You've got to be kidding."

"Nope," he said. "I'm serious. I can handle it. Can you?"

"You're a doctor," she teased him back. "You shouldn't let people do this to themselves."

"Let's go for it. Come on."

They paid for their dinner and giggled all the way to the sombrero. And, after it was over, they both wobbled off, panting and laughing, hand in hand, faces glowing.

"You look a little green," he commented.

"So do you."

He grabbed her hands again. "We'd better help each other along."

She gripped on to him. "I wish," she said out of the blue, "that we had brought Cody here."

He looked at her sadly, remembering everything now that stood between them. "So do I." He changed the subject. "I promised to win you an animal, didn't I?"

"Yeah," she said. "Come to think of it, that's exactly what you promised me."

"Well, come on, then."

They walked to the midway, where he spent a fortune buying chances to throw balls at milk bottles and shoot darts at balloons and throw dimes in bowls. Finally he was victorious. The man behind the booth handed Jennie a fat plush purple pig with a flourish. "There you go, young lady. Your young man certainly earned it!"

"Thank you, Michael." She shot him a little sideways grin that made her look sixteen years old.

"Do you know how much money I just spent on that thing?" he asked, eyeing it ruefully.

"I love him. I'm going to name him Petunia."

"Him? Petunia?" He threw his head back and laughed. Really laughed. But when he looked at her, he stopped because she wasn't laughing at all. She had tears in her eyes.

"Do you know how badly I needed this?" she asked him. The soft expression in her eyes caught at his heart.

It was everything he could do to keep from bundling her up against him again. But he wasn't going to do it here beside the ring-toss booth while she cried over Petunia the male pig. So he told her the truth. "I knew."

DURING THEIR AFTERNOON at Six Flags, they'd decided Jennie would start teaching Michael some of Cody's therapy the next day, at lunchtime. Michael parked the car, then stopped to admire one of the brightly colored paintings on the cement wall along the lot. Children staying at the hospital had done the paintings themselves, wonderful primary-color renditions of hopes and hurts.

How long, he wondered, *will it take Cody to be able to draw pictures again?*

As he boarded the elevator, Michael hated to admit he felt a little bit let down today. He'd been eager for some time to start learning Cody's therapy. But it was hard coming here after he and Jennie had had such a good time yesterday. For a few hours he had forgotten everything Cody was up against. He felt guilty for that. Guilty and afraid, because he'd held Jennie the other afternoon and he hadn't wanted to let her go.

The first person he saw when he walked into Cody's room was Jennie. Suddenly, he wasn't just scared anymore. He was terrified.

Their relationship had subtly changed over the past few days. He was attracted to her again.

He tried to pretend it didn't matter. After Cody got well again, Jennie would go back to drawing cartoons and ignoring anything that didn't advance her career. He'd go back to long hours with his practice and the hospital, taking duty calls at all hours of the night. Despite what had happened to Cody, he and Jennie were still the same people they'd always been.

At the sight of her, he remembered the day four years ago, when they had faced each other in the courtroom. Jennie had sat quietly, tears and anger in her eyes.

"Your honor," his lawyer had said. "The grounds for this divorce are irreconcilable differences. Both

Michael Stratton and Jennie Stratton have informed the court that the marriage cannot continue. There is no fault involved here, although Michael Stratton is the party who actually filed in court."

"Does Jennie Stratton agree with that statement?" the judge had asked.

Her lawyer looked at Jennie. Michael looked at Jennie. She hesitated ever so slightly, then she nodded.

"Yes, your honor," her lawyer had said.

And so, their marriage had ended. Once up a time, they had loved each other. Or maybe, they had only thought what they'd had was love.

"Hi, Jennie," he said quietly now as she turned toward the sound in the doorway. "Hello there, little guy." He took Cody's hand and focused all his attention on his son.

Andy Kendall knocked on the door right behind him, looking brisk and cheerful. "Therapy time," she sang out. When she saw both of them standing together, she smiled at her little patient in the big hospital bed. "Ah. Today my student is a teacher. So I just get to sit and watch." She sat down in the plastic chair and propped her feet up playfully. "Go for it, Jennie."

"You have to critique," Jennie told her. "I want you to watch me and tell me everything I'm doing wrong."

Andy inclined her head with a knowing smile. "Oh, I will."

Jennie laid her notes on the bed and surveyed a page before she started. Then she began to demonstrate shyly to Michael as she spoke. "This is how you do it. As you sit and talk to him, at least three times a day, you need to work his leg muscles like this."

He watched her for a while, then she stepped back so he could try it. It was almost funny, being so formal with each other today. Michael moved Cody's leg up and back, up and back, with one hand pressed firmly against the ball of his foot, the other gently bent around his knee.

"You're doin' it, Dad," Cody said. "You're doin' it just right."

From behind the three of them, Andy nodded, too.

"That *is* just right," Jennie told him. "Perfect."

"Aw," Michael said, not quite so afraid anymore. "Of course it's perfect. I wouldn't have it for Cody any other way."

"Now," Jennie instructed him. "Next we do this…and this…and this…" The lesson went on for over half an hour, while the two of them worked side by side. By the end of the session, Andy had left, giving them her approval, and Jennie was blowing streams of iridescent bubbles through a tiny blue wand. "Get 'em, kid, let's get 'em," Michael egged Cody on, relaxed now and totally engrossed in the movements as he and Cody tried to pop as many bubbles as they could before they wafted up over the bed.

Cody was giggling, then, finally, laughing, a great belly laugh as the room filled with bubbles. And just as Michael was deciding that this therapy session was almost as much fun as the day before at Six Flags, one of the biggest bubbles landed right on Jennie's head and sat there.

"Mom's got a bubble on her head," Cody cried. "Look, Dad. Mom's got a bubble sitting right on top of her."

"Get it off," Jennie said, not moving.

She raised a hand to brush it off but Michael stopped her. "No. Don't. It's a *sign.*" He made a pass over her head with his hands. "Stand there and see how long it'll stay."

"Michael, I don't want to stand here all day with a bubble on my head!"

All three of them just looked at each other. Cody snorted first, and pretty soon they were all laughing so hard their stomachs hurt. Jennie's bubble had long since been exploded into oblivion. And still they laughed.

It had been ages and ages since they'd laughed together like this. And, following on the heels of the incredible despair Michael had been feeling only days ago, it felt like a miracle.

He reached across Cody's legs and gripped Jennie's hand. How he hoped that she felt the miracle, too.

"Come on, Cody," Jennie said. "Let's try sitting up again. Can you support yourself with this arm?"

"Yeah."

"Watch this." She showed Michael how to prop Cody's arm against the pillow like a tent pole. "There you go. Let's see how long you can do this. Michael, time him."

Michael crooked his arm up so he could read the watch on his wrist.

I remember it now, Jennie thought. I remember why I fell in love with him. He cares so much about everything.

And I remember why I fell out of love with him. Because I decided he cared more about everything else then he cared about me.

At that precise moment, Cody started to wobble.

Jennie grabbed him to stop him from falling.

Michael grabbed him to stop him from falling.

They all grabbed each other. And then, even though their middles were still aching from the last onslaught, they all started laughing all over again.

MARK KENDALL STOOD in the doorway to Andy's apartment, hands in pockets, legs crossed, leaning jauntily against the jamb. He looked just like a kid ready to play a practical joke on somebody. But this was much, much better than a joke.

"Had to stop by," he told Andy, straight-faced, when she opened the door. "I've got this present for you."

"What is it?"

He pulled the white legal-length envelope from his jacket and handed it to her. Andy ripped it open impatiently, tearing the paper in little accordion-folded chunks. She pulled the two tickets out and stared at them in puzzlement.

He didn't say anything. He just stood there, waiting for her to figure it out.

"Sidekicks tickets? For tonight's game?"

"Yeah." Mark shrugged. "Just thought it was something you might want to be in on."

"What?" She hated to question Mark's motives. But she hadn't attended a game since Buddy Draper had retired. She didn't think she wanted to do it now. "What would I want to be in on?"

"You should be thanking me, you know," he said instead of answering her question. "This game sold out two weeks ago. I had to work miracles this morning to get tickets, especially after the paper came out with Harv Siskell's announcement."

"What announcement? What did Harv Siskell say?"

"Ah," Mark said, grinning.

"Well?" She couldn't help it. She almost shouted, he had her so frustrated. "What's going on?"

"Perhaps you should read the newspaper."

Andy rushed off to find the paper. Returning with it to the living room, she scattered it in sections across the sofa. "What exactly is it that I'm supposed to read?"

"Try the sports section," Mark suggested smugly. "Page eight."

She counted through the section with her thumb, then opened the page, shaking it once to dispense with the wrinkles.

"You see it?"

She scanned the page. "Just a minute...let me..."

Then she saw the headline.

Draper rejoins team, it read. *Former player to coach Sidekicks beside Harv Siskell.*

"Buddy's back," the story began. And, really, that was all she needed to know. "Mark! I don't believe it!"

"So," he said, still leaning against the jamb. "Maybe the guy listened to you after all."

"Buddy had a hard time listening to anybody."

"You never know," Mark pointed out, "what an impact you might have made on somebody's life."

She threw the newspaper at him, trying to cover the conflicting emotions churning within her. She felt happy and sad and frightened and excited all at once.

Mark abandoned his pose to dodge the flying object. "So what do you say?" he asked.

"I say he'll make a great coach. Coaches are good at bossing people around and not listening to a thing anybody tells them."

"Hey," he said, grinning. "I take exception to that. I'm a coach, too, remember?"

"Oh, I forgot that," she said, eyes wide, feigning innocence.

"No, you didn't." As he spoke, he fashioned page eight into a giant airplane and sailed it back at her. "You're making jabs at Buddy and me, too."

She sobered for a moment, looking down at the airplane by her feet. "I can't read the rest of the story."

"Doesn't matter. I'll tell you the rest on the way to the game. How do you feel about all this, Andy?"

"I don't know," she said honestly, knowing she could never sort out everything inside her heart just now. "I'm glad for him. And sorry it took this long in coming. I feel like he lost so much."

"Tonight's his first night back on the field. I knew you'd want to be there."

"You were right about that," she said, suddenly grinning and holding up the tickets. "Let's go."

"BUDDY! BUDDY!" the lady shrieked from behind him. "Good to have you back, Buddy!"

He turned and acknowledged her with a nod, then waved at another fan higher in the stands who was holding up a Welcome Back, Buddy banner to him.

Harv, standing with arms crossed, leaned sideways and spoke in his left ear. "See? I told you, didn't I? They haven't forgotten you in half a year. They won't for a long time."

"Tell me this isn't a marketing move by the front office, Siskell," he growled. He was already perturbed by the carefully orchestrated press releases that hit the stands this morning. "Tell me you really want me standing beside you telling these poor players what to do."

"I really want you standing beside me telling these poor players what to do."

Buddy stared straight ahead, assessing the opposing team's performance. "I should have known the Colorado Comets would play like this. Their keeper is incredible. Quicker than any I've seen."

Just then, the Comets' left forward kicked the ball toward the Sidekicks' goal. Miraculously, the keeper blocked and deflected the ball to the right side.

"All right, Buddy Draper!" somebody hollered from behind.

Buddy crossed his arms just like Harv and did his best to concentrate on the game. He still had a lot to learn. But though he didn't say anything to Harv, standing on the field with the huge lights swinging above was everything he needed, whether the fans remembered him or not. It was incredible what sensations this place brought back to him. The tart, earthy scent of the stadium, of fast food, of the players. The sharp surreal sounds of the whistle blowing and the crowd cheering and the glare of the lights. The players grunting with exertion and the smack of leather or leg against the spinning ball.

I may not be a player anymore, he thought, *but dammit, at least I'm here.*

The Dallas left forward, Chuck Kirkland, trapped the ball, took two steps and crossed the ball to the left side. Marshall Townsend, the striker, controlled the ball, trapped it, and passed it back to the defender. The defender passed it to the right forward.

"He's got a clear shot," Harv shouted, jerking his arms to his sides. "Take it, Spooner! *Take it.*"

Eric Spooner passed the ball back to Townsend. Marshall took the shot from what seemed like very far away. The Comets' keeper had plenty of time to prepare for it. He reached up and blocked it with his fist, smacking the ball off to the left side.

"No!" Harv pounded his fist against his open palm to accentuate each word. "No. No. No! Spooner could have made the shot. Why did he pass it to Townsend? What made *anybody* think Townsend could make that?"

"Townsend was going for the miracle shot," Buddy commented offhandedly. "If he'd made it, you'd have been slapping him on the back and telling him you were buying him a New York strip for dinner."

"No, I wouldn't have," Harv growled. "I would have let him have it either way. He turned down a sure thing for a chance at stardom. It was a stupid try. The only player I've ever had who could make those shots was you."

The discussion that ensued on the sidelines when the players came off the field was a lively one, full of Harv's emphatic "no's" and colorful cussing. Buddy stood rigidly by Harv's side, feeling that he had nothing to contribute. A few minutes into the discussion, he turned his head sideways a bit and, for one moment, he thought he saw a vision. She was climbing up the steps in the stands not far from him, wearing a bright red dress and carrying a bag of popcorn. "Andy..." But it couldn't be. How many Dallas women looked like that from the back, with rippling dark hair against their backs and shoulders set so square and broad?

She wouldn't be here. I know that. Not after everything that's gone between us. She'd be crazy and so would I to think it. Stop supposing she still believes in you more than you believe in yourself.

He straightened his back, shifted his gum to the other side of his mouth, and turned to the players. Harv had already moved down the line after finishing with Townsend. The team was just starting back on to the field. "Hey, man," Buddy hollered at Townsend, a teammate he'd played beside not so very long ago. "I only have one thing to add to that chewing out you just got from Siskell."

"Well," Townsend tensed up and spat. "Get on with it, Draper."

"If you try a shot like that one next time," Buddy warned him, smiling, "just be sure you're going to make it."

CHAPTER EIGHT

THE NEXT MORNING, as Jennie lay in bed halfway between sleep and wakefulness, the telephone rang. "It's me," Michael said without preamble. "I just received a phone call from Cody's doctors. They want us to come to the hospital for a consultation some time today."

Her heart stopped. "Michael? What is it? Is he sick again? What's wrong?"

"He's fine, Jen. Calm down. He's fine. But his doctors have written an evaluation on him. They're going to present the results and they want us there."

"What time?"

"They'd like to see us about nine-thirty."

"I'll be there."

When she arrived at the hospital, he was waiting for her in the lobby. "Am I late?"

"No," he said. "Just on time."

They stood there, looking at one another.

"We probably should sit down," he said to break the silence between them. How funny that yesterday the silence had been comfortable and the laughter had been so spontaneous. Today it was not.

They sat as though frozen, within hands' reach but not touching, barely breathing.

The seconds ticked by, until Andy entered the room and motioned to them. As they walked up the hallway toward the doctors' conference room, Michael didn't take Jennie's hand the way he had yesterday and the day before. The easy rapport between them was gone.

Michael had wondered if Cody would be at the meeting. He was glad now that he would not be. This wasn't the place for a child, certainly not one whose dreams hung in the balance of what the doctors might tell them.

The interns filed in one by one. Jennie glanced at Michael, wondering if he could still see himself in these somber young people who stood waiting to declare a verdict on their child. One of them handed Michael a manilla folder that contained the typed report.

"This outlines Cody's progress and will tell you what we expect from him during the next months," the intern began. "We will go over it with you verbally now. Tonight you can go over it together and contact us if you have questions."

So cold. So clinical. A little boy's limbs . . . their little boy's life . . .

"We can't promise you anything," the intern continued.

"Well," Michael said impatiently. "Tell us what you can. Please."

"We believe Cody's muscle control may come back over time, especially in his arms."

"And . . ."

"His legs may be more difficult to bring back."

"Which means?" Michael said grimly.

"Because we have to speculate on it now, we must tell you that, at this point, we believe Cody will *not* be able to walk again."

"What?"

"We speculate now that your son will not be able to walk in the future."

"No." It was too much for Jennie. "Don't say that."

She took one step forward and Michael grabbed her arm. "They might be wrong. Nobody knows, Jennie. Nobody. You mustn't lose heart. They have to give us their opinion, but it doesn't mean anything. Not really."

One of the interns continued. "We're suggesting surgery on his left leg. The orthopedic surgeon on staff examined Cody two days ago. She is concerned that the muscles' tightness could pop your son's hip out of joint. We think it's in Cody's best interest to sever that muscle before it causes a problem. But you've got to know that while severing the muscle will solve the problem with the bone, the resulting damage to the muscle will leave it permanently weak."

"No," Jennie whispered. She turned tear-filled eyes toward him.

Michael turned back to the interns, knowing from the sudden slump of Jennie's shoulders that he had to get her out of the room fast. "Thank you." He tucked the folder under his arm and steered her toward the door. "We'll go over this. Then we'll get back to you."

He didn't let go of her elbow. They walked out side by side, their heads held high, past the row of interns.

"You want to go in and see Cody?" he asked.

She shook her head. She couldn't bear that right now. "No. Not just now. I couldn't..."

"Come on, Jennie. Let's go for a walk." He wanted to take her outside into the beaming sunshine and into the fresh air, any place that might bring them both a moment of peace after the news they'd just received. As they started up the hallway toward the stairwell, they passed the small gymnasium where Andy and the other physical therapists conducted their sessions.

"Simon says," Andy's voice rang out, "put your finger on your nose."

Five children, all happy and sitting in line in wheel-chairs, touched their noses.

"Good," she said. "Very good. Now. Simon says wiggle your right hand."

Five right hands wiggled.

"Now, wiggle your left hand."

One left hand wiggled.

Jennie stood in the doorway riveted to the scene. She gripped Michael's forearms and hung on to him. He was her life preserver. "Michael." She looked up at him like someone drowning. "Please. Take me somewhere. Get me out of here."

"Come on."

He took her arm and they raced down the steps and burst through the polished glass doors.

SHE TOOK her first desperate, labored breaths of fresh air while Michael held her up.

"How can they say that?" she said, her voice raspy with pain. "How can they stand there and say that to our faces and expect us to accept that he won't walk again?"

He gripped her shoulders. "They had to do it, Jennie. They're doctors. They have to assess the situation as they see it."

"Who gave them the right to pronounce that sort of sentence on his legs? Who gave them the right to tell us what Cody can or can't do? *Who gave them the right?*"

"Jennie." He held her at arm's length. "Stop and think about it. *We* did. We gave them the right. We wanted to know what they had to say."

She looked into his eyes, his dear gentle eyes that had calmed her during so many storms, that had been as cold as death once, looking at her from across a courtroom. Today, in the blaring sun, they held every bit as much pain in their sea green depths as they had held then. Pain. And frustration. And anger.

Anger. She stopped short, realizing it for the first time.

"You aren't accepting what they're selling, either."

"I'm sure as hell not accepting it."

"Why?" And, in the moment she asked it, she saw him flinch. She could answer the question for herself. She could see it written plainly in his expression. "You've done that sort of thing, too."

He nodded. "It's always a judgment call. It's one of the most difficult things a doctor has to do."

For the first time, she understood what he had been up against all along in his work, and their marriage. She hadn't known that he'd made those sorts of assessments when he'd been an intern. That realization came as another blow. She had to wonder. *How much of a buffer could I have been for him then?*

"So there's hope..." she said instead, shakily.

"There's always hope," he said. "Don't let anybody fool you."

He hugged her around the shoulders as she went to him, nestling against him as he held her there. Despite her sorrow or, perhaps, because of it, she clung to him without reservation now, without restraint. And the emotion that soared within her made her feel as if she were balancing on the edge of a dangerous precipice.

Here was the attractive fair-haired boy she'd fallen in love with once.

Here was the grown man she'd grown disillusioned with and disappointed in.

Here was the man she wanted to kiss her more than she'd wanted anything in her life.

He hadn't shaved this morning and the prickles of hair left dark contours around a jaw that had once been less severe, not so firmly set and a mouth much more prone to widen into a smile. His eyes, the true green color of the grass after spring rains, spoke volumes. They told her what she instinctively had already known. He longed for it just as much as she.

She ran her hands up his arms, hungrily pressing the pads of her fingers into the smudged cambric of his shirtsleeves. She could feel the smoldering of his skin burning through the fabric, the rise in his pulse and her own.

He whispered her name. "Jennie." He combed through her wheat-colored hair with his fingers, raking it back from her face and holding it tangled between his fingers.

She pulled closer. She felt him catch his breath.

When his breath caught, it was as if time had stopped, as well. Ten years ago...six years ago...four...all melded into this one moment.

He bent toward her. His touch, not as soft as it once had been but grittier now, was more demanding. He purposefully moved toward her mouth, and she turned slightly, knowing how well their lips fit together.

"Dear, sweet heaven," he whispered against her mouth.

For a moment she was nineteen again and he was twenty-one and it was the first time they'd touched each other. He held her so close she could scarcely breathe. He traced her teeth with his tongue. She shivered. And, even as he did so, the kiss changed.

Neither of them was the same as they'd once been. A new desperation and demand enveloped them both, an irrevocable passion drawing directly from the past days and their love for the little boy who lay in the bed on a floor above them.

Jennie felt as if she were paddling under water, struggling to reach some flat, crystalline surface above her head. She could feel the pulse in Michael's throat hammering as hard as her own.

Then his hands went to her shoulders and he held her slightly away.

Jennie looked up at his face, remembering again the frightening decisions they faced.

"Michael?" she asked reluctantly. "What are we going to do about the surgery?"

He broke their gaze for a moment. He stared up at the clouds drifting by above them. "We're going to let them do it."

"No," she said shaking her head and looking determined. "We aren't."

"What do you mean 'no'? You heard what they said. The surgeon recommended it."

"She *recommended* it. Dr. Phillips didn't say it was something we had to do."

"Believe me, Jennie. The woman knows what she's talking about."

"But you said yourself it was a judgment call."

"An educated judgment call. Jennie, we'll have a meeting with her and discuss it. But I already know what she's going to say. The orthopedic surgeon here has a wonderful reputation. She's trained for years to deal with situations like this one."

But Jennie wasn't giving up. "I was in Cody's room when the surgeon examined him. She came Tuesday morning at 7:30 a.m. Andy hadn't even had a chance to come in and work with Cody's legs yet. He was stiffer than I've ever seen him. The doctor didn't see him at his best."

"Fine, then. We'll get a second opinion. Is that what you're telling me you want?"

"I'm telling you that even if we get a second opinion, I won't be able to agree to let them damage a perfectly healthy muscle."

"Jennie, the doctors wouldn't suggest it if they didn't think it was the best thing for him."

"Twenty minutes ago you told me there is always hope. Now you tell me there isn't any."

For the first time, Michael's impatience was evident in his voice. "That isn't what I'm telling you at all. If Cody's hip comes out of the socket, he could face all sorts of problems."

"But what if it doesn't?" she insisted. "What if we ruined Cody's leg muscle for nothing?" Why, just once, couldn't they agree on something as important as their son?

"You'll have your way no matter what happens. We have joint custody. They won't agree to surgery without both of us consenting. So I have no say in the matter, do I? No matter what I think?"

"The surgery would make it so much harder for him to keep moving forward. Everything I've been reading says we should avoid surgery at all costs."

"And everything I know," Michael told her stiffly, "leads me to believe we should follow the doctor's advice."

She stood before him, nose to nose, bristling with defensiveness. "Because you're a doctor, too," she said.

"Yes. Because I'm a doctor."

"You and that orthopedic surgeon may be doctors. You're also humans," she stated. "Humans make mistakes."

He stared at her angrily, his eyebrows in a tightly

knit curl, his face as hard as granite. "You aren't going to let me forget that, Jennie, are you?"

"Not," she said quietly, "as long as my son's future hangs in the balance."

CHAPTER NINE

CODY COULDN'T HAVE ASKED the question at a worse time. He looked right up at both of them that afternoon, his eyes wide and full of hope, and asked, "Do you *like* each other again?"

Michael stared down at his son, covering his pain with a blank expression.

Jennie stared, too. "Honey…" she said after a long, awkward silence.

"Cody…" Michael said just a half beat later.

"I *said*, 'Do you and Mom *like* each other again?'"

"Why would you ask a thing like that?"

"Because you're being funny around each other. You look at each other and then you don't look at each other."

Michael glared across the bed at Jennie. He'd look at her all right. He'd look at her with all the blame he could muster in his eyes.

Jennie glared back.

Sweet heaven, Michael thought. *What can either of us say?*

Jennie's pinched expression softened somewhat as she touched Cody's hand and sat on his bed. "Darling." Michael knew she spoke slowly because she was searching for words, trying to be as honest as she could with him. "Your dad and I will always care about each other, mostly because we share *you*."

She glanced at Michael and then down again.

At that exact moment, Michael and Jennie faced everything they needed to face. It was time to stand before Cody and answer the questions they'd been asking themselves each time Michael had held her close in his arms these past few days.

The answer came swiftly. "The together part of our lives is over, Cody," Michael told his son, steeling himself not to look at Jennie. At last, at last, she would know for certain where she stood with him. "Your mom and I tried to be married once and we couldn't be. That's how we have to leave it."

The little boy's eyes, eyes that had been sparkling with happiness only minutes ago, began to fill with tears. "But—y-you come here t-together all the t-time and laugh and I thought—I thought..."

"We're here together because of you, Cody," Jennie said calmly.

Each of them realized it at the same time. They should have known they were tiring him out. Now, his expression was exhausted and forlorn, as if everything seemed insurmountable. "But I don't like you being d-divorced all—the time. I want us to live in the same h-house. I want us to live in the same p-place. I get—mad having to move around all the time—and none of my friends know where I—a-am—when they want to come p-p-play," he sobbed.

"They know where you are," Michael soothed him, but even in his own ears the words sounded insincere.

"They know you live at my house on some days and at your mom's house on others. Lots of kids do that."

Cody's voice was rising into a wail. "B-but—I d-don't *w-w-want-t-t*-tooooo."

"Darling. Darling." Jennie tried to gather him into her arms but he wouldn't go.

"I w-w-want...to...b-b-be in our old h-h-house when we were all togetherrr-rrr-r-r," he sobbed.

"Son. Cody." Michael stood above them helplessly, feeling more helpless, if that was possible, than he'd felt when Cody had first gotten sick.

"Pleeease!" Cody cried, tears running down both sides of his face. "Pleeeease like each other again and then m-m-me and M-M-Mason can stay in the same p-p-place..."

A nurse stuck her head in the door. "Is everything okay in here?"

"Yes," Jennie said firmly, holding Cody's little head on her knees. "He just got upset about something is all. He'll be fine in a while."

Michael and Jennie sized each other up. Michael could feel everything built between them during the past few days, every faint hope, every vague possibility, shattering into bits.

"I'll go," Michael said. "I don't know what else to do."

"I'll stay with him," Jennie agreed as Cody wept into the lap of her denim skirt. "I think you should."

He shrugged into his coat and bent down to Cody. "Daddy's going to go now."

But Cody wouldn't turn to him. So he left, casting one backwards glance at the two of them, Cody and

Jennie, two blond heads bent together on the bed. Then, silently, he shut the door and headed for home.

THAT NIGHT, just after eight o'clock, Jennie pounded on his door. Neither said anything until he had hung up her coat and ushered her into the den. There each took up a position facing the other and squared off like prize fighters, each sorting through a welter of feelings and having no idea what to do about them.

"Damn it, Jennie!" He slammed his fist on the fireplace mantel. "I didn't know what to say to him! 'Yes, son. I've been kissing your mom in the parking lot. What do you think about that?'"

"Well, you couldn't be honest with him. After all," she said tersely, repeating his words from only hours ago, "it didn't mean anything anyway."

"You're right. It didn't."

"They had to call an intern and sedate him."

"Why didn't we see this coming?" he asked himself aloud. "We were idiots. *Why* didn't we see it?"

"There were a great many things we didn't see, Michael."

"Dammit," Michael slammed his fist one more time. "This shouldn't have happened. Dammit, I'm sorry."

"What are you sorry for?"

He looked at her. He didn't dare voice all the things he was sorry for. "I don't even know. For kids being so intuitive. For me being transparent." He shook his head.

"It was a perfectly natural assumption for Cody to make," she said quietly. "We have been there for him. We've been there *together*."

"I know that. We've misled him."

"Have we?"

He looked directly into Jennie's eyes. And, because he was aching inside and feeling cornered, he didn't think to soften his reply. "I would not fall in love with you again, Jennie. I would not fall in love with a woman who gives cartoons and a journalism career a higher priority than *people*."

"My career was never more important than *you*. I waited..."

"I'm not talking about me. I'm talking about Buzz Stephens."

"Oh, of course you would be," she said sarcastically. "Was that his name? It's been so long ago now that *I* don't even remember."

"I'm surprised you ever even *knew*. He wasn't a person at all to you. He was just some poor fool to ruin in the paper."

She threw her purse on the floor. "His controversial medical research was being funded by taxpayers' money. My readers had a *right* to know that. That cartoon series made one of the most ground-breaking editorial statements we ever printed at the *Times-Sentinel*. You never did understand how important that was to me. It was one of my first really *big* successes."

"All I *ever* understood was that Buzz Stephens and I were friends in med school. He was one of the nicest guys and the best doctors I'd known. Because of that article, the IRS delved into the finances of his private practice and caused him a great deal of grief and embarrassment.''

"I didn't do it to him, Michael,'' she argued hopelessly. "He did it to himself.''

"You might as well have run him out of Dallas on a rail. He had to start from the ground up and build a new practice in Amarillo. *Amarillo,* for God's sake.''

"I've had enough,'' she said as she advanced on him. "Did you hear me? I said I've had *enough.* I hate private practices. I hate internships. I hate med school. I hated waiting up for you all night long. I hated your patients. I hated being in love with you and thinking I'd grow *old* and we'd never get to spend time together. You weren't even there to drive me to the hospital when I went into labor with *Cody*...''

"I met you there,'' he threw back angrily.

"After you'd finished delivering someone else's baby. I didn't even have anybody there to help me breathe. I think that's the loneliest I've ever been in my life, lying in that birthing room waiting for you.''

"I know I did that to you,'' he said bluntly. "I would probably do it again. I'm a doctor. A good one. And sometimes that doesn't leave me with choices.''

"All I ever wanted...'' She started to say it but then let the words trail off. It was just too personal to her now and too painful. *All I ever wanted,* she wanted to say, *was to know that I was important to you, that there were times you might have wanted to choose me.*

The emotions she'd managed to shut away were now all coming to the fore. "I'm *glad* Cody forced this issue, Michael. I'm *glad* he asked that question out loud so I could hear your answer. I'm vulnerable right now and hurting and disillusioned. I am *not* going to let you hurt me the way you hurt me before. I am not going to make the mistake of thinking anything might ever be different between us. And I'm not going to let *any of this* hurt Cody."

"I also want to protect that child, Jennie. So help me, I am not going to let him have any more disappointments. He's been through enough already. And he's got so many more disappointments to come." They still hadn't told Cody about the interns' assessment of his legs. Or about the surgery they couldn't decide on.

"What are we going to do?" she asked him.

"I didn't think there could be anything more painful than putting him through that divorce. I thought we were doing it the right way...." He sighed and sat down, raking his huge hands up through his blond mane of hair. "I don't want him to see us together again."

"I know that, Michael." He knew she spoke the truth. The irony of it shook him. They had *started* this, begun to draw together, for Cody's sake. And it had hurt him instead.

They stood there for the longest time, while the minutes ticked between them.

Jennie shoved her hands into her pockets, doing her best to seem nonchalant, trying to pretend that pulling away from Michael wasn't hurting her. She turned away to look out the big window overlooking the backyard.

As Michael stood watching her, seeing everything she was trying to hide, he berated himself for past mistakes. *Dear God, I really wasn't there to drive her to the hospital.* He couldn't believe he'd done that. In an instant he counted a myriad of times he'd deserted her.

Jennie turned back and searched his face. In that one moment she had a vision of years before: his clear green eyes, the cocky grin, beside her, just above her at the altar. He had been so full of youth, so full of passion for the people and patients he would serve. She had been so proud of him because of it.

"I take thee, Jennie, to have and to hold, from this day forward."

To have and to hold.

She drew herself up, aching because of what she knew she had to say. "We'll schedule our visits so we aren't at the hospital at the same time."

He nodded, never speaking.

"Michael." Her voice was softer now. "He's reading too much into our being together."

"I know that."

"We were reading too much into it, too."

"Yes." They were toying with something that would be devastating to each other. They didn't dare risk it again.

"I've needed someone during all this, Jen. Someone who understood how much I loved Cody." *And I had no right to want you to be the one... because there were so many times when you needed me...*

She stared at the ceiling for a moment, shoring herself up for the rest of it, as he studied the fine ivory arch of her neck. "I've known for a long time," she said without looking at him, now, "that it would be too easy to turn back to you when something difficult happened. We've shared our lives..." She trailed off again.

"No," he said. "Not really. We shared a bed. I don't know that we ever shared our lives."

She looked at him solemnly, feeling as if she had just lost something very important. "You're right. We didn't."

Her purse still lay on the floor. She picked it up slowly and tucked it under one arm.

He stood up and held the door open for her. There was nothing left for either of them to say.

Except goodbye.

"Goodbye, Michael," she said as she stood close.

"Goodbye, Jennie," he said.

She was wearing the winter white wool coat she'd arrived in, her gold hair fanning out in ribbons around her shoulders. Now she felt like a little lost waif standing on his porch beneath the floodlight. But neither of them could do anything now that could help or make her stay.

CHAPTER TEN

ANDY KENDALL SAT DOWN with Michael and Jennie the next day, face to face, and told them exactly how much Cody's emotional outburst had cost him. "I'd say it's a setback for him physically," she said quietly. "He's exhausted today. Our staff has decided it would be best to let him rest. We'll start his therapy again in several days . . . when he's ready."

Michael slumped against the wall, his arms crossed, his head bowed, trying not to appear as defeated as he felt. "You tell us what you think would be best, Andy." How he was beginning to hate these diplomatic words. What would be best . . . give it a try . . . read the assessment.

"Perhaps you could time your visits so you aren't with Cody at the same time," Andy suggested cautiously.

"But what about his morning therapy session?" Jennie asked. "How will we learn what we're supposed to do for him?"

"You may have to take turns coming. That's the only way I can think of to get around it. I've given it quite a bit of thought."

"That's easy enough," Michael stated.

"I have something else to discuss with you," Andy added. "Something that might not be as easy to accept."

"We want to do everything we can to help him," Jennie said, her hands folded together in her lap.

"Tell us what we can do," Michael prodded her.

"I've had a long discussion with the child-life psychologist here at the hospital. We both agree that you need to begin thinking about Cody and his home life when he leaves the hospital. His world will need to be kept very, very stable."

"He has a stable home," Michael said quickly. "In fact, he has two of them."

"That's exactly what I'm talking about," Andy answered. "The psychologist and I think the two of you need to decide to keep Cody in one home for a while. At least until he's stronger. We both believe it would be for the best."

For the best. That phrase again.

Michael felt as if every bit of his power was being stripped away. And somehow, even though the woman sitting beside him had no more control over the situation than he did, he felt as if Jennie was winning a round. What Andy was suggesting undermined their joint custody agreement.

"This is what you think he needs?" he asked Andy curtly. "How do you know what's best for him? We love him. We've given him everything we know to give him. We've paid lawyers hundreds of dollars to work things out for him this way."

Jennie, too, could not remain silent. "We've tried to be careful," she said. "We've tried to set things up so we could all three live with them." She had known all those years ago that they couldn't make this decision alone. It had taken the lawyers months to come up with the original joint custody arrangement.

"We wanted Cody to have *everything*," Michael said, his voice gravelly with emotion. Sweet heaven, the conflicts they faced now were tenfold what they had been during the divorce. He repeated it again for good measure. "We wanted him to have *everything*."

And yet, Michael reminded himself. *Cody never would have had everything he really needed since the divorce. He never would have had both of us.*

EACH TIME Jennie stopped in to see Cody, Cody talked about Michael.

"Dad came to see me last night," he said from his pillow. Jennie always suspected he was studying her face to see her reaction.

"That's nice."

"He had a talk with Mason."

"Oh?"

"He said he'd come to see Mason again this afternoon about two."

"I'm glad." She had to be back at the *Times-Sentinel* then. "How are you feeling today?"

A toothy grin this time. "Fine. Andy's been telling me about the swim team again. She says I'm getting closer."

"Great. That's my Bear!" She nuzzled him. "I can't wait. I promise you right now I'll buy you a new bathing suit."

"Yeech." He made a face. "Do I have to go to the store and try it on?"

"No." She laughed at him. He was a lot like Michael. "I wouldn't dare put you through that torture. I'll pick it out for you. I promise."

"Good."

She started on his therapy and worked with him until after one forty-five. Michael was due back any minute and she had to get back to the paper. "See you later, darling." She bent and kissed him. "Have a good visit with Dad."

This time, when Jennie left him, she felt the same as all the times before. She felt as if she hadn't done nearly enough for her son.

"DID YOU SEE that request from the *San Antonio Sun?*" Art Sanderson asked her when she got back to the office. "They want to run some of your statewide stuff."

"I saw the request."

"We may consider putting you into syndication," he said casually. "I'll bet we could get several of the biggest dailies in Texas to pick you up. It would be a step up in your career, Jennie. And a coup for the *Times-Sentinel* because we have you."

"It looked interesting."

"You don't sound as excited as I thought you'd be."

"I'm probably not as excited as you thought I'd be. My mind's just been on other things, Art."

The phone rang on her desk. She picked it up. "Stratton here."

"Jennie? Andy Kendall from the hospital is on line three."

When was her heart going to stop pounding every time a call came from the hospital? "Thanks." She heard the line switch and she immediately pounced on Andy. "What is it? What's wrong?"

"Nothing's wrong," Andy said. "I needed to talk to you and I didn't have a chance today at the hospital. I didn't want to tell you these things in front of Cody."

"What things? What is it?" Then, she heard herself. "Oh, Andy. I'm so sorry. I'm just at the office and I—"

"It's okay," Andy said. "I didn't mean to scare you. I just need to tell you what I'm feeling about Cody. This is my professional opinion, Jennie. One more of these 'you may not agree with me but I have to tell you anyway' things."

"Let's have it."

"Okay." Andy paused and took a deep breath. "The orthopedic surgeon examined Cody again today. His left leg is worse. If we're going to fight against the surgery, Cody needs more therapy time. I discussed it with Michael, too. I can only give him so much. I have other patients to work with, too."

Jennie's heart stopped for a moment. "What did Michael say?"

"He's willing to devote more time if you are. But he probably doesn't see the urgency of this matter the way you do. He told me he thinks surgery is the best answer."

"I know that." She stared at the scattered piles of memos and letters and cartoons on her desk. She stared at the full calendar that hung on the wall beside her phone. All she could think of, as she stared at it, was that things on this calendar did not go away. When she pushed them back, just as she'd been doing these past weeks, they piled up and up on top of each other until they threatened to make the entire twelve months fall off the wall.

She was blatantly honest with her answer. "I can't. I can't do any more than I'm already doing." In her mind, she was ticking off the hours. "Maybe if I came in at night. That way I could spend another two hours with him." She already gave him therapy for an hour each morning every other day and another one every day after lunch. Art had been wonderful to help her work it into her schedule. "But Cody's always tired then." The logistics of it all were staggering. Add to that an eight-hour workday that sometimes spilled over into a ten-hour one. And, despite her crazy schedule, she was lonelier than she'd ever been in her life.

She laughed, a tired little chuckle that betrayed how defeated she felt. "Maybe if I gave up sleeping, I'd have time to do everything I need to do."

"Think about it, Jennie. I don't want to push you. But we've got to come up with some workable answer. I'll try to get in to work with him a third time this evening. I don't want him to lose what he's gained. He's doing so well."

"I don't want him to, either."

Jennie hung up the phone and stared at it. *Who am I?* she asked herself while she sat glaring at the receiver, thinking of Cody lying in the bed needing her. "How much further can I stretch myself?" she asked aloud.

"What's that?" Art asked, walking toward her. "Do you remember the meeting in my office? We've been waiting for you for ten minutes in there."

"I forgot!" She jumped up from her desk, banging the drawer with her knees, and went flying into his office. But as she sat and listened to everyone's comments, all she could think of was Cody. Staff members talked about problems they were having and things that had changed and cartoon opportunities the paper had missed while she had been gone. She somberly authorized Art to send some of her work on to the *San Antonio Sun*.

After the meeting closed, Art cornered her. "Jennie? Is there a way you can rearrange your schedule to be here at noon tomorrow? I've got a photographer setting up to do some group shots of the staff. I thought we'd do some of you alone, too, and send them on to the *Sun*. That works for everyone else."

"I can't do it, Art. I can't be here at noon. That's when I give Cody his therapy."

"You can't change it? You can't do it another time?"

"No. I already go once in the morning." She was on the defensive now and she hated it. She felt guilty about it all. "I can't go after two because Michael—" She stopped. She couldn't explain it. It was just too complicated for anyone else to understand.

"I wish you could work this out for me," Art said.

"I do, too. But I can't."

I'm being overly sensitive, she decided as she marched back to her desk in the press room. She took her frustrations out on a piece of pen-and-ink paper, shading in a cartoon she'd already designed. She didn't like it when she finished. She started all over again.

I'm not doing anything right, she berated herself.

How many times in my life am I going to have to choose between Cody and Art Sanderson?

The rest of it didn't matter. It didn't matter that she never had time to sit down and read a book or write to a friend. She didn't care that she didn't have time to putter in the garden or run or go out to lunch with friends. All she cared about was Cody.

She didn't know for certain whether Michael's words made everything seem clearer today... or if today gave her new perspective on his words.

I would not fall in love with someone who gives cartoons a higher priority than people.

She sighed for the umpteenth time. *Have I done that?* she asked herself. *Have I closed people out, did I close Michael out, because I was afraid to make myself vulnerable to him again? And did I use the* Times-Sentinel *to do it?*

She didn't know the answer. She only knew she owed it to herself to ask. *I'm losing control of everything else and Cody's going downhill, too. Cody needs me. More of me. All of me.*

She buried her face in her hands and scrubbed her palms against her scalp, frighteningly close to tears. She didn't know what choice she would have made four, five, even ten years ago. But she knew what she would choose today.

Three minutes later, she stood in front of Art's office, trying to appear casual. "Do you have a minute? I have to talk to you."

"Come on in, Jennie."

She did and closed the door behind her.

He leaned back in his creaky chair with a slight frown. "What is it?"

"I'd like a leave of absence, Art. I need some time away from cartooning."

"What? Jennie, after the career you've built for yourself? This syndication from the Texas dailies could grow into something phenomenal! Take my word for it. This is not the time to disappear."

"There's never a good time to disappear."

"You could go national in a few years. We could send you to Washington, D.C."

At any other time in her life, Art's words and talk of "might be's" would have tormented her. But not today...not now...not with Michael's words still echoing inside her head. "I know all those things, Art." Suddenly, she felt very, very tired and afraid. This decision was something totally new to her. She would never have considered it before.

Art took a breath and gave her his most genial smile. "We don't have to decide this today, Jennie," he told her gently. "Take the time to think about it. Give yourself some breathing room. You're putting all this pressure on yourself when you don't have to."

"I'm not putting pressure on myself."

"You're doing this because of what's happened to Cody?"

"Yes."

"You've got other options. Consider those. Hire a private nurse."

"A nurse isn't the same thing as a mom. Right now Cody needs a mom." And, to her surprise, the more she argued for it, the more she knew in her heart of hearts that she was right. "Perhaps someday I can come back to all this. But this career is not as important as my little boy. It never was and it never will be."

"I think you're making an emotional decision at a very bad time, Jennie."

"Cody needs me. He needs me beside him at the hospital. When he gets out, he needs me driving him back and forth to outpatient care. He needs me to do therapy about five times a day." And Andy was still talking to her about getting him on to Mark's swim team but they hadn't set a date for that yet.

"Do yourself a favor. Sleep on this. Don't do anything drastic."

"It isn't drastic, Art. It's just a leave of absence. It's something I have to do."

"It's bad timing."

She gathered all her strength. "If you'll give me a leave of absence, I'll take it, Art. If you won't, I'll resign. This is *that* important to me."

"God forbid, no! You can't do that. Jennie, your *career.*"

"It's going to be tough," she said, with a little smile. She could tell by his expression he was going to give in to her. "Cody and I'll have to learn how to live on a lot less money.'' A *lot* less. But it could be done. She would just have to stop serving microwave dinners and bake some real food like chicken and potatoes and meat loaf. And she was certain Michael would help her if things got too bad. ''It's worth trying, Art.''

He smiled sadly. ''I can see you think so.''

Before, this would have been the very moment she gave in to her own self-doubts. Now she knew how much was at stake for her and for her son. ''I do.''

''Okay,'' Art said. ''I'll give you three months.''

''Six months.''

''You're kidding.''

''I've never been more serious in my life. I can't *afford* to kid about this. I'm working at keeping my priorities straight.''

''Negotiating with you is like negotiating with a brick wall, Jennie. Don't say I didn't try to talk you out of this. So clean out your desk. I'll have to hire somebody else for six months. Stay in touch.''

She was practically beaming. ''I will.'' And then, abandoning her professional reserve, she hugged him. ''Goodbye, Art!''

He hugged her back, his expression rueful. ''Call me if you change your mind.''

''I won't,'' she called back to him blithely.

In forty-five minutes, her desk was bare. She loaded her car full of cardboard boxes of awards and port-folios and framed letters and was on her way... to a new life... a new place... where her son was waiting for her.

THE FIRST PLACE she stopped to relay her news was the child-life center on the bottom floor of Children's Medical Center. The hospital staff counselor, a young, energetic psychologist who couldn't have been more than a year out of school, told Jennie she'd done the right thing. "Thanks," she said quietly. "I know I did. I've never felt better about anything in my whole life."

She couldn't wait to tell Cody. "Hey, little guy!" she greeted him. "I've just done something *wonderful*. I quit my job for a while so you and I can hang around together!"

"Really, Mom?" He beamed at her, eyes enormous.

"I thought we'd play checkers on the bed and tell more stories and have more therapy," she told him. "What do you think?"

"I think you're the best mom in the whole world."

"Good," she said, kissing him. "That's exactly what I was hoping you'd think."

Andy swept out of the next room, clipboard in hand. "Hi, Jennie."

"What time does Cody need his next therapy session?" Jennie asked, as excited as a little girl waiting for a friend's birthday party. "I'm here to do it. And I'll be here tomorrow. And the next day. And the next and the next and the next . . ."

Andy started to grin. "What have you done?"

"Took a leave of absence. Told them if they wouldn't let me have a leave of absence I'd just quit."

"Good for you! Oh, Jennie, did you really?"

"I did. I blew my editor's mind."

"You've blown mine." Andy grabbed her arm. "Are you doing anything after you give Cody his therapy? I've got to go to the Galleria and get a present for my brother. Maybe we can go to lunch, talk about something besides the hospital and interns and surgery for a while."

Jennie laughed, a happy sound that let Andy know what a weight had been lifted from her shoulders.

"I'd love to go with you. It's been about a year since I've done anything spontaneous and gone shopping with a friend."

Later that afternoon, they strolled through the Galleria, watching the ice skaters spin on flashing blades, two friends now, two women on common ground.

Andy led them to a little shop filled with sports logos on rugs and underwear and dog collars and even Christmas ornaments. "Is your brother a football fan?" Jennie asked.

"No," Andy said, leading her to one specific corner. "A soccer fan." Everything on the shelves here was emerald green and white, emblozoned with the words: Dallas Sidekicks.

"Look at these." Jennie pointed to a collection of beer steins imprinted with the team's logo. "Those are beautiful. Cody had played soccer every summer. Has Mark always liked the Sidekicks?"

"No," Andy said, her voice quiet again, enough for Jennie to notice it. "He had occasion to meet somebody on the team. After that, he really became a fanatic."

"Who? Who did he meet?"

It was still so hard for her to say his name. "Buddy Draper."

"*The* Buddy Draper? Gosh, he was great! I'm not a big soccer fan myself but I loved watching him play. That was too bad about the car accident he had."

"Yes," Andy agreed tonelessly as she moved away up the next aisle. "It was." She took a box of steins from the shelf and started toward the register. "I'm going to get these. They're just right."

Jennie followed her. "Didn't he get hurt badly in the accident? He never played again after that, did he?"

"No. And no." Andy paid for Mark's gift. "He never played again. And he didn't get hurt badly in the accident. He got hurt just badly enough that he couldn't be the *best* anymore."

"Is that what you heard?"

"Yes. Sort of."

"What do you mean, sort of?"

"Are you ready to go?" Andy asked, perking up with some effort.

"I'm ready," Jennie told her. "Let's get back to the hospital. I'm ready for *therapy* again." She raised one fist and shook it like a muscle man. But as she followed Andy outside, she asked her again about Buddy Draper.

Andy realized she had no choice but to answer her new friend. "That's why *I* think he stopped playing. Jennie, he told me he wanted to play soccer more than anything. Then, one day, he decided he didn't want that anymore. I don't know what happened. He was doing time trials on the field and getting ready for the next season. Maybe the coach pushed him. I didn't want him to stop playing and I pushed him, too."

Something in her tone must have told Jennie there was more. "Why would a famous soccer player come to Children's Medical Center for therapy?"

"Because he already knew me."

"From before."

"From long before." And then Andy decided to finally tell Jennie the rest of it. "We were seeing each other."

They climbed into the car and slammed the doors. "Oh," Jennie said, looking embarrassed. "I had to ask."

"Yeah. You did."

Jennie shook her head. "Maybe you're lucky you never got any further than that. Look where marriage got me." But she had memories of Michael she would always treasure. And she had Cody, too.

Andy saluted Jennie with the bag of steins. "Right back where you started . . . and I started . . . I think." Then she sobered. "Can I ask a nosy question?"

"You can ask it. I might not answer it."

"You and Dr. Stratton? Did you ever think about trying things again?"

The hesitation wasn't even perceptible. "No."

"You're both doing so much for Cody," Andy observed.

"It's been a battle every step of the way. Look at the surgery. He wants it. I'm dead set against it. Look at two weeks ago when we upset Cody so badly." Yet, after Cody had come out of the sedation, he had been fine.

"Can I ask you something else?"

"What?"

"What happened in your marriage? What made things go wrong between you?"

It was Jennie's turn to sigh. "What happened between Michael and me was very, very subtle," she finally said. "When we took our wedding vows, it's as if we vowed to be in each other's lives but not in each other's hearts. We were so young. We thought a career and money and a rewarding life-style were supposed to come easy. A *relationship* was supposed to come easy. But it's not like that. It really never was, you know?"

Andy nodded. "Thinking back to it, I must have just grown disappointed in Buddy. I have to watch these kids trying so hard every day for every little victory they achieve. Buddy is so talented and I felt like he wasn't trying at all. I went through this time when I couldn't understand him anymore."

"Michael worked thirty-six-hour shifts during his internship at Parkland. I was supposed to be this newlywed with blushing cheeks, welcoming him home with open arms. I never saw him except when he was exhausted and strung out and too drained to give any attention to what we had. So I turned around and channelled all my frustration into my work. I worked the same horrible shifts he did, only I did come home for a few hours to sleep, which he couldn't do. Then, when I got pregnant with Cody, I thought things would be different. I thought the baby would make us both different. But it didn't. It just got harder."

"Didn't you ever talk about it?"

"Sometimes. But not soon enough, Andy. Not soon enough. I wasn't there when he graduated med school. He wasn't there when I went into labor with Cody. It's like we just quietly needed each other without crying out. And then, one day, there was just too much pain between us...so much pain...something we could never overcome. And we blamed each other for it."

"End of story."

"End of story."

"But you are both there for Cody now," Andy said softly.

"It's different," Jennie said, almost whispering, too. "Very different than it ever used to be."

CHAPTER ELEVEN

"BILL," Michael told his patient sternly as they sat together in the consultation room, Michael's white coat unbuttoned over his shirt and tie, "Your blood pressure's sky high again. Have you been taking your pills?"

"Did for a while, Doc," Bill Josephs told him smugly. "Then I decided they weren't doing me a lick of good. Didn't make me feel better at all. In fact, I started feeling a lot better after I quit those things."

Michael shook his head and wagged a finger at Bill. "You are the most stubborn patient I've got. If I didn't like you so much, I'd pawn you off on some other physician."

"Well, why take medicine if it doesn't make you feel good?"

"Those pills *do* take some of your energy away, Bill. For your heart's sake, you've got to keep your blood pressure down. Have you been resting?"

Bill nodded. "Yep. Feel like I'm four years old again but I'm doing it because you told me I had to."

"Good. Are you walking?"

"Nope. I've been riding one of my horses. And I've been fishing a lot. Figured that would make up the difference. You should see the seventeen-pound carp

I caught the other day. Biggest sucker to come out of Lake Sam Rayburn in a long time!"

"Have you been drinking decaffeinated coffee?"

"Don't ask me about the coffee."

Michael laid his chart down on his lap. What exactly could he write in his records about Bill Josephs after *this* checkup? "You've been drinking it."

"Of course I've been drinking it. Had to have something to jump-start me after those pills you gave me. They made me feel like Marge's old Aunt Enid."

"Is she a relative in Dallas?"

"No, sir." Michael saw Bill's eyes sparkling and he knew the man was about to crack another joke. "She died back in 1957," Bill said, chuckling. "That's why I don't want to feel like her."

Shaking his head ruefully, Michael wrote out another prescription and handed it to him. "I should call Marge in here and tell her you've been disobeying my orders."

"Don't do that," Bill said. "I won't ever hear the end of it."

"I know that. I'm giving you a reprieve. This is a different prescription. These pills aren't quite so potent. I think they'll work better for you. And—" he wagged a finger again, feeling like a schoolmarm "—if *these* don't work, call me and we'll find something that does."

Bill raised his eyebrows. "Thanks, Doc. I'd just as soon not get Marge involved in all this. I love that old woman but she's stubborn. Won't let me do things my own way."

"I know that. That's what I like about her. I know she'll make you follow my instructions."

"We'll see you next month," Bill said, putting an old tweed hat on his head. "Don't send me a bill. I'll pay out front."

"Shelby Landon's charts are on your desk, Dr. Stratton," his nurse told him as he followed Bill into the hallway.

"Thanks, Inez. Do you want to get the MMR ready for room four."

"I will."

"Thanks."

Michael went to his office, picked up the little girl's charts and thumbed through them. Clipboard in hand, he opened the door to room four and faced a young mother with a toddler in her arms. "Hi," he said smiling. He had delivered Shelby sixteen months ago. He took the little girl in his arms. "I can't believe she's grown so much." He held Shelby out from him so he could look her straight in the eyes. "Shelby," he told her, "you're going to be in college before we know it."

"Oh, no," her mother said, laughing. "Don't rush her. She's just learning to talk!"

He sat on his stool with Shelby in his lap. "Okay," he said jovially. "One thing at a time. We'll let you learn to speak first. We'll deal with the valedictorian speech later." He handed Mrs. Landon a pink page full of instructions. "Let's discuss this sixteen-month MMR inoculation."

"I'm concerned about the side effects," Shelby's mother said. "Tell me what to expect."

"Well," he said, tickling the little girl, remembering Cody when he had been her age. "You can expect her to run a low-grade fever. We'll give her a dose of acetaminophen. In about ten days, she could *possibly* have a light case of the measles. Chances of that are pretty small."

Inez came in to administer the injection and Michael showed Mrs. Landon how to hold Shelby in her lap with the girl's little leg securely tucked between her own. Shelby took the shot like every other child. She waited a moment, let the pain sink in and started to wail.

Michael held her again when Inez was finished. "There you go, little one," he said gently. "It won't hurt but for a minute."

Shelby looked right up at him and gave him a great big grin. Then she grabbed his glasses and started to chew on them. "Call me if you have questions," he told her mother. "I can always be reached at this office number." He scribbled his initials on the bill and handed it to Inez.

I do care about my patients, he thought. *But I don't care about them as much as I care about my family.* But it niggled at him now, the words Jennie had said. Because he couldn't be sure he'd always felt that way. If he was brutally honest with himself, he'd admit there were times he'd gone for days working and not thinking of Jen.

He shrugged out of his lab coat and shoved his keys into his pocket. "See you tomorrow, Inez," he called out to her. "I'm going to visit Cody."

WHEN MICHAEL GOT to the hospital, he told Cody about all of his patients, including Bill, and they laughed together. But for some reason, the laughter wasn't as much fun without Jennie around.

"Did you know you were gonna be a doctor when you were little? When you were my age?" Cody asked him as they sat watching TV.

"Mmm." Michael thought for a minute before he answered. "You know what? I guess I did." He gave one short little chuckle, remembering. "I shouldn't tell you this but I used to bring all kinds of animals home when I was a boy. I always tried to doctor them and make them better. I brought home frogs, a mouse and a turtle. I did okay until your grandmother found a dead cardinal under the bed."

"Oooh. A redbird?" Cody leaned forward intrigued, the television forgotten. "Did it die under your bed? Couldn't you make it better?"

Michael shook his head, remembering the boyish seriousness with which he had approached his task. "I was about your age, Cody. It was dead when I found it. I didn't understand some things then. I thought if I treated it I could bring it back to life."

"Even *I* know you can't do *that*."

"Well, I thought I could do it. It's one of the hardest things a doctor has to face, you know? That you can't bring anything back to life once its life has been taken away." He gripped his son's hand, feeling sudden tears rising in his eyes, pushing the emotion down within him. It was the first time he thought to be grateful, truly grateful, that his son was alive. "I love you, kid."

"I love you, too, Dad."

They squeezed hands.

"So what did Grandma do when she found the red-bird under your bed?"

"She hollered at me."

"Why? You were just trying to help it."

"She thought every bird had mites. And that bird did. She found mites all over the carpet."

"Mom would kill me if she found mites all over the carpet at her house."

"Your mom would kill *me*," Michael said, laughing. "She knows this story from way back. She'd know you were taking after me." He surveyed his son seriously, his heart filled with pride and sorrow. "You think you want to be a doctor when you grow up?"

"No. I don't want to be a doctor. I don't want to be gone from home all the time like you are."

His answer might as well have been a kick in the stomach. Michael looked away, trying to compose himself.

Was I gone so much that it even mattered to Cody? Of course. Of course I was. And it mattered to Jennie, too.

He turned back to his son. "What do you want to be when you grow up?"

"A professional snow-boarder."

"Right."

"Or maybe a professional roller-blader."

"Right."

"Or maybe—"

"I think you'd better stop," Michael told him. "You're going to give me nightmares."

"Or maybe I'll just be a professional bull-rider in the rodeo. Just like the ones we saw last winter when you took me to the stock show in Fort Worth."

"Cody..."

"Just kidding, Dad," Cody said, his little bowed lips grinning and his eyes smiling, too. And then he struggled to hold his arms out to Michael. "Love you."

WHEN JENNIE STEPPED outside the elevator toward Cody's room, she heard Michael's deep, booming voice from all the way down the hallway. "She hollered at me."

"Why? You were just trying to help it."

"She thought every bird had mites. And that bird did. She found mites all over the carpet."

"Mom would kill me if she found mites all over the carpet at her house."

"Your Mom would kill *me*. She knows this story from way back. She'd know you were taking after me."

She didn't intend to eavesdrop. She just didn't have anywhere else to go. So she stood outside, listening to them laughing, feeling cut off from them, until the door opened and Michael stepped out. Closing the door quietly behind him, he leaned back against the wall and wiped his eyes with the back of one hand. *Was he crying?*

It didn't occur to Jennie to be embarrassed or to slip away. She stood silently watching him until he realized she was there. He rocked forward on his feet, his hands in his pockets, and turned toward her.

She gave him a little shrug. "I was just about to go in and see him."

He jangled his keys in his pocket. Then he shook his head. "I'm sorry, Jen. I didn't mean for you to see me that way again. I'm trying to be stronger."

She took one step forward. "It's okay. It's hard for me, too."

Michael rode one thumb back over his shoulder, pointing toward the room where Cody lay. "*He's* the bravest one of all."

"No, he isn't," she said quietly. "He just doesn't know to be afraid."

Michael stared at the ceiling. "I want him to get better. I want him to grow stronger."

"So do I."

They stood for a moment looking at one another, each of them thinking it had been a long time since their wants had been so entirely focused on the same thing. "I asked Art Sanderson for a leave of absence this morning," Jennie said.

His eyes shot to hers. "You did?"

She nodded.

Michael stared at her in disbelief. "What did you say to him?"

"That my son was more important—" she looked at him pointedly "—than cartooning."

"That was it? That was all there was to it?"

"That was it. I cleaned my desk out this morning." She shrugged her shoulders, half disbelieving it herself. "I didn't even give them an hour's notice. I just took off. And that may have been the easy part. I'll have to learn how to get by on my savings for a while. I'll miss the money."

"I'll help you. You know that." In their divorce settlement, he'd agreed to give her alimony if she ever stopped working. He hadn't begrudged her that at all. But he couldn't believe she'd really done it. Until now, the *Times-Sentinel* had meant everything to her. "Jennie." He didn't have to say anything more. He knew she understood how much he admired her.

"I know. It's amazing, isn't it? I told him if he didn't give me a six-month leave, I'd just quit. And he *gave* it to me. Just like that." She snapped her fingers.

"But your job, Jen? It was so important to you."

"Cody needs more therapy."

"You know I'm helping with that."

"He needs more attention than ever now... especially if we're going to avoid the surgery."

"That's what you're thinking of? Avoiding the surgery?"

"It's what I'm always thinking of now."

"I see." Into his mind came the doubts once more. Had Jennie left her job to support Cody, or had she done it so she might win her way?

"I can always go back to the *Times-Sentinel* in six months or so. I haven't burned any bridges." But she didn't really know how long Cody was going to need her. Maybe six months. Maybe forever. She sighed. "I got to thinking you were right. I shouldn't have let my work become so all-important. Maybe I should have given Cody a higher priority a long time ago."

He just stood looking down at her, looking perplexed and slightly hopeful as she spoke. "I miss you, you know," he said finally. "It helped, spending time with you."

"I know," she replied softly. "Me, too."

CHAPTER TWELVE

"HI, CODY." His best friend, Taylor Cowan, stood at the foot of his bed. "We miss you at school. I came over so I could bring you some stuff."

"I miss everybody at school, too. What did you bring?"

Taylor emptied his pockets and came up with a roll of cherry Life Savers, three football cards with Dallas Cowboy players on them, a quarter—"for the video machines at the hospital," Taylor explained—and a letter from his teacher, Mrs. Bounds.

"Dear Cody," the letter said. "We want you to know we're thinking about you every day. Your mom called the principal and we know you were very sick. Taylor promised to deliver this letter to you. Someday soon, we'd like to bring the class to visit you. We take a tour of Children's Medical Center every year. It's a nice hospital. When you get home, our school has a special bus that will come to your house and pick you up. In geography, we're studying Africa. We're learning about a troop of baboons that lives in the desert of Namibia. They can survive without water by eating berries and figs. It has been an interesting study. Love, Mrs. Bounds." Right behind the letter was a piece of green construction paper, signed by everybody in his class, that said Get Well Soon.

"I'll get one of the nurses to tape this on the wall," Cody said.

"My mom says you can come over to our house and spend the night," Taylor said. "I asked her."

"I can't walk around very much," Cody told him.

"That's okay. We can still play."

"Yeah. I guess you're right. I'll ask my mom. Or my dad." He frowned slightly. "I don't know where I'll be. I'll probably be at Mom's on Fridays."

Taylor pointed at the big bunny sitting up on a shelf beside the bed. "You still sleep with him?"

"Yeah. But just when I'm at the hospital. I won't when I go home. To Mom's. Or Dad's."

Just then, Andy came in. "Well, hello," she said to both boys.

"This is Taylor," Cody said. "He came to visit me. He brought me a letter from my teacher and all this stuff." He made one sweeping motion with his arm that thrilled Andy. Two weeks ago, he hadn't been able to move his arms nearly as well.

"Looks like you're having a good time." She grinned at Taylor. "You want to stay while Cody has his therapy?"

"Yeah, sure." Taylor stood on tiptoe, leaning over, his small freckled nose propped right on top of the chair where he'd been sitting. "I do wanna see this."

Andy began working with Cody's left leg.

"How come you're giving me therapy now?" Cody asked. "I thought we always just did this in the morning."

"The orthopedist is coming to check you out in a little while. I found out an hour ago that she's got you on her schedule tonight." As she worked, she asked the boys more questions, not wanting Cody to sense just yet how very important this doctor's examination might be. "So, does Taylor live close to you?"

"He lives close to my mom. I'm going to spend the night with him when I get out of the hospital."

"Do you guys really sleep when you spend the night or do you talk all night long?"

Taylor started giggling. "We talk all night long."

"That's what I figured."

AN HOUR LATER, the orthopedic surgeon arrived to examine Cody, flexing Cody's toes and rotating his leg while Jennie and Michael watched from opposite sides of the room. Andy had called them both when she'd seen Dr. Phillips' schedule.

"Don't know," the surgeon said as she splayed the bones of Cody's foot apart with gentle pressure. She watched closely as he flattened the limb against the heel of her hand. The examination lasted a few more minutes. When it was done, Dr. Phillips asked Michael, Jennie and Andy to accompany her to an empty lounge. Turning toward them, she glanced at Jennie, then her eyes leveled on Michael's. "I have to tell you, I still think surgery is the best option for the boy," she told them seriously. "I think it would be best. But it's fair to tell you that there's room here for doubt."

Jennie drew a deep, deep breath, holding it for an interminable length of time. Michael felt his annoyance growing. Why couldn't Dr. Phillips decide something? Why couldn't she just tell them what was right and best for Cody? Why couldn't she just end it all by saying: "Dr. Stratton. You're always right. She's been wrong all along. For Cody, surgery is the only way out."

Andy stepped forward and addressed Dr. Phillips boldly. "Cody is as limber as he can get. If you can't make an assessment this way, I'd suggest a series of X rays. We'll know how the bones are angling if we do it that way."

"Is the patient up to doing X rays tonight?"

"I don't see any reason why not."

"I'll order them."

"Okay." Andy didn't know whether to turn toward Jennie or toward Michael, so she spun around to include them both. "I'll go in to the X ray room with him. I can keep him limber, and I can help hold him in position."

Michael and Jennie nodded, and Dr. Phillips left the room.

Michael paced back and forth like a caged cat. He stood gazing out the window for a moment, then he brought his fist down on the radiator. It wasn't hot enough to burn him, but, still, he was so angry he didn't feel any heat at all. "She did not tell us anything," he said. "She didn't tell us *one* damn *thing*."

"I pushed her when I suggested the X rays," Andy said. "Dr. Phillips will still have the final recommendation. This way, the two of you will have something concrete to examine, something you can look at and *see....*"

What Michael could look at and see right now was the woman directly across the room from him, standing ramrod straight, her shoulders at a slight angle to him. It seemed as if the disagreement over Cody's surgery represented everything in the world that stood between them. And, in a way, it did.

She must have felt his eyes on her. She looked up, caught his glance, then looked away again. "Yes," she said, her cheeks turning red. "It's a good idea. Thank you, Andy."

Fifteen minutes later, someone from X ray called them all down. Michael and Jennie stood outside the doorway while Andy went in with Cody to ready him for the procedure. Then they followed their son and Andy down to the X-ray lab on the first floor.

"This is just dandy." Michael poked both hands into his pockets. He jangled the assortment of keys and coins there. He was desperate to find something to do with his hands. "All this time as a doctor and I never knew how helpless a *patient* feels at times like these. That woman should have been able to tell us *something*."

"You aren't the patient," Jennie reminded him. "You're the patient's father."

"It's the same difference."

She said softly, "Sometimes I think it's even worse."

He let out a deep, shuddering sigh. "You know I only want the best for him, don't you?"

She smiled sadly, wearily, looking once more into Michael's eyes. "And yet, we're at odds with each other..."

He had to say it. "You could agree with me, for once. You could change it then."

But she was shaking her head. "No, Michael. Not about something as important as this."

A pause. "You never were willing to compromise."

She bristled again. "Is this the point where you remind me of all my bad character traits?"

"That isn't what I'm doing."

"You're telling me I'm stubborn."

"I'm telling you," he said, "that it took eight years and a deadly disease for you to finally realize what your priorities are."

"Damn it, Michael! Think about me! This all began because I needed something to fill my hours the way the hospital filled yours! Don't you think I look at that little boy in there and know I made a mistake when I let the paper take over my life? At first all I wanted was to be there for you, Michael." She said it again as if to make certain he'd heard her. "It was *all* I wanted."

"Then where the hell were *you* when I needed you, Jennie? There were weeks I'd come home from the hospital needing you and you might as well not have even been there."

"I said at first," she replied tonelessly.

Her controlled stoicism only made him angrier. "Did you *once* stop to consider that I had no other choices then? Did you once stop to consider that we might not have any choice now?"

She backed up against the wall, eyes half closed, looking utterly drained, almost ready to slide down to the floor. "No," she told him forlornly. "No, I didn't stop to consider that. I'm sorry."

"Well, you should be. You and I both know things don't always work out the way you want them to. You can't take this Pollyanna approach to Cody. You've got to *accept* what he's facing. And, when you do, then we have to discuss *real,* practical solutions. Do you think I—"

"I said I was sorry."

"We're getting Cody the best care possible. Everything that can be done for him is being done."

"You only have that much confidence because you're a doctor," she said. *Because you're a doctor.* Her favorite line. But, this time, he didn't hear quite so much accusation in her voice. "I know the doctors are doing their best, and so are we. But we're both seeing things in black-and-white here when there might be a thousand gray areas we're missing..."

The door to X-ray swung open and out came an intern pushing Cody's wheelchair. Andy followed close behind him.

Michael and Jennie both waylaid her at once.

"What did she say?" Jennie asked.

"When will we know something?" Michael asked.

"I only spoke to Dr. Phillips briefly. She came in to sign the orders. She has surgery first thing tomorrow morning, and she won't have time to look at these until her office hours are over tomorrow."

"It's still going to be over twenty-four hours before we *know* anything?" Michael felt ready to hit something with his fist again.

"At least."

"She didn't say anything at *all?*" Jennie asked. "She didn't give you any indication which way she was leaning?"

"Not about the surgery." But then Andy brightened. "She *did* say one thing."

"What?" they asked in unison.

"She spoke with the interns on Cody's case. No matter what she decides to recommend about the surgery, she agrees it is time to release Cody. It's time for Cody to go home." And she turned to follow the intern and Cody, her footsteps brisk along the corridor and around the corner.

HOME. *Home?* And which home might that be? Michael and Jennie hadn't managed to sort that one out yet. They'd been too preoccupied with Cody's surgery.

"We'll have to decide, won't we?" Jennie asked.

Exhausted, they stood just staring at each other. "There are times," Michael said succinctly, "when I wish I could just give up... when I could let my defenses down... but I can't."

"I know," Jennie agreed. "There's no end to it."

A long bench lined one wall of the corridor. She sat down. Michael sat beside her.

"I'm selfish and I know it." She studied the spackled ceiling as if it were the most intriguing thing she'd ever seen. "I can't give him up, Michael. I want him *home* with *me.*"

"I can't do it, either. Jennie, I fought for him harder than I've fought for anything. He's my life, Jen. He's the only thing I've got. You know that."

She nodded.

"We're moving forward, I guess." She gave him the slightest glance and a wry smile. "If we can't agree, at least we can be honest with each other."

"Yeah," he said. His voice sounded cracked. He cleared his throat and tried again. "Yeah." Clearer this time, his voice still soft, but low and disconcerting.

Just as she was about to stand, Michael reached out and caught her elbow. She gasped in surprise and turned her head slightly away.

"Jennie?"

She hesitated fractionally before answering. "What?"

"I wouldn't put you through this," he told her softly. "I'd stop hurting you if I could."

"It seems there's no end to that, either."

"It should have been over a long time ago," he said, increasing the pressure on her elbow.

"But it isn't," she replied, the tears pooling in her eyes. "It won't ever end."

His thumb was rough on her bare arm and she shivered. "Perhaps—" She didn't lift her face, yet he knew she could feel him watching her "—someday it will."

His words still hung between them when they rose finally. Neither spoke in the elevator or during the walk back to Cody's room along long corridors. Michael remained painfully aware of Jennie's body close beside his.

"Michael, I've got an idea." She would never have suggested this, would never have even considered it, except for the things Michael had said about stopping the hurt. "What if Cody still changed houses but we gave him longer in each place? What if he spends two weeks with me, then two weeks with you? Then we could go back to the other schedule when he's stronger."

"Two weeks with you? Two weeks with you first?"

"I didn't say that. I was just giving an example."

They'd stopped two doors from Cody's room. "Maybe. It might be an answer."

Andy stepped out of Cody's room, her clipboard pressed to her chest, and shut the door behind her. "Tomorrow at 6:30 p.m.," she told them. "Dr. Phillips will meet you in her office. She'll be able to tell you something then." Then she scurried off to another appointment. Jennie wondered fleetingly if she ever found the time to go home.

"ANDREA KENDALL was right to suggest the X rays," Dr. Phillips told Jennie and Michael the following evening. "I liked what I saw there. At the present time, Cody has at least a thirty percent range in his muscle movement. That's borderline. It doesn't mean surgery is out of the question . . . say in the next three months or so. But, for right now, I have to say we'd be better off to leave well enough alone."

"You mean it?" It never occurred to Jennie to say "I told you so." She was too happy right now to even think of it. Three more months. Three more blessed months. If she worked hard enough until then, the surgery might never happen.

Jennie and Michael went to Cody's room and carefully explained the situation to him. They had thought he might be frightened, but he just grinned.

"I told you, Mom," Cody said, his tousled blond hair sticking straight up from his cowlick like the crown on a rooster. "I told you I'd show Dr. Phillips a thing or two. See. Here's one." He pointed to one leg. Then he pointed to the other. "And here's two."

Michael left the room before Jennie. But five minutes later, after Jennie had kissed Cody goodnight, she found Michael still waiting for her.

"Hey." He was leaning against the wall just outside the door. "You were right, at least for the time being. You should be rubbing it in."

"Rubbing it in?"

"I'm glad that you were so stubborn," he said, allowing his gaze to linger on her for the longest time. "We might have done the wrong thing."

She realized that, in his indirect way, he was apologizing to her. "Thank you, Michael," she said. She didn't really want to leave him now. She wished they could go someplace and celebrate.

"We'll have to deal with it again," he reminded her kindly.

"If I've learned anything through this—" Jennie spread her hands wide, palms up "—it's to take things as they come. I'm going to work my butt off and I'll worry about that part of it when it gets here."

"What did Andy say?" he asked.

"Three days. He'll be leaving the hospital in three days. I'm going to hire a lady to do some of the housework. That way I can spend extra time with Cody on his therapy."

"I've hired a nurse to stay in the house with him and do his therapy with him while I'm gone."

"Michael . . ." So it was coming to this again. "Let him be with me first. I'm going to be *home*."

When he heard her words, his face fell. "Jennie, I can't. You know that. I want him, too." The thought that came to her then plunged him into despair. *He doesn't trust me with him. And that's what we lost between us so long ago.*

The physical attraction was easy.

Trust wasn't.

"Jennie," he said. "Can't you let go some? I'm not going to let what he's gained so far slip away. And I'm not going to let him slip away from you." He nodded, as if he wanted to make her copy him and nod, too. "He'll be okay. He's a resilient kid. He's certainly proven that."

"Then let him come with me. I've got him all signed up for swim class. I can start taking him next week."

"So can I."

"You mean the person you *hired* can start taking him next week."

Really that wasn't the issue and they both knew it. He was willing to let Jennie come and help if she wanted to. But they'd both decided long ago that when the time came for Cody to leave the hospital, it would be best to keep their lives separate.

"This is ridiculous, you know," Michael told her. "We're both adults." He was rummaging in his pockets again. While she watched him, he pulled out a quarter. "I'm not so sure we aren't both wrong. Cody will get along with whatever we decide, unless we drive him nuts doing it."

"He's withstood a lot. I don't see any reason he should have to go through more conflict."

"Then are you willing to try it this way?"

"You want to *flip* a quarter for him?" she asked, aghast.

"I want everything to be perfectly fair for both of us."

"Nothing in life is fair, Michael. One of us will win. One of us will lose."

"This is the best way I can think of." And, suddenly, for Michael, that seemed very, very important. She recognized that he wanted to be completely equitable for both their sakes. "We probably should have done it this way when we got divorced. We wouldn't have ended up knowing so many rich lawyers."

She waved one small hand in the air. "Do it then." She gripped both of her elbows with her hands and squeezed. "This will decide it." She made a vow to stick by the result of the coin toss, no matter what the outcome.

"You call it, Jennie."

"I will."

Michael held out his hand, closed his eyes and sent the coin flying.

"Heads," she called as the quarter flew through the air. It hit the tile floor, bounced twice, then rolled across the terrazzo. It spun around three times in smaller and smaller concentric circles. Then it finally fell.

They walked over to it together, each of them peering to see what it was, before he bent to pick it up.

Jennie said it aloud first. "Tails." Her voice broke but she gained control of it. "He goes with you."

"Tails." Michael looked torn between joy at his good fortune and sympathy for Jennie. "Jen . . ."

"You said it yourself." She shrugged but he knew she was devastated. "It was an unbiased way to decide.

"You and I," she stated simply, "have always been out for ourselves. Since the beginning and maybe even before that. You got what you wanted. No matter what I sacrificed, he's going home with you first."

Michael had no reply. "I'm sorry, Jennie," was all he could say. "I know how much you love Cody."

"You don't know what's inside me, Michael. You never did. You never tried to know."

He closed his eyes at the sting of her words. "If I had tried, Jennie, you wouldn't have let me."

She looked up at him, her face still as a statue, her features so stiff they might as well have been etched in marble. "What does it matter now, anyway?"

MICHAEL DIDN'T SEE Jennie again until three days later, when she came to the hospital on the morning of their son's discharge.

"Well, Bear," she said as cheerily as if she were sending Cody off to camp. "Be good for your dad. Make sure he takes you to swimming on Tuesday. Andy's brother will be there. It'll be fun. If you need something and your dad's not around, call me. Sound good?"

"Yeah."

She rumpled his spikes of hair so close to the color of her own. "Love you."

"I love you, too, Mom."

"Your dad's going to bring you to group therapy with Andy these next two weeks. Be sure and work hard."

"I will."

"Where's Mason? Do you have Mason?"

"He's in the suitcase. Dad packed him."

"This kid weighs a ton," Michael said as he stood with Cody draped across his arms. "Do you mind if I set him in the car?" He gave her a reassuring smile, trying to say with his expression what she would never accept in words. *I know this is hard for you. I'm glad you came.*

"No," she said. Her laughter sounded too happy, forced and brittle, like something that might break. "I don't mind at all. You two had better get out of here."

He hoisted Cody higher. They were halfway to the car before Michael heard Jennie running behind them.

"Wait!" she called out breathlessly. He turned to see her trailing a plastic bag from F.A.O. Schwartz in one hand, her face pink. "I forgot! I've got things for him."

Michael reached his car. He tried to fit his keys in the lock but couldn't while he held Cody.

"Here... Michael," she sang out as she caught up with them. "Wait. Let me get the door, okay? Here." She took the keys from his hand and quickly unlocked it.

"Thanks, Jen."

He bent in and settled Cody on the passenger side.

"I forgot all this stuff," she said, still panting slightly. "Presents." She handed them in to Cody, then backed away. "You can open them when you get home, Cody. I know you two are in a hurry now."

Michael leaned back against the sleek fender of his black BMW and crossed his arms. "We aren't in that big of a hurry. Now that I've gotten him into a seat, I mean. He can open them here if he likes."

No words of agreement came from Cody. They both looked to see him already ripping open the first box. "A new bathing suit!" the little boy cried. "Gee, Mom, this is great!" He held it up to show Michael the fire red suit with the green plastic palm tree on one leg. "This thing is really stylin'!"

"It *is* a great suit," Michael said, conceding to her good taste where boys' clothing was concerned. He couldn't keep from grinning at the teenager vocabulary coming from the eight-year-old's mouth. "His friends will certainly think he's stylin'."

She smiled. "I thought so, too." She lowered her voice so Cody couldn't hear her next comment. "It's two sizes smaller than his old one," she said, "but he's lost so much weight that he needed one that fit."

Cody held up the next surprise from her, a huge poster of Troy Aikman, quarterback for the Dallas Cowboys.

"For your wall. At your dad's house."

"Good. I need new stuff for my walls." Cody pulled out the last gift.

She shrugged again, deciding she'd gotten very good at doing so lately. "I guess I overdid it, huh?"

"No," Michael said. "A mom can't ever overdo it with her son."

"I'm just so happy he's going home from the hospital." Going home. Not coming home.

Cody had the box open now. Out came a little wooden box of dominoes and a gigantic squeeze tube of Where's Waldo? bath soap. *"Wow,"* he exclaimed, holding the tube and reading the instructions. "'Finger paint gel soap. The fun way to color yourself clean.'"

Michael cocked his head to one side, looking at Jennie with an amused, doubtful grin.

"It's red," she said in explanation to both of them. "You use it in the bathtub and you smear it all over yourself and it cleans you."

Michael raised one eyebrow, still teasing her. "You're sending this stuff to *my* house? Thanks."

"I bought it last week so Cody could have it at my house but...I—" She floundered for words "—I thought 'why should it have to stay here?' I thought he might want to smear red around everywhere...your house, too...."

"Oh, good, Mom," Cody said with delight. "I'll bring it with me when I come to your house, too."

Jennie could feel the telltale signs of emotion beginning to emerge, the reddening nose, the sharpening of her voice. She had to blink rapidly to hold back stinging tears. Michael must have noticed, too.

"Better get out of here." She kissed Cody again, this time as quickly as she could manage it, right on the end of his upturned nose. "Love you, kid."

"Love you, too, Mom. See you in two weeks."

She didn't answer. She'd already turned and was walking toward her car.

Michael buckled his seat belt then leaned back, watching her retreating figure out the window as it grew smaller and smaller. She wove in and out of the parked cars in the lot, looking blindly for her own. She found it at last and climbed in. Only then did he put his own car in gear and drive away.

CHAPTER THIRTEEN

FANS FILLED THE SEATS around the Sidekicks' indoor field, settling into the ring in bright, random patterns of color. As the crowd increased, the noise and the chants rose to an echoing cacophony around them.

"Don't know what we're going to do with the stats this season," Harv grumbled as the electric excitement buzzed around them. "Five wins and eight losses don't look so good on the record books."

"No," Buddy conceded. "They don't."

"I need a miracle player on this team and I need him now. I just don't know where on earth he's going to come from."

I do, Buddy thought, but he didn't say it. *I know exactly where the miracle player's coming from.*

During the past three weeks, Buddy and Marshall Townsend had been getting together, sitting around the video room with feet propped on the coffee table, watching effective soccer plays. If anyone had asked him to define it, Buddy would have said they were participating in "mental exercises." But, luckily, no one had asked.

"Just don't know what's wrong with my game lately," Marshall had said, stretching lazily and crossing two arms behind his head before he settled into a new position. "I can picture you making these incredible shots. Remember that cross-field shot you made during the Boston game? I *dreamed* about that one."

Buddy nodded knowingly. He knew how frustrating it could be when you weren't performing as well as you knew you could. The same thing had happened to him plenty of times. But he suspected Townsend's problems stemmed from the fact that he wasn't mature enough to face the mental pressure of the game. It would come in time, though. He knew that, too.

"I picture *you* making those incredible shots. I *saw* you making them one after the other. Then I picture myself and it's just *me* and it doesn't seem reasonable to want those things anymore."

Buddy shook his head, smiling to himself. *What a sage I am,* he thought. "Life isn't always reasonable, Marshall. So stop trying to play it out that way." How many times had Andy Kendall told him this very same thing? "You've got the right idea but you're going about it wrong."

"I am?"

"Your brain controls your body," he said simply. "If you make yourself *see* the right things, you've got it made." *If I say this to many more people,* he thought with an odd quirk of humor, *I'll end up believing it myself.*

Sports medicine, he reminded himself. *This is nothing but psychological sports medicine. But Andy had used it with her kids, too.*

"I learned that a while back," he said. *From someone I cared very much about.* "I think it can work for you, too.'' Strange that during rehabilitation after the accident, he'd forgotten so much of this.

''I'd like to try it,'' Marshall said. ''Anything that will help me make those impossible shots.''

What do I tell him now? What would Andy have told him? Buddy let his mind travel back, back before the accident, back when he had been a superstar at soccer, back when there had just been Andy.

''Come on, you!'' They were skiing at Breckenridge, the snow so light and dry around his boots that it had reminded him of the flakes of dried paper he saw in all the store windows in Dallas at Christmastime. Andy'd waved at him with a wide arc of her arm. ''All you do is point your skis downhill and you *go*.''

''That sounds easy enough,'' he'd said blandly, peering down the hill. ''It just doesn't *look* easy enough.''

''You can do it. If it looks like you're going to run into a tree or a person, you just fall down.''

''Something tells me I'm not getting the traditional ski lesson here.''

''You get,'' she said, swinging her curly, dark ponytail at him, ''exactly what you pay for.''

''That's what I was afraid of.'' He used his poles to push himself downhill toward her. ''So I do this? Just go downhill and if I start running... into...somebody...'' Here his skis passed right over hers and, as he continued on, he grabbed her tightly, hanging on to her the way a frightened child would hang on to its mother's legs. ''...then I just fall...'' And here she started screaming and giggling at him all at the same time, pushing him to try to get out of his grasp.

"...down..."

Kerplop. They both landed face first in the snow.

They thrashed around a bit, laughing. Andy spit snow out of her mouth. "I think I'd recommend a professional lesson," she said, deadpan. "This doesn't seem to be working."

Buddy looked at her and grinned the grin that had made him tremendously popular with female soccer fans. Her cheeks were as red as crab apples and her nose was three shades brighter. He could see two matching reflections of himself in her snow-blotched Vuarnets. "I think it's working just fine."

"Get off," she demanded, giggling. "Get off!"

"You aren't being very persuasive, and besides," he'd said, grinning at his own reflection in her glasses, "I don't think I can."

Their skis were so jumbled up and lying at such odd angles to each other that they would never get them untangled.

"Instructor!" she shouted from where she lay in the snow. "Instructor! This man needs an instructor! Help! Help!"

At that point he'd pulled her toward him, and kissed her so she would shut up and not embarrass him any further.

Someone had come along soon after and had mercifully untangled them before they froze that way. After that, she had stalwartly refused to give him any more free lessons. "Enroll in a class," she told him, kissing him quickly on the lips to punctuate it. "Now. Before you kill somebody. Like me."

He had signed up immediately, and three hours later he knew how to traverse a hill and turn and draw himself to a crude, skidding stop with a snowplow. Rejoining Andy, Buddy persuaded her to take the lift to an intermediate hill with him. Andy had still skied circles around him. "How are you doing that?" he'd asked her.

"It's easy," she'd called back as he did his best to follow in her tracks. He was trying to decide whether it would be more fun to concentrate on his own turns or to watch the turns she was making up ahead of him, her hips swaying with every stem christie she made.

He'd decided to match her turn for turn. He attempted to follow her but hit an icy spot, headed straight downhill and lost control. As she helped him up one more time, he realized he'd better stop concentrating on Andy's hips and start worrying about staying alive. "I tell this to the kids at Children's all the time," she'd said then. "Picture yourself doing something exactly the way you want to do it. Now, as you ski behind me, picture yourself doing it perfectly, traversing the hill with the skill you want to have. Every time you turn, picture perfect stem christie turns. You won't believe what good it'll do, Buddy."

By the end of the day, he'd been able to keep up with her. And when he got back to the Sidekicks to start playing again, he'd found himself picturing plays, completed plays, successful goal attempts and victories.

Andy's concept was foolproof. It worked. What she had taught him meant everything to him until the accident, until he let it go.

It's funny, he thought, *that I'm sitting here beside Marshall Townsend watching tapes and trying to help him* grasp the idea. I know very well what I'm doing. In explaining it to Marshall, I'm trying to grasp it again for myself.

"Marshall," he said. "I wish I could take you skiing. I could make you understand this if I could get you up on a ski hill."

"Oh," the player said. "I ski. Had a great vacation in Vail just a couple of months ago."

"That's just it, then," Buddy said, excited now, figuring they were getting somewhere. "Control of the ball in a game of soccer is just like control of your body while you're skiing a slope. Now, picture yourself skiing perfectly," he instructed.

"Okay. But what does skiing have to do with playing soccer?"

"See it as a rhythm to catch, controlling the ball, trapping it and passing it. Then follow through all the way in your mind. See yourself shooting past the goalie and driving in the score."

"Makes sense to me."

"Research conducted at Stanford University has shown that an image in your mind fires your nervous system exactly the same way as actually doing it. When you picture *me* making a shot and compare that to what you think *you* can do, that jinxes you, Townsend. Focus only on what you want to have happen. Then, when things get tough out there, don't pull in your horns. Risk it. Put yourself on the line instead of working to minimize your losses.''

"Ah!" Marshall leaned forward and snapped off the play tape. "Buddy, I can honestly tell you I've never had a coach like you before."

Now, today, as he stood on the edge of the playing field, Buddy's own words echoed in his mind. "Risk it. Put yourself on the line instead of working to minimize your losses." But he hadn't listened to his own advice when he'd given up his career playing for the Sidekicks. He had minimized his own losses.

No wonder Andy couldn't accept that from him.

He pulled his billed hat out of his pocket and slapped it on. Marshall Townsend's opportunity could very well come on the field today. Buddy had seen the player's incredible improvement and excellent moves during practice the past week. "Harv asked me what's gotten into you," he commented to Marshall now as they made ready for the game. "I told him you've been working after hours. He's gonna faint when he sees the results of all your hard work. Never *if* anymore, only *when*.''

The Sidekicks took the field at 2:00 p.m. As the play swung into full action, Harv and Buddy both kept busy substituting players on the fly and adjusting their plans. The afternoon, as always, moved quickly. With ten minutes left to play, Spooner stole the ball from a San Diego player, quickly moving it outside then passing right to Kirkland. Kirkland controlled the ball perfectly, moving it toward the far end of the field.

Spooner freed himself first, dancing forward with a half turn, controlled the ball and shot. San Diego's keeper deflected it with two hands high over his head and the ball bounced back to Marshall Townsend.

Not yet, Marshall! Buddy thought. *But almost! Almost!*

As if his friend had read his mind, Marshall dribbled the ball for five steps, looked straight toward the net and faked a shot.

Now! Buddy thought. *You've got it!*

For one moment there might as well not have been anyone or anything on the field except for Marshall Townsend, the spinning black-and-white leather ball, the San Diego goalkeeper and the net.

"No!" Siskell shouted, pounding his palm with his fist. "He's going to try that confounded left long shot again! No! No! No!"

Buddy said simply, "We've been working on this, Harv."

Marshall took one more step and kicked. The ball shot forward half the length of the field, an inch above the ground, going at least ninety miles an hour.

The keeper dove for it frantically but he had no way of gauging its velocity. He was just a breath too slow. The ball whizzed past him in a flash of black-and-white. It landed and lodged itself neatly in the left side of the net.

"Goal! Dallas Sidekicks!" the announcer hollered so loud you could hear him ten blocks away.

The crowd went wild.

The team went wild.

No one stopped to count how many months it had been since someone had made such an impossible shot. But Buddy knew.

"It was Townsend! Marshall Townsend!" Harv turned and gave Buddy a hard high five. "What a play! *What* a play! So help me, tonight I'm going to buy that boy a New York strip for dinner!"

CODY LOVED his new swimming class. He loved going to the big indoor pool, jumping in and feeling the water all tingly and cold around him. When he was in the water, he felt almost as if he could swim. But he couldn't quite manage it, so he just pretended he was a frog instead, using his hands to push and splash.

His dad had come home from the office today to bring him. There was a lady that came to his dad's house during the day to help take care of him. But his dad didn't spend too much time away right now.

Cody liked it that Mark Kendall had introduced him to all the other kids on the swim team. He liked the thought of making new friends who hadn't known him before. He didn't know if his old friends at school would like him anymore since he couldn't walk around. His new friends were good because they liked him just the way he was.

In the class they took turns on a kickboard while Mark helped them splash in circles through the water. They played all sorts of water games together, diving for rings and pitching balls and closing their eyes and looking for each other. There was a little girl named Megan who could swim really well. Somebody told Cody that she'd won a race. She liked his swimsuit. She said she thought the plastic palm tree changed colors when it got wet.

At the end of the class, his dad was really happy. He heard him say to Mark Kendall: "I believe in this program one hundred percent. Andy's been telling us this would be good for Cody. And I believed her. But I didn't know it would be *this* good."

"I liked it, too," Cody told his dad in the car on the way home. "Do you think my bathing suit changes color?"

"What?"

"The palm tree. When it gets wet. I think it changes color."

"I'm not sure, kiddo," his dad said, kissing him.

"Megan thinks it does. She saw a shirt that does it on TV."

His dad smiled. "You want to go to the office with me? This would be a good day to come, if you're not tired. You can meet some of my patients."

"Yeah, Dad! I want to—"

"Okay." His dad switched gears. "We're on our way."

WHEN THEY GOT to the office, Michael introduced Cody to Inez, the nurse, and Chris Bell, the receptionist. Cody made friends with the kids in the waiting room and even got to sit in on one of his dad's appointments. "This is my son, Cody," Michael said, introducing him to Bill and Marge Josephs. "I didn't think you'd mind if he sat in with us."

"Not at all," Bill bellowed in his Central Texas twang. He said "at all" in one word. *Atall.* "You figurin' on growing up to be a doctor some day, son?"

Cody sat up straighter. "I don't think so. People keep asking me that question but I'm not old enough to have it all figured out yet."

"Guess what," Bill said, leaning toward him conspiratorially and pointing to the rows and rows of wrinkles around his eyes. "I'm not old enough to have it all figured out yet, either!"

"Let's get this over with, Bill," Michael said, pointing toward the examining table. "Get right on up there and let me have a look at you."

"Good luck catching him," his wife teased. "He's moving so fast these days, I have a *horrible* time catching him and making him do what I want."

"Honey," Bill said, "it's all in your frame of mind. When there comes the time that *I* want to do what *you* want me to do, then I'll let you catch me."

Michael shot a grin at Bill. "Been feeling good lately, huh?"

"The best. Been feeling like a kid. Got so much energy, I don't know what to do with it."

"Right," Marge said, winking at Cody.

"Can't decide whether to go fishing or go golfing or go dove hunting or just hang out with the boys. And I've got these two horses named Dan and Kimbo that need riding all the time." He leaned down close to Cody. "You like to ride horses? Have your dad call me up and we'll take you out for a ride."

"Hard decisions," Marge interjected. "Too bad you don't consider fixing the doorbell as one of your heart-wrenching choices. Or how about finding the leak that's ruined all my soaps underneath the bathroom sink?"

"But, *Marge,*" he said in the exact same tone of voice Cody used when he said "But, *Mom,*" "I'm *retired.*"

"Okay. Let's check you out now," Michael said again. Bill hoisted himself up onto the table. "Good." Now the room was silent while Michael noted Bill's blood pressure and listened to his heartbeat. "Your blood pressure's lower. Your new medication must be working," he said after he completed all the tests. "You *are* taking them like you're supposed to? And you're following my other instructions?"

"He's doing everything you told him just like he does everything *I* tell him," Marge confirmed.

"Ma-a-arge," Bill drawled. "Don't give me away now. Yes, I'm taking those confounded pills."

"It's for your own good, you old coot," she said.

"Ma-a-arge."

Michael shook his head at both of them while Cody laughed. They put on quite a show. "Bill," he began. Then he glanced at Cody again. Cody made him see the humor here in its proper perspective. He walked over to his stubborn patient and slapped him on the back. "Bill, you're in good shape. You're eighty-four years old, you've got a heart that's getting stronger, your cholesterol level is low and it's clear that you're moving fast enough to keep Marge on her toes. I'm not going to lecture you about this, but keep the coffee down to two cups a day if you possibly can."

"I can do that, Doc," Bill said, guffawing. "I surely can."

MICHAEL AND CODY TALKED about Bill later on that
evening on the way to Michael's first therapy session
with his son. "Dad," Cody said as Michael lifted him
out of the car and carried him to the gym. "That guy
was funny."

"Oh, he's a character, all right."

Cody's arms clamped around the back of Michael's neck. "I liked him."

"Me, too," Michael said, glad to think of something besides the upcoming therapy. For weeks he'd
wanted to be a part of this. Now that the time had
come, he felt totally inept. He'd performed therapy
with Cody often alone in his room. But he'd never
been able to arrange his schedule so he could take part
in the groups. Jennie had always done it. "A doctor's
not supposed to have favorites but I've got to admit
Bill's one of mine. He always makes me laugh when I
need it most. He's a good friend."

"His wife made me laugh, too. She ought to do like
Mom. Mom always calls the plumber when we get a
leak under *our* sink."

Michael's warning signals shot up. He wasn't about
to let himself be drawn off in *this* direction. "Bill was
very sick a while back. But he had surgery and now
he's doing much better."

"Sorta like me, Dad?" Cody asked as they bobbed
along.

"Yeah," Michael answered. "Sort of like you."

Andy met them in the hallway and took Cody's face
in her hands. "Boy, have we missed *you* around here
lately. How are things at home? How are you feeling?"

"I'm feeling real good. Dad took me to his office today and I got to meet all the patients."

Andy winked up at Michael and instantly put him at ease. "What a great way to spend your first week out of the hospital. Visiting a doctor's office."

"Oh, it was fun. I got to meet Bill Josephs and Dad checked him all over and his wife kept teasing him because he wouldn't fix things..."

Other children began gathering for the session. "Come on in, you guys," Andy called, beckoning to them. Turning back to Cody, she said, "Mark said you did *great* at swimming."

"It was fun."

Michael found a chair where he could set Cody down. For the next twenty minutes he watched while Andy showed each child how to paste funny ears and noses on pieces of paper to form faces. Next she led each of them in a rigorous clown pantomime. Michael was laughing and Cody was sweating by the time they finished.

"Now it's time for the parents to join in," Andy said, nodding at the adults. "Bring your son or daughter over here and find a comfortable place on the mats." She turned on a cassette tape of light pop music and instructed them. "Start with the arms. Like this."

Michael hated to admit he was hopelessly lost. Jennie had spent hours writing down these directions for him. He had them beside him now. But reading directions and actually performing hands-on therapy in the middle of a room full of people were two entirely different things. He grasped Cody's leg just atop the knee and began to maneuver it. He moved the leg again…again…before his son cried out. "Ouch, Dad! You're hurting me." The little boy was biting his lip, trying his best to hold the tears back.

Stricken, Michael dropped Cody's leg. Around him the other parents continued to work with their children's muscles. "Cody, I'm sorry, son."

"It's okay, Dad."

A light film of sweat covered the little boy's face.

"Your mother never would have let that happen. She knows how to do this better than I do."

"Dad, don't worry. It didn't hurt that much."

"Kiddo. I'm *really* sorry."

Andy appeared at Cody's side. "Need some help over here?"

"I'm hurting him," Michael said.

"Here. Let me show you." The physical therapist knelt and took Cody's leg in two competent hands, rotating his ankle just a bit. "When you're doing a group exercise like this one, you want to work the muscle at this angle. See? Like this." The leg moved better for her, like a glider on a track, to and fro, to and fro. "Now. You try it."

"I'm almost afraid to."

"Don't be afraid. It always seems scarier than it is."

Michael stepped up again and did exactly as Andy showed him. "That okay, son?"

Cody nodded.

During the remainder of the session, Andy had to help him through six more exercises. Michael's thoughts, as he worked, came unbidden: *I'm lost in this without Jennie.*

Michael knew now, more than anything, what he had to do. He waited that night until Cody's breath became deep and heavy before he summoned the courage to telephone her. He sat in the huge chair beside the hearth and dialed the number from memory, a number that once had been his own.

It rang four times before she answered. "Hello?"

"Jennie." He hesitated. "It's me."

Total silence. Then a quick "Hello, Michael."

He didn't say anything else. He couldn't. He didn't know how to say it.

She sensed his wariness and suddenly panicked. "Michael? Is he all right? What's wrong?"

"You ask me that every time. Cody's fine, Jen. Just fine." *But no thanks to me,* he thought wryly.

She breathed a sigh of relief. "You scared me. It always scares me when anybody calls."

"I didn't mean to scare you."

His heart started pounding. Why had he done this? Why had he been so all-consumed with this crazy idea of calling her? Without confessing to her how totally inadequate he felt, he had absolutely nothing else to say. "I wish we could go back to Six Flags," he said at last.

"Me, too," she said quietly.

The silence came again. "I'm sorry, Jennie," he said. "I shouldn't have done this."

"Michael." He heard it in her voice, then. She was glad he had called her.

So he opened up to her, knowing he couldn't turn back. "I got lost in the group therapy session today," he said simply. "I got into that place and I didn't know how to do anything."

JENNIE SETTLED HERSELF more comfortably, putting aside the hand towel. "You haven't done a group session with him before, have you? You'll do better after you practice with him." She was honestly saddened that the scheduling and the split-up of therapy had worked to Michael's disadvantage. She couldn't really picture Michael being incompetent at anything. She felt a stab of sympathy for him she didn't dare acknowledge. She felt certain he had tried to do his best.

"Oh, Michael."

He sighed, a long, lonely sound that immediately revealed to her how lost he felt.

There was no stopping it. She knew now what she would do. *He needs me,* she thought with a triumphant thrumming of her heart. *Everything else might be lost to us. But he needs me for this.*

Her question, when it came, came in a whisper as hushed as the flicker of a bird's wings. And she knew, even as she asked, that she was making herself vulnerable to him again.

"You want to go together on Friday? I could stand beside you and give you the crash Cody course."

She pictured him rocking from nervousness in his huge, comfortable recliner and now stopping, leaning forward. "What about Cody?"

"You'll have to explain to him that I'm coming to help him and not to be with you. You've got to make *sure* he understands that. Just tell him it's because you did so badly in class today and you want to do better. Tell him it's the only thing we could think of to help you.''

He gave a little humph of indignation and said softly, ''I'll make sure he understands that much. We'll have a man-to-man talk.''

''Be gentle with him,'' she said, still quietly. Then: ''That's it, then.''

''Are you sure this is the best thing to do, Jennie?''

''Yes,'' she said solemnly, knowing full well everything she was risking. ''I'm sure.''

CHAPTER FOURTEEN

As JENNIE STOOD beside the window waiting for Michael and Cody to pick her up, she felt as if she'd stepped into a bottomless chasm that might swallow her whole.

It had seemed perfect and right, though it had been difficult, when they'd spent time together at the hospital and made decisions for Cody when he was ill. Today, however, signaled a new phase in their relationship with each other, and with their son. Today each of them would stand in the other's territory, side by side, and Cody would see them doing it.

She started when she saw the BMW round the corner. She grabbed her purse, trying to quiet the loud thudding of her heart.

"Hey, Mom!" Cody called as she climbed in behind him. "How are ya?"

"I'm great," she said, kissing him. "You've grown again. You look bigger than you looked the other day." She glanced at Michael's reflection in the rearview mirror. "Are you two ready for this?"

"Yeah!" Cody said happily.

"As ready as I'll ever be," Michael said. And Jennie decided that Michael sounded happy, too.

"Good."

Cody jabbered all the way to the hospital. He talked about swimming and spending the night with Taylor and his new friends at the pool. He talked about the golden labrador puppy, Jehosophat, who had moved in next door.

Jennie started worrying. Cody seemed far too animated. Was he again hoping that she and Michael would reconcile?

I shouldn't have come. I knew I shouldn't have come.

The drive to the hospital seemed an eternity. When they finally arrived at the gym, and had set Cody down to visit with his friends before class, she cornered Michael. "Did you talk to him?"

"I did."

"What did you say?"

"That you and I were going to be together today to help him with his therapy. That you and I didn't see each other at all except when we wanted to help him. That you and I—didn't *want* each other anymore."

"Good," she said, even though it was painful to hear him say it that way. "I didn't know exactly how you were going to put it."

They started back toward the group of children and parents. "I wanted to make sure he understood," Michael said, searching her face for any reaction.

She didn't give him one.

For Jennie, it was a welcome reprieve to begin working with Cody again. She watched first while he traded paper noses with the other children at the table until he found one he liked. He smeared glue on the paper and attached it to his picture. When it came time for the parents to participate, Michael carried Cody over to the mats. Then he obligingly stepped back so Jennie could work with him. She motioned to Michael to squeeze in next to her.

"I'll show you how," she whispered conspiratorially. He felt a rush of gratitude for her. "It's a snap. You'll get the hang of it and you'll be the best one here."

"There isn't much chance of that."

"Oh yes there is."

The first few exercises went well. Michael learned the correct angle and placement of Cody's feet, hips and knees. But as Jennie began to work with Cody's arms, she could feel him tightening up against her. "Hey," she said to Cody as Michael looked on. "What are you doing? Your muscles are getting tight, little one."

"I'm starting to hurt."

"You've got to push ahead through this part."

"I'm getting tired," Cody said, beginning to whine. "I don't think I can."

"Of course you can!" She was searching inside herself now, doing her best to find the right words to inspire him. "I know it gets tough. But you're a tough kid. Your dad needs to see how well you can do these things so he can learn them, too."

She felt Michael's reassuring hand on her back. She closed her eyes and sat back on her heels, easing into his touch, forgetting for a moment where she was, who she was, who *he* was.

It feels good, so very good, she thought, *to have someone support me.*

For the rest of the session, the three of them laughed and told jokes. And, as they drove home together, Cody fell fast asleep in the back seat of the car.

"He worked hard today," Jennie said quietly after she'd turned around to check him. "He deserves a good rest."

"He does."

Michael glanced across the car at her. He smiled, just a little smile, but it meant the world to her. "You make a wonderful therapist, you know it? I loved the joke you told him about the elephant stuck in the peanut butter jar."

"I *had* to get him to move his legs." She grinned at him. "Something tells me you aren't going to let me forget that one for a long time."

He winked at her. "I'm not."

The drove on in silence, but this time the silence felt comfortable between them. Michael pulled the car up in front of her house. Before Jennie had time to reach for the handle, he'd parked the car and jumped out. "I'll walk you to the door."

"It's not dark. And this isn't a date. You don't have to walk me to the door."

"I want to."

She climbed out, deciding not to make an issue of it. He strolled with her up the walk and waited while she dug her keys out of her bag. When she turned to thank him, he grasped her forearms with gentle, certain hands. "Jennie. Please—"

"Michael—" She glanced back at the car and saw Cody sleeping there, his lashes resting against his cheeks as lightly as gauze. "I don't think—"

He held up a hand, stopping her words. "You have to know this," he said, persisting. "You have to know how much I needed you today. You have to know how much it meant that you came."

"I think I know." Their eyes met in the growing darkness. "I was afraid, though."

"I thought you might have been." He gave her a half smile, a bittersweet smile made more melancholy because he tilted his head at her like their little boy. Then, without another word he drew her close, his arms tightening warm and strong around her.

"I just wanted to do this again," he whispered. He held her as he had never held her before, like a drowning man seizing a life raft. "Oh, Jen, I've missed you."

"Me, too."

Their eyes met again and held in the dimness of the porch light.

"Michael," she said very softly as she reached up and took his face in her hands. "I very much want you to kiss me."

As though it were the most natural thing in the world, as though it weren't the very thing they'd been fighting so fiercely, he took her into his arms and kissed her for a long, long time. When he stopped, they were both breathless.

"Should I tell you I'm sorry for this?" He searched her face.

"Why should you be sorry?" she asked him. So he kissed her again before letting her continue. "I'm the one who asked. I wanted—" She stopped. "I don't know what I wanted—I just—"

"I know," he said, touching her chin with one finger before he pulled her close one last time. "I know—"

For minutes after that, they stood fiercely entwined, not moving, Jennie burying her face against Michael's chest, where she could hear his breath. And even after he drove away and she stood there alone, she could still feel the strong, steady beating of his heart.

THE TIME SOON CAME for Cody to move back to Jennie's house. She cleaned all that day, dawdling about the house, straightening things she'd already straightened twice, rearranging pillows on the sofa, pausing in the doorway to Cody's room and just looking at it.

Michael arrived at five-thirty. "Hi, you two!" She held the door open for them. "I thought you'd never get here." She ruffled Cody's hair. "It's about time you started hanging around this place again."

"I'll be glad to be hanging around this place, too."

She looked up and past her son's head. "Hello, Michael."

"Hello, Jennie."

For a moment they stopped, a little awkwardly.

"Well," she said, clearing her throat abruptly and stepping back to make way for them. "Come on in."

"Thanks." Michael moved forward to deposit Cody on the couch. "The place looks good."

"Thanks. I cleaned all day."

"Can I see my room?" Cody asked.

"Sure," Jennie told him.

"Here," Michael said, bending to lift him.

Jennie touched Michael's elbow. "No. Let me try."

"You sure you want to?"

She nodded. She'd have to carry him around plenty soon enough. She might as well start while Michael could help her.

He stood behind her while she gave Cody a tight, giant hug and lifted him. "Agh," she groaned, teasing him. "You've been growing again!"

"I'm trying to grow!"

They made it up the hallway without knocking the walls down. They only ran into two things, a watercolor painting of bluebonnets that swung crazily on the wall when they bumped it, and Lester the cat, who squalled as if he'd been mortally wounded when Jennie stepped on his tail.

"Oh, Lester," she sighed. "I didn't even know you were down there."

She plunked Cody down on his bed and propped pillows all around him. "Is this good?"

"Yeah."

She stood back, giving him some room. "You want us to stay with you?"

"Naw. I just wanted to come in here and remember everything."

"Okay." She wasn't certain she and Michael should go. "You'll call me if you need me?"

"I'll call you."

"He'll be okay," Michael reassured her. Then he turned to his son. "I guess I'll go, Cody."

"Okay, Dad. Thanks."

He bent down on his knees. "You be good for Mom, you hear?"

"I will."

"You'll remember everything we talked about?"

Cody nodded.

"Okay. Love you, son."

"Love you, too, Dad."

This was the hardest part for both of them, telling him goodbye.

Jennie followed Michael along the hallway. "You're going to miss him, aren't you?"

"Terribly."

He turned to face her. He had nothing else to say but he couldn't quite bring himself to leave.

"Can I come pick him up and continue to take him to Andy's sessions?" he asked.

"You want to?" she said, surprised. She'd figured that, with Cody gone, he'd go back to spending long hours with his patients and at the hospital.

"I *do* want to," he said. "We've been doing fine in there—" He shot her a sheepish grin "—now that I know what I'm doing. Thanks for coming with us."

She turned and looked out the window at nothing. "You're welcome."

He watched her for a moment. Then he stepped up behind her. "Jennie? What is it? What's the matter?"

"Nothing."

"It isn't nothing. I can tell."

"Why do you try to read my mind?" she asked. "Why do you think you know me so well?"

"Because I do," he told her. "I can't help it." Then he asked her very quietly, "Are you afraid to have Cody here?"

She turned slowly to face him. "I am." Then she took a deep breath and said in a rush, "I don't think I'm ready for this, Michael. I'm so ashamed to be afraid. But what if I do things wrong with him? I'm not afraid *of* him. I'm just afraid I won't be good enough."

"You will be good enough. You're the one who taught *me,* Jen. And I think I felt just as inadequate as you do."

"Did you?"

"Yes."

As she watched the man who had been such an integral part of her life for so long, she realized she wasn't being completely honest. "There's more to it than that, Michael. It's more than Cody. It's you. I'm realizing that, when I'm afraid, I'm depending on you. I've started *needing* you again. And that frightens me just as much as anything."

We're both so fragile, he thought, *we're willing to need anybody, even each other.* He took another step closer to her, his fists clenched, his knuckles white knobs beneath his skin, frowning. "You're overlooking one thing," he said finally. "We didn't *choose* to need each other again, Jennie. But now we do. You're Cody's mother. And, beneath it all—" Here he paused and seemed to struggle with himself. "—beneath it all, I don't think God could have picked anybody better for the job."

It took several seconds for his words to sink in. Then the tears welled up into her eyes. "You really think so?"

"Yes." He took another step nearer.

She crossed her arms and rubbed her forearms in an unconsciously protective gesture. "You don't know how badly I've needed to hear that. I've felt so inadequate. Like it was ridiculous of me to think I could even *try*. And then, when he went home with *you*..."

"I know that hurt you," he said. "I hated to hurt you like that. And then you accepted it like it was something I'd done all the time."

"It was. A long time ago, you hurt me all the time. And so I turned around and hurt you, too."

He shook his head. "But no more, Jennie. We aren't going to do that to each other anymore."

"I was thinking about the other night," she said slowly.

"When I kissed you?"

She nodded. "Michael—I—"

"Don't talk." One more half step and he stood only inches away, a head above her, looking down at her, the only man she had shared a bed with, and wedding vows. He reached for her then, gripping her elbows with warm sturdy hands, and pulled her to him. He slid his hands up her arms towards her shoulders, savoring the delicate, devastating softness of her skin.

She gazed up at him, lips half parted, eyes wide and innocent as a child's. "I don't just need you," she whispered against his lips. "I want you, too."

Oh, how easy they'd all said it would be, to want him again.

With that, he took her lips with his own, wildly answering her words with his kiss. She rose on tiptoe to meet him, clasping her hands around his neck. She could feel his pulse there, racing almost as violently as her own. "Don't say that—" he whispered against her lips "—unless you mean it."

His hands traveled the length of her as they kissed, touching her in secret places, bringing back memories, all of them achingly familiar and sweet.

The only thing sturdy enough and strong enough that she could cling to was him, this dear, precious man she had known forever, who felt like a rock against her now, his heart thrumming in an exquisite echo of her own.

She remembered a hundred nights of lovemaking with him. She remembered one fall when they'd gone to East Texas to cut firewood and they'd tumbled around on the ground in the acorns. She remembered loving him as they had lain in their bed in their first little apartment in Dallas. She remembered watching him sleep one of the last nights they'd been together, his back an insurmountable mountain that marked his edge of the bed, when she had thought, "I don't know him anymore. And he doesn't know me."

Jennie knew the price of commitment so well. What she felt for Michael now was no romantic illusion. This seemed very, very different, something she'd never experienced, a sort of womanly wanting that made her feel as if her heart would burst.

"Jennie." He was trailing kisses around the base of her neck. They'd both totally forgotten about the little boy waiting in his room. "I have to get out of here." He said it in a hoarse voice that revealed exactly how desperate he was.

"I don't want you to." She found the hollow of his neck with her lips and she burrowed there, drinking him in, thrilling to the feel of him. His flesh tasted of salt.

She felt as if she'd rather die than see him go. But she knew she had to let him walk away.

CHAPTER FIFTEEN

JENNIE HAD STARTED drawing again, making funny sketches for Cody and jotting down little stories. Tonight she started drawing caricatures of Cody's new friends on the swim team. Cody watched, entranced, while she shaded them all in.

"The swimming has really helped you, Bear." She scrubbed the paper with a dull pencil. "Look. Here's you. Here's your fabulous new bathing suit that changes color." It didn't really but they were pretending it did. "And here's Megan."

"That's great, Mom!"

"Sometimes I wish I could do something more to help. All these other people are helping *you*. . ."

"I bet you could help. I bet you could help Mark get more kickboards so we could invite more kids."

"You don't have enough kickboards?"

"No. We have to wait *forever* to get a turn on them."

"If Mark had more children, could he purchase more supplies?"

"I don't think so," Cody said. "We were griping about taking turns one day and Mark said he doesn't have enough money for everything he needs."

"Really? I wonder if he needs help getting money?" She remembered hearing about all the tax cuts and the budgets that were affected. And suddenly, as she sat sketching a swimming pool with children coming up out of the water, she knew exactly what she would do.

After Cody went to bed, she telephoned Andy. "Mark's program has never been funded by the government," Andy explained. "But even if it had been, things would be tougher now, I expect."

"Andy," she asked, her heart thumping with excitement, "would Mark let me organize some sort of fund-raiser? The *Times-Sentinel* is always looking for public service projects to be involved in."

Andy's voice brightened. "Mark would love it! If he had more money, there are so many more things he could do. He could put together a brochure so he could reach more kids. He could get more equipment. Would you really do something like that?"

"I'd love to. I'll phone Art first thing Monday morning and then I'll talk to Mark when I take Cody to swimming," Jennie told her. "Consider it done."

HARV SISKELL RETIRED from the Dallas Sidekicks in the middle of the season with a huge party and a five-tiered cake. Buddy Draper was named his replacement. Buddy's career as head coach of the Sidekicks had begun.

On the morning he was scheduled to coach his first game by himself, Buddy stood on the field midway between the two goals, having pulled his zippered satin jacket more snugly around him, his hands jammed into the pockets. The sun was just appearing over the

Dallas skyline and, outside, the day was frigid, one of those wet winter days in Dallas that makes you feel as if the cold has penetrated your bones.

Buddy crossed the huge building alone, the soles of his shoes squeaking against the floor as he made his way to the half line. In seven hours, the stands would be full again and he'd embark on yet another new phase in his life. He had already come so far now, he could scarcely remember what it felt like to be a star player.

He looked to the left and the right, running the game plan through his mind, hoping he had considered everything, and that he could make Harv proud.

Buddy loved game days more than anything. Each game day was like taking a big test—one you passed every time you won.

He went into his office and tried to convince himself that this was just another game, that no one would remember it, that it didn't matter that this was his first outing as a professional head coach. But, try as he might, he couldn't manage to relax.

By the time the fans began to arrive and find their seats, a little bit after noon, Buddy felt like a fish out of water, gasping for breath.

Today they were scheduled to play the Tacoma Stars. The Stars were already in their locker room, laughing with comradery, when Buddy headed down the hallway to find the Sidekicks. When he walked in, they were all waiting for him.

"Here's the coach!" somebody hollered.

"We've got to make this happen for Draper!" somebody else shouted.

Marshall Townsend pitched him one of the practice balls. "So do you want the game ball today, Coach?" he asked with a wide grin on his face.

"Only if we win."

He gathered them into a group and gave them their instructions for the day. He talked to them about effort, passing and control. It was everything Harv Siskell had always talked to him about, everything that had once made a difference in his life. That and the positive thoughts Andy had shared with him.

Andy. How many times had he thought of her lately? How many times he had wondered if she'd come to watch him at one of the games. Every week, thousands of people watched him and his team. Every week he pretended to himself that one of the fans might be her, that she might be ready to forgive him and willing to accept the decisions he'd made.

Just before game time, he and his team gathered in a big circle, put their right hands together and bellowed, "Go, Kicks!" as they lifted fists to the sky. The crowd roared as they raced out onto the field. And, after a few minutes of raucous warm-ups, the clock just below the huge MISL banner read 2:00 p.m.

The visiting Stars took possession of the ball for the kick-off at center line. For the next forty-five minutes, the players crisscrossed the field in wild patterns, the striker made two shots, the keepers switched places and the press drove Buddy bananas. He felt as if they never took the cameras off him once during the entire first half. He needed to concentrate on the game and on what to tell his players. There were several times when Marshall Townsend passed the ball with a one-touch shot when he should have controlled it more.

"Marshall, no," Buddy said to his player after authorizing a substitution. "I want you to concentrate more than that. It looks like school-yard soccer out there."

"Sure, Coach." Marshall shot him a grin. "You sound like Harv."

"I'm *supposed* to sound like Harv."

Marshall went back in three minutes later. As the last fifteen-minute period began, the scoreboard read Tacoma 4, Dallas 3.

A Tacoma player belted the ball toward the Sidekicks' goal, but once again the keeper blocked it. He punted it to the right side of the field. The Tacoma forward trapped it. He took two steps forward, then crossed it to a player on the left side.

When Marshall got the ball, he too trapped it, jealously controlling it himself for several steps before he passed it backward to the defender. The defender in turn passed the ball back to the right forward. And Dallas's right forward, Eric Spooner, took the shot.

Tacoma's keeper blocked the ball with his fist. The ball barely missed the outside post and rebounded. Chuck Kirkland was right beneath it, already anticipating its return pattern. The ball flew through the air several feet above the ground. As Buddy watched, with his heart stopped, his fists clenched, he knew the only thing Kirkland could do was volley it.

The left forward poured every effort into the motion as he sprang from the ground like a giant cat, whipping his foot out in a fierce kick that sent the high ball straight back into the goal like a guided missile.

Score. Dallas.

Fans jumped up and down in the stands, hugging each other and cheering. The television cameras from WFAA and KTVT moved in ever closer. But with three minutes left in the game, while one of the Sidekicks' best defenders sat waiting in the penalty box, Tacoma turned the tide around by scoring again.

The Sidekicks and Buddy couldn't recover from that. When the last whistle blew at 4:25 that Saturday afternoon, the score stood Tacoma 5, Dallas 4.

"Buddy Draper!" the sports reporter from Channel 11 called to him as he started toward the locker room. "Do we have time for a short interview?"

"Certainly," he agreed. He spent five minutes with the reporter, telling the people watching he thought the Sidekicks had expended too much energy early, and that perhaps the players had placed too much weight on the game because it was his first. He was pleased with his players' performances and told everyone so. And, just as the cameraman changed to a different angle and the reporter asked one last question, Marshall Townsend loped up beside him. "Guess you don't want the game ball since we lost, huh?"

Buddy wasn't sure how to answer that. The cameras glinted at him. He turned away to collect his thoughts. And that's when he saw her. Andy stood ten rows above him wearing a red dress that looked vaguely familiar, her dark hair lying in soft curls around her shoulders, her eyes meeting his just as he'd always imagined they would, every game, from any place in the stands.

He forgot Marshall's question. He forgot the sports reporter from KTVT. He even forgot the huge cameras and the boom mike that hung just above his head. "Andy?" he called out. *"Andy?"*

She pattered down the steps toward him, looking mildly surprised and even a little unnerved by his reaction.

"Hey, stranger," she said, grinning, as she leaned over the railing and took his hand. "It's nice to see you."

"You look good."

"You, too."

The reporter had taken the cue and had ambled off. The photographers switched off their cameras and somebody turned off the mike. "You still give good interviews," she said quietly.

"Don't know about that." He smiled. "What are you doing here?"

She shrugged. "I don't really know. It's crazy, I know. I just—needed to know how you were doing."

"I'm doing fine."

"I know that. I—mean—I would have known that from all the stories I've read. Marshall Townsend is doing a good job taking your place. He's one of the best strikers I've seen."

"He's gotten better," *Thanks to you,* Buddy thought. But he didn't dare say it. He asked what he thought was a safer question. "Is this your first game this season?"

She shook her head. "No. I've come to several."

Chuck Kirkland came out and took his elbow. "Come on, Coach. We're all waiting for you."

He searched her eyes wordlessly.

"Go ahead," she said, taking one step back. "I didn't mean to keep you."

"You aren't keeping me," he said. "I'd like to stay here and talk. I wish I could."

"Buddy." She said it so softly he almost couldn't hear her. "It was awful good to see you again."

The players surrounded him, moving him toward the lockers. He couldn't say any more to her. But just as he entered the locker room, he caught one last glance of her as she stood high in the stands, gathering her jacket, watching him.

"So? What did you think?" Marshall asked, teasing him the moment he arrived back with the team. "Are we gonna have to throw this game ball into the trash? Or are you gonna take it home?"

In his head, Andy's words reverberated like a victory bell. *I've come to several.*

He held out his hand for the game ball.

"Guess I'd better take this home. Good effort, guys," he told them all. "It's an afternoon I'll remember my whole life. Thanks."

He pitched the ball into the air and caught it.

JENNIE CALLED Art Sanderson first thing Monday morning. It didn't take her long to convince him that the *Times-Sentinel* should be a corporate sponsor for the swim team fund-raiser. Art discussed it with the marketing staff and called her back almost immediately.

"We like it," he said. "How much will you be willing to do for this? Are you going to organize it? What do you have in mind?"

"I'm thinking of doing a variety show that spotlights the kids on the team," Jennie explained. "We'll have musical numbers and skits interspersed with appearances by several Dallas celebrities."

"What celebrities are you thinking of?"

Jennie thought about it. "I'll have to talk to several and see who's willing. Maybe Troy Aikman from the Cowboys. Maybe a local disc jockey and the weatherman from Channel 8."

"Let us know what you come up with. When it comes time for publicity, the *Times-Sentinel* will handle it."

"I'd like to do some drawings for the ads," Jennie said. "We can print up posters, too. I'll donate any artwork you need. I've got some great drawings of the swim team."

"What about music?" Art asked her. "I assume we'll need that, too."

"Let me talk to somebody at the symphony," Jennie suggested. "I'll bet we can get some of the instrumentalists to donate their time."

"When you're finished with this major project," Art said conspiratorially, "maybe you'll consider coming back to work."

"Ha." She gave a little laugh. She'd been wondering when he was going to bring that up again. "I don't know, Art. Don't count on it. I've got accustomed to staying around the house with this little boy."

"I had to try, you know," he told her.

"I'd be disappointed if you didn't."

MICHAEL SAT at the huge country oak table in Marge Josephs's kitchen. "What a great breakfast, Marge," he said, leaning back and stretching. "It's been a long time since I've eaten like that." Everything had been delicious. Fresh grapefruit from the Texas Rio Grande Valley. Venison sausage from the deer Bill had brought in last fall. An omelet filled with tomatoes and green peppers and onions from the Josephses' garden out back.

"Well, Doc," Bill said. "We wanted to do something nice for you. You've done so much for us. And breakfast is our best meal of the day."

"You can say that again," Michael agreed, grinning. "This was great timing, too. I can still go in and work a full day."

"Come on out back," Bill said, scooting his chair away from the table. "I want you to see my horses."

Michael followed Bill out through the screened-in porch and past about a hundred old fishing rods. They walked out through a rickety grape arbor to the corral. Bill whistled, and the horses whinnied and came running. "This here's Dan. And this mare is Kimbo. Anytime you want to use these horses and go riding, Doc, let me know. That boy of yours looks like he'd make a fine rider. They need somebody to exercise 'em."

"Cody's ridden some. His mother loves horses."

"His mother can ride, too. Kimbo's a fine horse for a woman." Bill stopped and cocked his head at Michael. "You still married to that boy's mother?"

Michael shook his head. "We divorced four years ago."

"Too bad," Bill said. "Too bad. Ain't nothin' better than living with a good woman, Michael. Makes you live a *long time* having somebody like Marge taking care of ya. I recommend it highly."

"Thanks, Bill." Michael slapped him on the back. "I'll remember that advice."

They went up to the barn, where Bill showed Michael his chickens and his rabbits. "I keep the rabbits around here for the grandkids," he said. "They're more fun than the cats. The cats out here go wild. They live under the barn and catch mice. The kids can't get their hands on them."

After a final tour of the house that included a long description with photos of the Josephses' grandchildren, Michael was ready to leave. He hugged Marge goodbye. "Thank you," he told her. "The memory of this breakfast will keep me happy a long time. I don't know of any other doctor who's as lucky as I am."

"You plan on coming out here a lot," Bill told him. "People love to come out here and just *be*. You plan on bringing that boy, too."

"I will," Michael said, shaking Bill's hand. "I really will."

"Morning, Bear," Jennie said, hugging Cody in his bed. "How'd you sleep?"

"Good," he said. "I dreamed that you and Dad took me to the fair."

"Did you?" she asked, kissing him on the nose. "We did that once. When you were a little boy. We

took you to the Texas State Fair." She hugged him
close once more and lifted him from the bed. "You've
got to come to the kitchen and eat breakfast. I've got
surprises for you."

"What are they?" he asked when she had him
halfway there. The two of them struggled up the hallway.

She settled him in his chair, gave him a steaming
mug of cocoa and a bowl of oatmeal. Then she sat
down across the breakfast bar from him. "I talked to
Art Sanderson this morning, my editor from the
newspaper, and we're going to do a big show to help
your swim team."

"That will be *great!* Can I be in the show?"

"You sure can."

"You think Dad will come and see it?"

"I know he will. He'll be so proud of you, he won't
be able to stand it."

"So is that my surprise?" he asked.

"That's one of them."

"What's the other one?"

"Andy called this morning. She wants you to come
to the hospital today to attend a special class."

Cody frowned. "What kind of class?"

Jennie took both of his hands in hers. "It's a class
so you can learn to use a wheelchair."

"I don't need that. I don't need a wheelchair."

"You do, darling. Just for a little while."

"No."

She couldn't believe her ears. "Cody—"

"I don't want to go."

As she dressed him that morning, she knew he was still angry with her. But she had no choice. He was getting heavier for her to carry every day.

"My legs are working *fine,*" he said to her as she adjusted him in the car. "I've worked so hard." By the time she got to the hospital she was worried. She hadn't even considered he might react to it this way. Perhaps he was frightened. Perhaps he'd concluded that they were putting him in a chair because they were giving up on him.

She labored into Andy's office with him and sat him down.

Andy recognized immediately that there was a problem. "Cody? What's wrong?"

"Why does Mom think I need one of those chairs? I'm getting along just fine."

Andy did her best to reason with him. "You'll be able to get around the house better. You won't have to depend on your mom and dad for so many things. You can even go back to school."

A nurse pushed the chair in to them. It was entirely different from what Jennie had expected. It folded out, was lightweight, had red metal arms and a bright striped canvas seat. "Cody," Jennie said. "It's great! Look at it. Everybody at school will want you to give them rides on this thing."

"No." Cody was gritting his teeth, his face beet red. "Get Dad. Mom, get Dad. *He* won't make me do this."

"Dad's at his office."

"I don't care."

Jennie had never seen him so determined. "Dad will agree with me, Cody. You wait and see."

"Dad will not make me sit in that thing like I'm a sick person."

"You aren't a sick person." *Oh, Cody*, she thought. *Believe this. Because if you do, you'll make it so.* "You're a healthy little boy who's getting closer and closer to walking every day."

"Dad!" he kept hollering. "Get my Dad!"

CHAPTER SIXTEEN

NO AMOUNT OF MANEUVERING or cajoling on Jennie's part was going to get Cody into that chair. Andy tried too, and so did one of the interns. But Cody sat there, crying, stubborn as a mule, and refused to unbend his legs. He would have fallen to the floor if he had to so he could prove his point. Thirty minutes later, exhausted and defeated, Jennie finally telephoned Michael.

"I'm sorry," the receptionist told her. "He's with a patient right now. Can I have him call you back?"

"No." Jennie was past the point of exhaustion and disappointment, and was almost ready to break. *Isn't it funny?* she thought. *I've handled so many big things with Cody. And it's this little thing—this one day—this chair—that's going to break me.*

"He can't call me back. This is Jennie Stratton." She didn't identify herself further. She didn't want to say "his ex-wife." But she couldn't say "his wife." "Can I just hold for him? Can you get him on the phone as soon as he leaves his patient?"

The receptionist sounded dubious. "You may have to wait a while."

"I'll wait," she said.

She waited in Andy's office for fifteen minutes. She could still hear Cody crying in the next room. Every three minutes or so, the receptionist came back on the line and asked her, "Do you want to *continue* holding?" and she'd say, "yes."

Then finally, finally, she heard his voice on the other end of the line. "Jen? It's you, isn't it?"

"It's me."

"How long have you been on the line? She should have interrupted me for you! I can't *believe* she made you wait so long! You should have told her who you were."

She smiled at the sound of his voice. Her entire body relaxed. It was so good to know she could call him like this. "It's my fault. I didn't know exactly how to tell her who I was." *I don't know who I am to you,* she wanted to say. *I don't know how to classify us together anymore.*

"What is it?"

"I need you. I don't know what to do." She told him about the chair. "I don't know whether Cody's scared he can't do it right or whether he thinks we don't believe in him anymore. Or maybe he thinks we're pushing him back into things too fast."

"Why don't you ask him?"

"I'm not sure he could answer even if I asked the right questions." She could still hear Cody crying through the closed door. "He keeps asking for you and saying *you* wouldn't make him do this."

"I *would.*"

"What if I bring him to the phone? I could try to calm him down enough so he could listen to you."

"No," Michael said. "I'm coming down there. I'll cancel everything for the afternoon. You stick with him and tell him I'm on my way."

True to his word, Michael arrived within the half hour, still dressed in his doctor's coat and the little plastic badge that said Michael Stratton, M.D. He walked immediately toward Cody, stopping only long enough to squeeze Jennie's arm in a gesture of support.

"What's the problem, son?" He stooped down beside Cody.

"I—don't—want—one—of—those—chairs—I—want—to—wa-a-a-lk—" Cody wailed.

"You think if we get you in a chair that we'll stop helping you learn to walk again?" Michael asked.

"I—don't—*knowwww*—"

"That isn't what we'll do at all."

"I—don't—want—one—of—those—chairs—" Cody kept wailing.

"Hey, kid," Michael said kindly. "Your mom and I have gotten you this far. You've got to trust us a bit, okay?"

"I—knew—you—wouldn't—make—me—do—this."

Little rivulets of tears ran down Cody's cheeks and Michael handed him a tissue. "Tell me, Cody, when is the last time you wanted to take the easy way out of something? That isn't what you need right now. You've got to try these new things." Cody blew his nose with a great honk that made them all smile again.

Michael turned to Andy. "Can you have someone bring in a chair that's big enough for me?"

Andy grinned. "Sure thing, Dr. Stratton."

Michael eased himself into the chair as soon as the hospital aide brought it, strapped himself in with the seat belt, and began to manipulate the big, shiny wheels. He went the wrong way at first and winked at Jennie. "I've never actually *done* this before."

"I didn't figure you had," Jennie said.

"Dad," Cody said, smiling in spite of himself. "You're being goofy."

"I'm not." Michael kept spinning around. "This is fun." He kept spinning until he made himself woozy. "Cody, this is great!"

Jennie was getting dizzy just watching him.

"Actually," Cody commented, still dubious, "that looks like it *could* be fun."

"It is," Michael said, grinning. "But, better than that, look how fast I can go." He shot across the room as fast as he could until he came nose-to-nose with the little boy. "And I can stop on a dime."

Jennie treasured what Michael was doing for their son. Her emotion was so reassuring, so *certain*, that she didn't even try to chase it away.

It would be so easy, she thought, *to fall in love with this man again.*

"Come here," Michael said, holding his arms out to Cody. "Let's try this together. I'll let you work the wheels, okay?" He unfastened his own seat belt and lifted Cody with ease. "There you go."

They sat in the chair together with Cody at the controls, turning the wheels carefully so the shining spokes moved opposite each other just the way Michael had showed him. Michael whispered something in his ear and, all of a sudden, Cody made the chair shoot forward. Together they banged into the wall.

"No!" Michael said, laughing, as they backed away from the wall and gave it another shot. "No reckless driving or I want off of this thing!"

"Oh, Dad." In a little singsong voice. "Chicken!"

"I'm not a chicken. I'm just smart. If you're going to drive like that, you get your own chair."

Cody motioned toward the bright little chair that stood ready, waiting for him. "I might like my own chair."

Jennie thought her heart would burst as she stooped down toward Michael to unfasten her son from the big chair. As she hugged Cody to her, she felt so close to his father that she said impulsively, "With you teaching him to drive, we'd better take out extra insurance."

He looked her straight in the eye, deathly serious. "I don't know of any company around that would consider us a good risk."

No. A bad risk at driving. A bad risk at marriage. She looked straight back at him. "I'm sure you're right." *We aren't a good risk. We never were. But I think we're changing.*

And suddenly, her feelings didn't seem so impossible anymore. They didn't seem crazy at all.

She lifted Cody, and Andy held the chair steady while she lowered him into it. As soon as they had him buckled in, Cody and his father shot out the door like streaks, shouting about racing each other up the hallway.

"Don't run over the staff!" Andy called after them. "We need everybody we've got!" But Jennie knew they were already too far away to hear her.

"Mark will love this story!" Andy said, laughing. "I've never seen a dad use this technique before."

As they started toward the hallway themselves, they heard Michael shout, "Green light!" and they heard somebody else scream.

An intern stuck his head inside the door. "Andy Kendall! Are these your two patients out here?"

"Oh, no," Andy said, her eyes widening. "Yes! One of them is. The little one."

"Well, the big one just ran into one of the fourth-floor housekeepers."

"Ha!" Andy said, laughing. "I'm not responsible. The big one isn't my patient!"

"Just an overzealous dad, I'm afraid," Jennie added.

"Come on," Andy said. "We'd better get out there before they get somebody else!"

By the time Andy and Jennie caught up with them, Cody was learning to turn corners and weave in and out between furniture in one of the waiting areas. Michael was relinquishing his chair to one of the nurses. "They made me turn in my vehicle," he said, shrugging.

"I don't blame them," Jennie said, shaking her head and laughing.

"Seeing as you aren't on two wheels anymore," Andy said, "I've got to get back to the office and do paperwork. Cody's missed the class for today. He can work for a while in the hallway. This is good for him."

"Thank you, Andy," both Michael and Jennie said at once. Then they stood together, side by side, watching Cody negotiate around a flowerpot containing a silk dieffenbachia.

"How about that?" Cody shouted when he cleared it. "Just how about that?"

"All right, Cody!" Jennie said.

"Good job, son!" Michael said at the same time.

Cody started to go around again. That's when Jennie turned to face Michael and found him gazing down at her, gazing down with such longing in his face she could scarcely comprehend it.

He reached for her hand. She felt her face turning hot. She felt her breath catch in her throat.

Cody reeled around the plastic couch and started off up the hallway again. "Look! I'm going faster!" he hollered. "And faster and faster and faster..."

Jennie looked after him, worrying about him and anyone who might unsuspectingly step out into the hallway. She took a step forward but Michael held her back, his hand tightening over her own. Before she knew what was happening, he'd swept her into his arms and was twirling her around, right there in the hospital hallway for everyone to see, even Cody. She thought he was exhilarated because of his success with Cody, but it was more than that. "This is crazy, Jen," he said after he'd set her back down on the floor. "I can't help it. I love you, Jennie. I don't know what we're going to do about it, but I love you."

"You're telling me that *here? Now?*"

"I am."

She looked up at him, tears beginning to fill her eyes. Even now, she didn't know if she trusted him. She didn't know if she trusted herself.

Cody came roaring up the corridor toward them. "Dad!" he was saying. "This is—" But he stopped when he saw them, watching them as they held on to each other, their faces full of longing and regret.

"Momma?" he asked, his voice sounding like he was frightened again, or lost. "What are you doing?" Then, as realization dawned, he started shouting questions, as full of happy excitement as if he'd just interrupted Santa Claus putting toys beneath the tree. "Are you *kissing*? Did I see you *kissing*? Do you *like* each other?"

"No, honey," Jennie said, pulling away. "Let's get your things from Andy's office. It's time to go home."

"I can do it myself now. I know how," he said, still eyeing them both. "I think you were kissing. I think you are *liking* each other."

"I know you know how," she said, ignoring his other statements. She knew their expressions and the way they were clinging to each other must have spoken volumes.

"Jen." Michael touched her arm again as soon as Cody was gone. "Meet me tonight. We've got to talk. We've got to come to some—understanding—about this."

She glanced after Cody. "I don't think we can."

"Can't Cody go visit a friend? Wangle him an invitation to Taylor's house." Michael sounded desperate. "Just for supper. Just so we can finish this."

She gripped his hand tightly but, even then, she couldn't stop her own trembling. "I'll do it. He wants to go to Taylor's."

For Jennie, the afternoon seemed endless. Cody whined and zoomed around the house in his chair, knocking over a lamp. Finally... finally... came the time to take him to his friend's house. Jennie had arranged the visit earlier. Cody was invited to eat with Taylor and play and show his best friend his new chair. And in the end, Linda Cowan had insisted Cody stay and spend the night with them, too.

Jennie left him sitting in his chair with his overnight bag draped across his lap. She held him close for a minute, feeling horrible about leaving him. But he was happy. Linda was making sloppy joes, his favorite, for supper.

She rushed back home to dress. An hour later, she met Michael at Brennan's. When she saw him, all thoughts of Cody left her. They sat at a cozy table for two in the corner, the little dancing candle on the table making his skin and hair glow like gold.

"You know where I want to go after this?" he asked, gripping her hand and grinning like a little boy. "I want to go to Fair Park and look at all the buildings again. It's been so long since I've been there."

She gave a little tinkling laugh, a laugh that during the past month had grown familiar to him. "Cody had a dream about the fair this morning. I told him we went once."

"The fairgrounds will be deserted this time of year. I thought it would be a nice place to walk off this dinner."

"I think so, too," she agreed. So, after they finished coffee and cheesecake, they drove to the place that held so many memories for them. It was late, almost nine-thirty, and the humidity hung heavy in the air. As they strolled, taking their time and holding hands like teenagers, Jennie gasped in admiration at the beautiful art deco buildings.

"I never noticed the buildings before," she said, whispering for no other reason than the night was so soft around them. Above them, it was hard to tell where the Dallas skyline stopped and the thousands of twinkling stars began. Even the doves were silent and Jennie guessed they must have already roosted for the night in the lovely old elms and live oaks that lined the Esplanade. "It's always covered with people and exhibits and little kids with corny dogs in their hands. I've never been here at night like this. I didn't know that, beneath it all, it was so beautiful."

In silence they walked through the Grand Allée du Meadows behind the Dallas Civic Garden Center. They still didn't speak as Michael led her to the massive old Hall of State and they stood gazing up at the restored golden Tejas Warrior at the entrance.

"Hidden beauty," Michael said quietly as they stood gazing up at the statue. "Or maybe not so hidden. Maybe people just don't take the time to stop and see when they're here."

He wasn't looking at the statue anymore. He was looking at her. She felt lovely and desirable and strong. As if, with Michael by her side, she could master anything.

He brushed her cheek with the back of his hand. "Oh, Jen. You're so beautiful."

She closed her eyes against his touch, reveling in it. When she felt his fingers brush against her lips she opened her eyes again, seeing so much hope in Michael's green eyes and so much need that emotion threatened to overwhelm her.

She stood on tiptoe and wrapped her arms around his neck and kissed him, full on the mouth and hard. Then she whispered his name and he clasped her to him so tightly she could scarcely breathe.

"This is crazy," he whispered to her as he buried his face in her hair.

"You've said that several times today." She kissed his neck.

They broke apart then and walked farther in silence, but after a few minutes he said, "I don't know what I'm going to do."

"It doesn't matter what you're going to do," she said softly, feeling the same desperation in her heart, and not knowing how to overcome it. "We have tonight. Tonight is all that matters. Just think about tonight." Not the past months. Not the past ten years. And not tomorrow. Definitely not tomorrow.

They stopped at the entrance to the park and looked at the myriad of stars glistening in ripples against the length of the reflecting pool.

Michael stepped up on the marble ledge of the pool and reached down for her. She stepped up beside him. He bent to kiss her again and she rose to meet him, standing atop the pink marble. She gazed up at him, at his thick blond hair that looked almost silver in the moonlight, his gleaming sea green eyes that were so often unreadable but that, tonight, seemed to mirror the stars.

She reached up with long, gentle fingers and touched the strong square line of his jaw. "I don't know what I'm going to say to Cody," she told him. "I don't know how to make him understand what he saw today."

"I'm not sure that I understand it, either," Michael said. He took her face in his hands, tenderly stroking her cheeks with his fingertips. "I just know that I love you. You've given him so much, Jennie. I've watched you sacrifice so many things for Cody."

"But it wasn't a sacrifice," she told him. "I did those things because I *wanted* to do them, because I loved him so much."

"I know that," he said quietly. "But I needed to see it."

He combed her hair back with his fingers and she touched his face again and suddenly she wanted so much more, so much more for tonight, so much more for their lives. He kissed her fiercely, over and over again, and she met him with a passion of her own, ignoring tomorrow when she would have to tell Cody, for his own sake, that she and Michael were nothing more than friends.

"Jennie—" He whispered her name between the kisses over and over again. "Jennie—Jennie—Jennie—"

She wanted to lose herself in him. She wanted this to never stop. She wanted to always be surrounded by this feeling of Michael . . . the rough skin at his jawline where his beard was already starting to grow...the place on his neck where his curls turned under...the fuzzy stray hairs at his temples that felt like down under her fingers...the way his aviator jacket smelled and creaked like new leather.

"Come home with me tonight," he said ever so softly.

"I don't know," she said, faltering. But she did know. She wanted it more than anything else in the world.

"I want you to come home with me," he said quietly. "I want to make love to you."

"Yes," she said so softly her words were scarcely more than her breath against his skin.

Jennie had known, in her heart of hearts, that it would come to this. She knew what she felt for Michael was so much more than desperation, so much more than familiarity or ease, so much more than even the romance that had brought them together ten years earlier. Tonight she wanted to give him everything. It would be the only chance she would have.

She met his gaze in the darkness and said again, "Yes, Michael. I'll come with you."

The decision made, things became magnified all around them. The stars shone twice as brightly. The water in the reflecting pool shimmered and danced as if with the same insistent primitive rhythm that pulsed warmly through Jennie's veins. As they walked toward the car, Michael started to laugh again and drew her into his arms. "I can't believe this! I can't believe, after how far we've come, how long it's been..."

But they were both different people now and he knew it as well as she did.

When they reached his car, she climbed in and, before he closed the door for her, he bent down and kissed her again. This time, she giggled.

"What's so funny?" he asked as he climbed in beside her. But he was grinning, too, as he turned the key.

"Us! We're like two kids who've finally escaped from their parents. And I'm thirty-one years old and you're thirty-three."

"Ah. You make us sound ancient. We're just kids," he said, laughing now. "Just fresh out of school."

"Not quite."

It took twenty minutes on the expressway before they reached his house. Michael solemnly opened the car door for her and took her hand in his. They walked across the front garden together and Jennie felt in an odd way as if they'd just been married again. *I, Jennie, take thee, Michael...to have and to hold...from this day forward...or even just for now, tonight...*

In her mind's eye, she saw the lovely little spot where their wedding ceremony had taken place. A white clapboard church out in the country with a huge old bell hanging in the front steeple and redbud trees practically groaning with pink blossoms lining the walk. How long ago that seemed. And how relevant now, the vows they'd once made.

They mounted the steps together and he closed the door behind her as she stepped inside. Michael encircled her waist with one arm and paused to look into her face searchingly before they walked slowly up the hallway together to his bedroom. On the way, they passed the threshold to Cody's room. Jennie stopped. "Oh Michael," she said, her voice scarcely more than a whisper. "I don't think I can do this."

Slowly, he nodded. "You don't have to, Jen. I wouldn't force you, not if it's what you decide..." All this murmured into the golden veil of her hair, as he unleashed it from the barrette that held it away from her face. He kissed her neck and her hair and her breasts as she reached out for him.

She smiled through the tears in her eyes. "If I could do it again, Michael," she whispered, "I wouldn't run the cartoon about Buzz Stephens."

"I know," he whispered back. "I know." With his mouth, he hungrily began to nudge open the neck of the pretty cream blouse she wore. Jennie treasured it all, wanting this night to last a lifetime. "I love you, Jennie. I think I've always loved you—I shouldn't have ever—let—you—"

But she silenced him with her own mouth, caressing his lips with exquisite movements. He gathered her into his arms and carried her to his bed. Gently he laid her down and slowly began to pull her blouse away. Slowly he unfastened her skirt, then undid her lacy bra.

She combed through his hair with gentle fingers, brushing away the waves at his temples, seeing the desire on his face. With her hands she sought and held and cuddled until she, too, felt the powerful rise of passion. She wanted him desperately... needed him now more than she'd needed anything in her life.

"Jennie," he said as he kissed her ear and then held himself away from her so he could see her face. And, when he did, she could see all of the questions in his green eyes. Ever so softly, as gently as a butterfly lands, she reached up and ran her hand down the line of a muscle in his face. When she touched him, he relaxed. It was all the answer he needed to know. Her gray eyes met his and she nodded.

"My darling," he said. "I want you—"

"I know," she whispered. "Me, too."

He peeled off the last of her clothing and, as she lay before him, a thousand memories came to mind. Jennie on their wedding night, her skin as luminescent, her expression as fragile, as the lace on the exquisite Natori nightgown she wore. Jennie pregnant with Cody, her belly and breasts round and full, her body bewitchingly sensuous as she lay before him, ripe with his child.

He pulled away just long enough to discard his own clothes, then laid himself beside her and held her very close, so close, as if to meld his very flesh with hers. Then, with a hunger so great he could hardly bear it, he eased himself over her and pressed inside her, pushing himself deep, deeper, as Jennie clung to him.

She trailed little kisses all around his neck and his ears and his face. He could feel the cool wetness there and he knew she was crying. He moved gently with her, even though his desire was so great that it was tremendously difficult to be tender. They rocked together with the eternal motion, until Jennie rose up beneath him and cried out his name.

Michael let himself go then, holding his hips firm against hers, coming against her with a strength as ungiving as granite. At last, at last, he pressed his forehead hard against hers as he felt the heat shoot through him. He seemed to float along with it, letting it fill him, letting it fill Jennie, too, as he yielded himself to her.

They clung together, their damp bodies drying in the cool night air, drifting, for what seemed like forever. Michael opened his eyes later and found her nestled against him, her eyelids resting against her cheeks like gossamer, her hair fanned out all across his pillow. "I love you," he whispered. He knew she didn't hear him. She looked like a sleeping child, peaceful and cuddled into the crook of his arm.

She shifted slightly, and he kissed her again. It seemed like a lifetime before he could pull away from her. "I love you, Jennie," he said again, his breath teasing strands of her hair like a gentle breeze. But she didn't answer him, as he propped himself up on one elbow and gazed down at her in the massive French mahogany bed.

CHAPTER SEVENTEEN

"YOU KNOW what I was thinking?" he asked her.

"No," she said, smiling slightly. "What were you thinking?"

"About all the times we've been together—like this—and how beautiful you are right now. More beautiful than I ever remember." It was true. He had seen her like this, held her like this so many times. But he had grown and so had she. Being with her now seemed different. Her body's curves were fuller, richer, and he couldn't ever remember having loved her with so much passion.

"It's amazing, isn't it?" She reached up and touched his face wonderingly. Then, when he nodded, she pulled him to her and kissed him. Her hands began to rove and she laughed as he gripped her to him. "I want more and more of you—"

"Me, too."

"I shouldn't stay all night," she said, sighing. "Cody's spending the night at Taylor's house. He was letting Taylor have rides in his wheelchair when I left. Linda said they'd be fine, but if anything should happen—"

"Don't go yet," he said, beseechingly. "Just stay another hour. That isn't much, Jen."

She burrowed down into the bed, resting her head on his arm as peacefully as a baby.

Michael eventually disentangled himself from the sheets, went downstairs naked and returned with a plate of cookies. "Here," he said, picking out a big one for her. "Eat this."

"I'll get crumbs in your bed."

"That's okay." He took a big bite of one and climbed back in beside her. "It's worth it. I need to keep your strength up, you know."

"*You* need to keep *my* strength up? Ha!"

"Yeah." He gave her a rakish grin.

"You—" She bopped him with her pillow. He grabbed her elbows and she collapsed against him, giggling, as she kissed his neck and chest, dribbling cookie crumbs all the way. By the time she got down to his navel, Michael was on fire for her again. He took her hair and held it in bunches, groaning while she trailed her lips across him, and they made love again, this time slowly, each of them savoring the miracle of it. Jennie whispered his name over and over again against his skin and, for the hour, they forgot about their son and everything that stood between them.

It was three in the morning by the time she pulled herself away. "Thank you," she said, leaning over him and letting her long hair hang down around his face like a curtain. "Michael, thank you."

"Oh, Jennie," he said, holding her face, wanting to remember the way she looked now always. "My Jennie."

The last thing he wanted was to take her home. But she rolled away from him and began to get dressed. A few minutes later, he found her in his bathroom, brushing her hair with his wooden brush, and crying.

"Jennie . . . honey . . . what is it?"

"I gave you this—brush—f-f-for—Christmas once."

He nodded, taking it from her hand. "You did."

"I'm so glad you s-s-still—have—it—"

He wiped her hair away from her face. "I've kept it a long time."

But when he looked into her eyes, he saw fear.

"What is it? What's wrong?"

"I'm—so—scared," she whispered.

As he answered her, he began to stroke her hair. "Oh, Jen. Is it Cody?"

She shook her head, holding the worn mahogany brush handle, balancing it in the palm of her hand. "It isn't just Cody. It's all of us. If this didn't work—if—we—tried—it—again—and—it—didn't—work—"

He knew where her words were leading, and that her fears were justified. "You're afraid for us."

She nodded. "Tonight was so wonderful and I wanted it so badly. . . . I couldn't try this and have it—not—work—again. I think how it would feel to lose you all over again and I couldn't bear—everything—to stand there watching it hurt—all—three—of—us."

"Jennie." He knelt on the carpet before her. He'd been so certain of his feelings today, so certain of her response to him tonight. He didn't want her to pull away. He'd given her everything he had to give.

For the first time he recognized just how gravely he'd hurt her once, and just how far she still needed to come. "I'm taking you home. It's almost four in the morning. It will seem different after you've slept."

When he let her off at the front door of her house, she was still upset.

"What would happen to Cody," she asked, "if we tried again and it didn't work? How would he feel if we did this to him all over again?"

"I don't know, Jennie," he said, his heart aching for all three of them. "I just don't know."

LINDA DROVE Cody home at ten-thirty the next morning. Jennie was on the phone making plans for the swim team fund-raiser. He rolled right in, set his overnight bag down beside the mantel, waited until she hung up and accosted her.

"I thought about stuff last night," he said to her as he steered his chair into the kitchen. "I couldn't sleep."

He parked right in the sunlight that streamed in beside the table. "I saw the way you and Dad were at the hospital yesterday. Taylor's mom and dad were looking at each other the same way last night."

Jennie gripped her coffee cup and closed her eyes against the hot steam rising from it.

"Cody," she said aloud. "I've got to talk to you about Dad and me. You have to try and understand something, okay?"

"Maybe I don't want to."

"You *have* to." She knelt down and met him eye-to-eye. "Your Dad and I tried to be married once and it didn't work. We hurt each other and we hurt you. I don't think it would be very smart of us to let that happen again to any of us."

At that moment the telephone rang. She picked it up without thinking. "Hello?"

"Jen," Michael said. "It's me. Meet me for lunch."

"I don't think that's such a good idea," Jennie said carefully.

Michael realized that Cody must be listening. "Not a good idea now? You want to do it later. Can we have dinner tonight?"

"I don't think so."

He understood. His heart turned to ice. Despite what Jennie felt for him, despite what they had shared last night, she wasn't backing down. The fear was winning. She was silent for a long moment. Then, finally, she whispered, "I won't do it." Meaning a myriad of things. *I won't meet you for lunch. I won't meet you at all. I won't acknowledge that what happened last night affects my life in any way.* "I can't. Don't ask me. Please."

He said nothing for a while. Then: "I don't know what to do, Jen. I don't want to hurt him. I know you don't, either. But everything I'm feeling is real. I don't think I can put it aside for him anymore."

Jennie felt tears smarting in her eyes. She couldn't explain how she felt to Michael now. Not with Cody listening.

As she stood clutching the phone and watching her son, she couldn't help but remember the hurt, the sheer disbelief, on Cody's face when they'd told him about the divorce. "I *don't* want Daddy to go," he'd wailed as he stood beside the front door clutching both Mason and Michael's leg.

"He *has* to go, honey," she'd said gently, bending down to his eye level and trying to make him understand. "Next week, after Daddy finds another house, you can go and be with him *there.* You'll be the luckiest little boy I know, Cody. You'll have *two* houses instead of one."

He'd stomped the foot of his fuzzy, footed pajamas. "I don't *want* two houses. I just want this house. With *Daddy* in it . . ."

After Michael had left that night, Cody had cried as if his heart would break. He fell asleep finally, exhausted, at midnight. But by 2:00 a.m. he was awake again.

"Momma! Momma!" he'd screamed from the darkness of his room. "There's a monster outside. He's eating my house—"

"Cody!" She'd run up the hallway, almost as frightened by his outburst as he was by his nightmare. "Honey." She'd gathered him into her arms and crooned to him. "It's just a dream. Just a bad dream."

Sobbing, he'd crawled into bed in his mother's room and held on to her. It had been weeks before he was able to sleep through the night.

Never again, she vowed. Never again would she stand before the same little boy and watch his face crumple while she told him his family was disintegrating.

"This has already gone too far," she whispered to Michael now. "I wish I could just turn everything off and not *want—*" she caught herself "*—so many things.*"

He answered her quietly. "You're being human. And caring. You're doing this because of how much you love Cody."

Jennie didn't answer.

As they hung up the phone, she turned to face Cody. *How ironic,* she thought, *that the very thing that is bringing us together, our love for our son, is exactly what's going to keep us apart.*

CODY DIDN'T LIKE the swimming lesson much today. Nothing was going right. His mom had been grumpy all day. She got off the phone and she'd made him hurry when it came time to put his bathing suit on. Cody didn't like to hurry. He didn't hurry very well anymore. When his mom saw he wasn't getting everything done he.was supposed to, she'd put his bathing suit on herself. He felt as if he were three years old.

He'd stared out the window all the way to the pool, feeling sad and not knowing why. He wanted to do everything right for his mom and for his dad, but sometimes he wished he could just stop trying so hard. Sometimes he wished he could just be a kid again, and things could be the way they used to be.

When he got to swimming, Mark wanted him to put his head underwater.

"I don't want to do that," he said.

"Come on, Cody," Mark said. "You did it plenty of times last week."

"I just don't want to do it today."

"If you blow out as you go down, you won't get water up your nose."

"I don't care if I get water up my nose." He rubbed his eyes with the back of his hand. He felt tears wanting to come out.

"Cody? Bud?" Mark asked. "What's wrong? Is there anything I can do to make you feel better?"

Cody shook his head.

"Do you feel like you're getting sick?"

Cody shook his head.

"Your mom's going to be here in a minute. She can take you home and maybe you can lie down."

"I don't want to lie down."

"Then why aren't you working harder today during swim class?"

"I don't know. I just don't feel like doing anything today."

When the time for kickboards came, Cody waited on the side and shook his head every time one of the other kids offered him a turn.

Mark took him in his arms and tried to get him to dive for rings. "This is your favorite game. You're the best on the whole team at this!"

"I don't care if I'm the best. I don't want to."

"So," Mark said. There was one little drop of water hanging from the end of Mark's nose. But even that didn't make Cody feel like smiling. "Are you just going to quit trying altogether?"

"I think so," Cody told him.

"WHAT'S UP WITH CODY?" Mark asked Jennie when she arrived. "He wouldn't do anything during class today. I've never seen him like this."

"I don't know what's wrong," she lied. She knew exactly what was wrong. But she wasn't willing to share it with Mark. "Maybe he's just disappointed with the way things are turning out."

"But he was doing so *well.*"

At that moment, Andy strolled up to them, and Mark told her what had happened in the class.

"Jennie," Andy said, taking her aside. "You've got to motivate him to start working again. If he doesn't he's going to lose everything he's been working for."

"I know that," Jennie said. "I just don't know how to make him do it."

"Has something happened we should know about? Do you know what's made him turn inside himself like this? He isn't acting like himself at all."

This time, Jennie nodded and Andy saw the discouragement welling up in her eyes. "Oh, Jennie." She touched her friend's shoulders. "What is it?"

"It's Michael." She told Andy some of the past days, what had passed between them at the hospital, everything that Cody had seen.

"Oh, dear," Andy said, sighing. When she spoke, she seemed to be picking her words very carefully. "The risk of hurting Cody may be a risk you have to take. You and Michael have learned to be strong for each other. You probably never got that far the first time, did you?"

"No. We didn't."

"I think you two owe it to yourselves to find out—how you've changed—how those changes could affect your feelings for each other."

Together, they watched while Mark did his best to tow Cody around the pool. The little boy had no exercise during the session at all.

"Someday Cody will be grown up," Andy said. "Someday you won't run into Michael at therapy anymore. Someday you won't *have* to be strong for each other. And what will you have left? A lifetime, Jennie. A lifetime to wonder if you and Michael could have built something for yourselves again."

"You think so?" Jennie asked. "You think we should risk it all again?"

"I do," Andy said solemnly. She told Jennie more about Buddy. About the accident. About how she couldn't forgive him for not pushing ahead. "People change over time, Jennie. Some for the good and some for the bad. But people don't stay the same. I've watched Buddy's career lately in the newspapers and it's incredible what he's done." She had to stop to swallow a lump in her throat when she said it. "I wish I hadn't expected everything at once."

"Well," Jennie noted quietly, "if it isn't too late for Michael and me, maybe it isn't too late for the two of you."

"Don't you see, though?" And this time, the threat of tears was in Andy's eyes. "I lost faith in him then. He knows it. I don't think there can ever be a coming back from that. I don't know."

As they stood together by the pool, Jennie reached out with both hands and hugged her friend. "I don't know, either, Andy,'' she said. She was thinking about Michael.

BILL JOSEPHS SAT on the examining table and bit his lip while Michael listened to his chest. "There's not anything wrong with me, Doc," Bill said finally. "I know those pains came from something I ate for dinner last night."

"You can't be too careful," Michael told him as he moved around to his back and listened to a different area.

"Marge keeps sending me over here. I hiccup and she tells me I need to see you. Frankly, I think she has a crush on you. That's why she always insists I come to this place."

Michael stood up and let his stethoscope drop to his chest. He couldn't hear Bill's heart anymore anyway; he couldn't listen to the thumping of a patient's heart and the patient's opinion about things all at the same time. And Bill Josephs had plenty of opinions about everything. Instead, Michael smoothed his hair back exaggeratedly. He knew exactly how to get his old friend's goat.

"You think Marge really likes me, Bill? Is that why she had me out for breakfast? You know, if it wasn't for her bringing you in all the time, I wouldn't have a practice at all. You and Marge are the only reason I can pay all my bills."

"I'm that way to everybody," the old guy said, winking. "That's why my momma named me *Bill*. You should *see* all my bills. During my lifetime, I've kept half of this country in business. I've got this nightmare I get to heaven and St. Peter hands me a list of all my charges. Please pay in advance.''

Michael chuckled. "It could happen." He flipped Bill's chart open and made several notes. "But I doubt it. Generally, God doesn't work things out that way with us."

Bill grinned. "Let's hope not. If it was that way, I'd never get in up there."

"Well," Michael said, as he clapped his friend on the back. "You go back and tell Marge you aren't going to have to worry about St. Peter for a while, anyway. From what I could hear, your heart sounds fine."

"I'm going to let Marge pay the bill for this," Bill said, chuckling.

"You do that." Michael smiled as he scribbled the charge on the business form and handed it to his receptionist.

"No matter what's wrong with this old body," Bill said, "I always feel a little bit better after you've checked it over."

"Bill—wait—" All at once, he knew what he had to do about Jennie.

No matter what's wrong with this old body, I always feel a little bit better after you've checked it over.

Bill's words had just given it to him right between the eyes. *Bill trusts me. And so help me, Jennie, you can trust me, too.*

"What can I do for you, Doc?"

"I've got a favor to ask. A big one."

"I'm good at favors," Bill told him. "What is it?"

"Can I borrow your horses? Dan and Kimbo? I'd like to take somebody riding."

"Your boy?"

"No. My—a friend."

Bill raised his eyebrows. "A *woman* friend?"

"You might say that."

"You takin' my advice, Doc? You going out and lookin' for a good woman to take care of you when you get old?"

Michael laughed and nodded his head. "You might say that."

"You say the word. You've got those horses any time you want them. You can borrow the rabbits, too, if you think they'll impress her. And I've been thinking about getting one of those potbellied pigs."

Michael's grin broadened. "No potbellied pigs or rabbits. All I want is the horses for one afternoon. I'll call you and set it up. You tell Marge this office visit is on me. No charge."

"No charge?" Bill practically guffawed. "You mean you aren't gonna bill me?"

"Nope. You're free and clear. Use the money and take Marge on a date."

"That isn't such a bad idea," Bill said, pulling on his battered tweed hat and shaking Michael's hand. "I'll do that."

CHAPTER EIGHTEEN

CODY'S SWIM THERAPY went even worse the next day.

Mark tried to coax Cody to work from the water.

Jennie tried to coax Cody to work from the poolside. From what Jennie could tell, Cody had just stopped trying.

"Cody—please—" she pleaded with him.

She remembered his first day of kindergarten. He'd been afraid to go and had refused to let go of her hand. She felt as helpless until the teacher had knelt down beside him and offered to show him Hannah the hamster. The teacher had let him feed Hannah a bite of nectarine. After that, he'd been hooked.

"Please, son," she said now. "You've got to do what Mark says."

You were doing so well... But she didn't dare say that aloud to him.

"I just wanna go home," he said to her, flopping over into Mark's waiting arms. "I don't want to do this again. Ever again."

"Darling," she told him. "You've got to *try.*"

"I don't want to try."

She felt miserable as she helped him to the car and drove him back to the house. She didn't blame Michael. She certainly didn't blame Cody. She blamed herself. She sat up late that night, reading books, trying to concentrate, but all she could think of was Cody, his failures and her own. She didn't know how to motivate him or where to turn. And Mark had already told her he didn't have the answers, either.

At nine she went in to check on him and found him fast asleep. She sat beside him on the bed, stroking the cottony yellow strands of his hair. Now, here, the tears fell at last... where no one could see her... where no one could share the discouragement she felt. Why wouldn't he work? Why had he given up?

"Cody," she whispered as she wiped her wet cheeks with the back of one hand and studied his sleeping, peaceful face. "Cody. Son. Please. You just need to try."

ART SANDERSON STUDIED the sports page with the trained eye of a perfectionist, making certain the layout looked clean, that none of the headlines bumped together, and that everything made sense.

With his red pencil, he circled two things. One, a headline that bumped up against another one so it looked as if it read: "Local runner takes first in 100 mph plunge off hillside."

The second item he circled was a small box on the third page. "Swim team for special kids makes waves with water therapy." He was glad to see they were already running promotional articles for the fund-raiser. He wanted this group to have good play in his pages. The article should have been given better placement. He wanted it closer to page one. He'd talk with his layout staff about both this afternoon.

He picked up the phone and called Jennie. When she answered the telephone, he could tell something was wrong. She sounded subdued, not like herself at all.

"How are the fund-raiser plans going?" he asked.

"Going really well. I've got several celebrities but I need more."

"You've done well. You ought to sound more excited about it than you do."

"I've had a thousand things on my mind. The fund-raiser's been on the back burner during these past few days—" She paused, knowing full well that the best thing for her mental fatigue right now would be to jump headfirst into this project. "—but I'm coming along. I need two more famous people and I'll have it."

"Jennie. Are you okay? You don't sound like yourself. Maybe you need to come back to work."

She had to smile. Subtlety was not Art's strong suit. But when she spoke, her words were serious. "Cody's reached his breaking point, I think. He was doing so well for a while that he got all our hopes up."

"Jennie," Art said suddenly. "I've got another idea for you. Do you know anything about Buddy Draper?"

She gave a little start and then grinned. "The Dallas Sidekicks' new coach?" She knew a good deal about Buddy that other people *didn't* know.

"What do you think about getting him involved in this project? I'm betting he'd do it," Art commented, "considering what he went through himself. You know. Special kids fighting to be winners. Buddy Draper fighting to be a winner. That sort of thing.''

Jennie's mind was already racing. Here was the idea to lift her above her discouragement with Cody, her desperation about Michael. Why hadn't she thought of it?

Andy was going to kill her. But fairy tales came true all the time. *So,* Jennie asked herself, *what are good friends for? To give fairy tales a little push start.*

"I like it, Art," she told him, trying to sound composed and professional when what she really wanted to do was jump up and down. "I'll let you know when I get something put together with him."

She hung up the phone, buoyed once again by the plans for the show, and carried Lester the cat back to see Cody. "Hi, Bear," she said gently, her eyes sparkling as she laid the purring cat in his lap. "What are you doing?"

"Sitting around," he said. He didn't even look at her.

"Darling," she said, kneeling down beside him. "I don't know what to say or do to make it better."

"There isn't anything."

"I've got some great ideas for the swim team fundraiser today. Let's work together. Why don't you come in here and do your book report while I make phone calls?"

He'd started back at school just two days before, not to his old school but to a special school in Plano. The teachers there helped kids who had been out of school for a while to catch up with their studies. "Has something happened at school? Are you wishing you were back in Mrs. Bounds' class?''

"No," he said, shaking his head. His nose started to turn red and she knew he was about to cry again. "I don't miss my friends. I talk to Taylor all the time."

It was time to take a different tack. This gentle pleading hadn't worked with him at all. "I'm tired of the way you're acting, Cody," she told him, standing up abruptly. He started at the change in her voice.

"I'm acting fine," he retorted.

"No, you're not. You're making *me* feel bad because you won't *try*. Well, I refuse to feel bad anymore, young man. You aren't being fair to yourself or to me. You just think about it. You sit there and figure out what's so wrong you have to give up. Then you figure out how to tell me, Cody. Because that's what you're going to have to do before anything gets any better around here."

She turned on her heels and left him sitting there in his wheelchair, with Lester the cat still purring in his lap.

"YOU SHOULD DO IT," Marshall Townsend told Buddy as he stepped out of the shower in the locker room and toweled himself off. "This swim team sounds like a great cause to support."

"They should have asked *you*," Buddy replied. "You're the star player these days." But there was more to it than Marshall knew. Much more. They were talking about Mark *Kendall's* swim team.

At first, when Jennie Stratton had phoned him this morning, he'd actually wondered if Andy had engineered this. But he'd quickly realized Andy wasn't involved. And suddenly he'd found himself wishing that she was.

"I just don't know if I have the time, Ms. Stratton," he'd told her. "I'm honored to be asked. I'm honored to be included with a list of guests this impressive. I know the swim team is a worthy group. I've heard Mark Kendall works wonders."

"I just don't know if I want any more media attention," Buddy told Marshall now, trying to cover for himself. "Things have finally started dying down."

"Don't tell me you've gotten tired of media attention," Marshall said wryly, running the towel wildly over his head. "You've always thrived on it."

"Nah. Not so much anymore."

Somebody hollered at him from the front office and told him Jennie was on the phone for him again.

"What did you decide?" she asked him.

"I haven't decided anything," he told her pointedly. "You told me you'd give me some time to think about this."

"I'm calling again to convince you that you have to do this, Mr. Draper," she said, the excitement in her voice beginning to wash over him, too. "My editor at the *Times-Sentinel* has just given me permission to do a series of cartoons to promote the event. And I'd love to do one of you—flattering, of course—" she added, laughing. "We'll have cameo appearances from all the other celebrities. But you're the perfect person to be our master of ceremonies for the show."

"You're sure about that."

"I wouldn't be bothering you like this if I wasn't."

He wanted to consider it. But what would happen between him and Andy at this posh media event?

"Well, you've talked me into it. I'll be there," he said, as Marshall walked into the front office and shot him an A-okay sign. "Let me know when you'll need me."

"I'll send you a script and a list of the acts," she told him gleefully. "You don't need to follow the script, though. You can ad-lib all you want to. It'll be fine with us."

"Ad-libbing?" he asked, chuckling and wondering about Andy again. "You'd better watch me close if you're going to let me ad-lib. Or else I'll probably get myself into lots of trouble."

THE NEXT MORNING just after the little van had come to pick Cody up for school, a pickup truck pulling a horse trailer pulled up to the curb and stopped. Jennie heard the commotion and she peered out through the lace curtains to see who it was. Out stepped Michael clad in faded jeans and an old blue flannel shirt she knew he'd had forever. He looked so handsome and so familiar. She opened the door without giving him a chance to knock.

"Hi," he said. "I knew you'd be home. I tried to call but the phone was busy."

"I've been working on the show for the swim team." She smiled, stifling the almost unbearable urge to throw her arms around him and hug him hard. The last time they'd been together alone, they'd made love.

"Can I come in?" he asked finally.

She gave a little tinkling laugh. "Oh, do." She stepped back and he entered and, as he stepped onto the carpet, she noticed the gray antelope boots he was wearing. "You make a good cowboy."

"Yeah," he said, grinning. "All I need's the hat."

"Everything's coming together for the fund-raiser. It's going to be quite a production. Mark's already got the kids practicing, too."

"I think you should work on the fund-raiser tomorrow. I've got two horses out there—" here he put on his best cowboy swagger and voice "—that are just hankerin' to take you for a ride across the blacklands of North Texas."

"Oh, no!" She started to giggle. "You're crazy. You know that?"

"I'm more sane now than I've ever been in my life. Get into your jeans. I need a change of scenery. We're going for a ride."

"Michael."

She didn't think she should go, but she wanted to more than anything.

He saw all her doubts on her face. "Come on, Jennie. I'm not taking 'no' for an answer. The horses are all loaded up and waiting. Don't turn me down now."

She considered. "I've got to get back by 4:15. That's when the van brings Cody back from school."

"That's fine. We've got all day. We'll beat the traffic back into town."

Jennie changed quickly and rejoined him downstairs, her heart thumping like a schoolgirl's all over again.

"These are Bill Josephs's horses," he told her as they climbed into the truck. "You remember him? He's been my patient a long time. They used to have a ranch over on Preston Road. Now they have a little place out past Mesquite."

"I do remember him. His wife's name is Marge?"

"That's him. They don't use the horses much anymore. He said he'd love for us to take them out and give them some exercise."

"So...where are we going?"

"You'll see."

"We need to make plans for Cody to come to your place. You want me to bring him over on Sunday?"

"Let's talk about that later."

He just kept driving. He drove them far north of Plano to a pretty house atop a knoll that had acres and acres of land and a perfect white fence lining the driveway. Down past the house on the other side of the drive stood the corrals. He backed the trailer in and climbed out to unload the horses.

"This place is beautiful," she said, climbing out of the truck and crossing her arms over her pretty blue sweater. "Are the owners patients of yours, too?"

He shook his head. "Nope. Just somebody I know." That was all he intended to say for now.

She stepped over to the side of the knoll and looked across the pasture that was just now beginning to tinge with the green of early springtime. "You can see for miles."

He came to stand beside her, leading a horse. "That's pretty much what Texas is known for, away from the city."

She turned to him, only a breath away, her skin as soft and pink in the cool morning air as the embroidered roses on her sweater. It was everything he could do to keep from kissing her. But he wasn't going to do that, not while he still had so much to tell her.

He handed her the reins to Bill Josephs's chestnut mare and he lifted her easily so she could mount. She kept the horse still, waiting for him, while he led the other horse, a dun, out of the trailer. But he waved her on. "Go ahead, Jen. I'll catch up with you."

"You don't mind?"

He shook his head.

She kicked the horse and they were on their way. "See you in the pasture!"

Michael watched them both for a moment, smiling at the two bouncing ponytails as they disappeared just over the knoll. He saddled up his own horse and hurried to catch up. "Hey, you!" he called as he galloped up beside her. "I didn't know you were going to ride across half the county!"

"This feels wonderful," she called back, laughing. Her wheat yellow hair was streaming back behind her and she had tears running down her cheeks from the wind. "I know it sounds wild," she told him, "but I feel so *free* out here. Everything has been weighing on me. But out here the weight is just gone."

"You needed that."

"I needed that."

They rode along together in silence. It was one of those precious days in early spring when the black earth and the tender sprouts of grass poking up through the brown smelled herbal and rich and full of promise.

"What are the horses' names? Did Bill tell you?"

"He told me," Michael answered her, smiling. "He treats these horses like they're his children. Your horse is Kimbo. Mine is Dan."

"Cody would like to ride sometime. Do you think Bill would let him?"

"Bill's been suggesting it." Michael chuckled. "Bill has a lot of suggestions."

She tilted her head at him and grinned. He loved watching her. She looked like one of the little sparrows that kept twittering and rising from the pecan trees around them. "Dan is a pretty common name, but I wonder where he got 'Kimbo.'"

"I think he named her after his daughter."

She laughed. "An honor, I'm sure." She laid long, slender fingers against the horse's neck. "You're a good girl, Kimbo. A fine horse."

They rode farther, neither speaking.

"You want to race?" Michael suggested.

"Do you know something I don't know?" she asked him. "Which one of these horses is faster?"

"I have no idea. That's why I wanted to race. We could find out."

She leaned low over the chestnut's neck. "Okay. Let's find out." Before he knew what was happening, she was galloping ahead of him like a Kentucky Derby jockey and the distance was spreading.

"Hey!" he hollered. "I didn't say 'go!'"

"No." she shouted back, pulling even farther ahead. "I did."

He spurred Dan and the horse leapt forward. Michael felt as if he were flying as he pounded after her. The distance began to close. Up ahead, he could hear Jennie laughing and urging Kimbo on. "Come on, boy," he whispered. "Let's get her."

Dirt flew up in clods from Kimbo's racing hooves. Jennie's ponytail was long gone. Her hair flew out from her head like a banner.

He'd just about caught up with her. They raced together across the field toward an unknown goal, running just for the joy of running, the horses flank to flank, the sweat pouring from beneath their saddle blankets despite the cool day.

Dan inched up now, slowly, slowly, until his nose bobbed up and down directly beside the horse he challenged. And then, at long last, the nose went past and the race was over. "I won! I won!" Michael shouted as he pulled up. He winked at her. "That was the finish line back there."

"No," she said in her soft Texas drawl. "There wasn't a finish line. I just wanted to see how far I could go before you won."

"Ha!" he said, throwing his head back and wiping sweat off his face with a shirtsleeve.

"We got pretty far," she added, grinning.

"Thank you," he said, "for letting me win."

"Thank you," she said, "for the race."

"There's a creek up ahead. We probably ought to let these guys rest and have a drink."

"Sounds fine to me," she said. "You know the lay of this land pretty well, Michael."

"I've walked it several times."

They came toward the creek. The horses began to knicker as soon as they saw the water. Michael and Jennie loosened the reins and the horses lowered their heads. Dan and Kimbo snorted and sucked water with such relish it made Michael smile. "Sounds like a herd of elephants drinking here instead of two horses."

"We ran them pretty hard." But she didn't really participate in the joke. Her mind was somewhere else, on Michael's thigh in fact, as it rubbed her own in the saddle. The horses stood hindquarter against hindquarter and as Michael bent down to watch their heads, two drops of sweat glistened against his temple in the sunlight.

Jennie's senses were suddenly filled with him, filled with the nearness of him, with the warm gamy smell of the horses, the creaking of worn leather. And Michael, the beautiful, powerful presence of him here beside her, his hair wet with exertion, curling wildly at his neck the way it always did after they made love.

She reached across and touched his hand where his fingers lay open atop the knotted reins. He jumped as if he'd been seared.

He turned to face her. "They've had enough to drink, I think," he said quietly. "We'd best get them out of this creek."

"Sure," she said, looking away from him, sorry she'd touched him, sorry she'd allowed herself to feel anything, as Kimbo's head came dripping up out of the water.

He turned his horse back toward the house and Jennie followed him. They'd ridden without saying anything for what seemed like forever before he turned to her. It was time he told her what he'd brought her here to say. "I'm giving you full custody of Cody, Jen."

"What?"

"My lawyers have been working on it. All they need is your signature."

Jennie stared at him, shocked. She pulled the horse to a full stop. "I don't understand. After everything you fought for, Michael? Why? Why now?"

"Jen," he said, stopping Dan just beside her. "I've watched you give Cody everything you had to give him."

With tears in her eyes, she nodded.

"Well, I want to give him everything, too. I don't want him to have to go back and forth between us. I want him to have one home, one life, where he belongs."

"Until he's stronger?"

"No. Until forever. In a home where he belongs."

"Why, Michael? Why now?"

"Because this is the best way I know to give him as much as you've given him. And I think he deserves that much from me, too."

"But...Cody..." It was all she could say. She reeled from the enormity of his sacrifice.

"We've talked. Last Thursday when I took him to therapy at Children's, we had a long discussion. He wants it, too, Jennie. He told me he'd rather live with you as long as I come visit him and we still do things together."

The tears began to course down her face. Michael thought he might cry, too. But he didn't regret what he was doing.

I want her trust, he thought. *And I want her to love me.* Love, different in countless ways from what they'd shared before. Love, free from suspicion and guilt and jealousy. Not romance but love, tempered to strength on the anvil of what they'd shared—a broken marriage—a son's illness—a binding faith.

"I'm afraid," she told him quietly.

"Because you'd have him all to yourself?"

Reluctantly, she nodded.

"But you won't be by yourself," he said, his own tears threatening again. "I'll be there, too. I'll always be there for you and Cody. Remember that."

This time, it was Michael's turn to reach across the horse and touch Jennie's hand.

"Michael," she said, "I don't know what to say."

"You don't have to say anything."

She gripped his hand, held on to it as tightly as she wanted to hang on to him. "I guess 'thank you' would be a good start."

"As good as any."

Gently, tenderly, he lifted her hand, their fingers intertwined, until the back of her hand rested against the cool skin of his cheek.

For a moment she looked entranced by the simple gesture. Then she uncurled her fingers and ran them lightly along the curve of his ear and down the tendon at his neck.

"Oh, Michael . . ." she whispered.

He looked into her eyes for one long second, holding his breath, waiting for her to say something more. But she didn't.

She sat silently, the tears still glittering in her eyes.

He released her hand.

She pulled it away and gripped the reins, still feeling the insistent firm press of his fingers there, still feeling the velvet softness and the pulsing vein where she'd trailed her own fingers against his skin.

Michael kicked Dan and turned the horse back toward truck and trailer.

Together he and the animal galloped across the sweet green grass.

JENNIE SAT MOTIONLESS for a moment watching them. The muscles of both horse and rider surged in waves like the water, while the grass blew to and fro in erratic lacy patterns where they passed.

He looked for all the world as if he were running away from her, away from everything he'd just given her, away from the melding fire that burned in the touch they'd shared, away from the life and the son that held them together.

Jennie reined her own horse in a circle, kicked Kimbo, leaned forward in the saddle and followed him.

CHAPTER NINETEEN

THE TIME CAME for Cody to try to stand on crutches.

"I'm worried about him," Andy told Jennie at one of Cody's swimming sessions. "He should be ready for crutches by now, and he isn't. But if we don't let him try them out now, if only to show him what we're working toward, I don't know if he'll ever get there."

"I hate for him to try and fail, Andy," Jennie told her honestly. "If we ask too much of him and he can't do it, he'll be discouraged."

"Or it might just make him start trying again."

Andy cleared out all the equipment from the gym at Children's that morning, leaving only the tumbling pads and parallel bars, which she placed in the center of the room. Jennie drove Cody to the hospital and Michael met them there. Michael and Jennie watched anxiously as Andy and an assistant lifted their son from the wheelchair, one of his little arms wrapped around each of their shoulders, and maneuvered him toward the equipment.

"Here you go, kiddo." Andy told him as she helped him circle his fingers around each bar. "This is it. Time to stand up and show all of us what you're made of!"

"I'm a kid," Cody told Andy. "You know what I'm made of. Skin and stuff."

"More than that," Andy shot back at him. "I've seen you work. I know what you're made of. Good stuff. Good dreams. Dreams that are gonna make you try and do this thing right." She nodded at the assistant and the man took on the full brunt of Cody's weight. Andy stepped out between the bars in front of him. "Now. It's time. Let's see you straighten those legs and put some muscles to use. There you go. Ease it down. Think about what you're doing."

Cody's eyes locked with Andy's. Jennie and Michael held their breath. Cody's legs buckled beneath him and he began to sink. Andy caught him and helped pull him back up.

"No," Andy said. "Not like that. Think strong. Think legs of steel. Decide you're a robot, like C3P0 on *Star Wars,* and you've got to lock your knees and raise yourself as tall as you can."

"C3P0's a *droid,*" Cody argued, obviously trying to keep everyone's mind off the task at hand.

"Whatever he was," Andy shot back, "he stood strong and tall and helped Luke Skywalker."

Andy nodded at the assistant again.

He relinquished his grip on Cody a second time.

"Now, Cody," Andy urged. *"Now."*

Beside the door, Michael gripped Jennie's hand in his own.

"Please, Cody," Jennie murmured. "Please try."

"Come on, son," Michael chimed in. "I *know* you can do it."

Cody's knees turned inward...outward...one outward and one inward again...and the little boy's posture started to crumple. Again the assistant rescued him.

"That was better," Andy encouraged him. "You balanced a little bit longer." She knew she had to encourage him. Cody had one more chance. If he couldn't do this, she wouldn't do much more with him today. They were all expecting an awful lot of him. It was best if they didn't tire him out. "I want to see you try it one more time."

"I don't want to try again," he said, whining.

"I remember when you used to try everything. You do this and you'll be back on the right track, kiddo. You just wait and see. You'll be *so glad* if you try."

This time, Andy's words seemed to spark something within Cody. He shook his head and squared his shoulders and sighed as he tried again.

"That's it...." Andy egged him on. "Come on...come on..."

Michael clenched Jennie's hand so fiercely she scarcely had feeling in it anymore. She gritted her teeth and held her breath as she silently prayed for Cody.

"You can do it, Cody," Andy whispered to him. "I'm proud of you! I see you trying! I know you can!"

For one instant...maybe less than an instant...it seemed that Cody was bearing the brunt of his own weight. His legs wobbled...once...twice...and he lost his balance. He began to topple. The assistant moved to grab him but he missed.

"Ooof," Cody grunted when he hit the ground. And, as Michael and Jennie ran to him and Andy lifted him up, Cody began to cry in earnest.

"I hate this!" he bawled as tears of frustration streamed down his cheeks. "I hate my legs. I hate my head. I hate having to *fight* to make things work right. I hate this." He started pounding the mats with his hands. "I—hate—this!"

"Cody, son," Michael said, reaching out to him. "Your mother and I—we hate it, too. But it's got to be done. You've got to keep fighting. If you do, you won't believe how far you can go."

But Cody would hear none of it. "I don't care what you and Mom think. I don't care what you and Mom do!" he shouted. "You two are the dumbest parents alive. You don't even understand."

Michael felt his anger rising. He did his best to keep it in check. "You watch yourself, young man. I don't want to hear that tone of voice from you again."

"You aren't being fair!" Cody shouted at him. "You and Mom aren't being fair!"

Jennie knelt beside them both. "Cody. We want to understand you and help you with everything you're going through. But you've got to try to help us."

A new flood of tears began. "That's just it, Mom! That's always it! All you tell me anymore is try. Try, try, try—I'm sick of the word try."

"That's because we know what's best for you," they said together, precisely in unison. It would have been funny if Cody hadn't been so upset.

"You tell me to fight all the time and to *try* and wish for one thing and you tell me not to fight and to wish for another," he cried at them. "All the time I can see that it's you and Dad who aren't trying...."

At his words, Jennie's face went ashen. And here, Cody buckled his knees up beneath him—a very promising movement as Andy saw it—buried his face against his legs, and continued to wail. "It's you who won't try. It's you. And it's Dad. So I decided I'm not going to try, either."

Andy sat beside him, holding him as he hollered with frustration. But there was nothing she could do. At last Cody was telling them all what was wrong.

"Oh, Cody," Jennie whispered, devastated. "Is that it, then? But it's such a different kind of trying."

"It doesn't matter, Mom," Cody told her. "It doesn't matter that it's different. Because it's what I want more than anything else in the whole world."

ON THE AFTERNOON of the fund-raiser, Andy stood backstage at the gigantic pavilion where the show would be held, directing five little girls from Mark's team and putting the finishing touches on a routine Jennie had suggested. They were doing a funny skit in which they all wore bright yellow leotards and danced with soccer balls.

The show was only hours away. The *Times-Sentinel* had yet to announce who the master of ceremonies would be. The newspaper had billed him all week as a "local celebrity" and a "must-see attraction." Even Jennie was keeping it a secret.

"We decided that would be part of the fun," she explained when Andy questioned her for what seemed like the ninety-ninth time. "Everybody will come to see who the mystery celebrity is. I guarantee they won't be disappointed." She shook her head and gave Andy a little grin. "*You* won't be disappointed, either."

Now, as Andy worked on the dance with the kids, she pushed a bright red headband up over her bangs, readjusted her own black leotard and motioned for them all to follow her. "Vanessa. When you kick, turn just like this, okay? She couldn't tell them to point their toes. They hadn't yet mastered that skill. Now. Let's try it again. One—two—"

Just as the music began, one little girl lost control of her soccer ball. It rolled across the stage before anyone could grab it, and it disappeared into the wings.

"Oops!" Andy stopped the routine and ran to get it. "Hang on, you guys," she said, laughing as she fumbled around in the dark. "We can't go on without our props."

Suddenly, a big hand reached out of the darkness and handed the ball to her. "Is this what you're looking for?"

"Yes." The ball rolled into her arms and she clasped it to her chest. Her eyes tried to focus in the darkness. She couldn't see who was speaking. The voice sounded familiar.

"Didn't know there would be soccer balls in the show tonight," he commented offhandedly. "Must have something to do with the master of ceremonies."

Andy's eyes adjusted. She caught her breath.

"Buddy?"

She couldn't believe he was standing there, this close, chuckling and talking to her.

"Buddy." She said his name again just to convince herself he was real. "*What* are you doing here?"

"This is where they told me to come. I'm in the right place, aren't I? For the swim team fund-raiser?"

"You're coming to the show? Then you're supposed to be in the audience." Her heart was pounding and she couldn't think. "And you're early. It doesn't start for another hour."

He chuckled again, a warm, melodious laugh that brought back a thousand memories. "No. I'm not early. I'm *in* the show."

"You're *in* the show?"

He wrinkled his nose and nodded. "Yeah. Is that okay? Are you going to kick me out?"

She still couldn't believe it. At that moment Jennie walked up to them. "Oh, good, Buddy. Here you are. I've been waiting for you. Do you have any more questions about the script?"

"One or two things." They talked briefly. Jennie answered his questions and told him when to introduce everyone and in what order. "We're opening the show with the soccer ball routine," Jennie said, glancing at Andy for the first time, as if Buddy's presence meant nothing to either of them.

When she caught the glint in Andy's eyes, she grinned back, hoping Andy wasn't making plans to strangle her. But from the way Buddy kept glancing away from the script and gazing at Andy, Jennie was willing to bet things were going according to plan. "At the end of the routine, Buddy will run out on stage and we'll introduce him. That's how everybody will find out that Buddy Draper is our 'mystery master of ceremonies.'"

"Even me?" Andy asked her pointedly. "Is that how I'm supposed to find out, too?"

"No. Of course not you," Jennie said, laughing. "Because you've found it out now."

But Andy didn't even hear that last remark. She was looking at Buddy and he was looking at her as if only the two of them remained in the world.

"You didn't know I was going to be in the show?" he asked her. He was struggling with every memory he held of her and with the incredible urge to reach out and touch her creamy skin, her thick, dark waves of hair.

"I didn't know."

"Ms. Stratton phoned and asked me. In fact, she phoned me several times."

"You let her talk you into this," Andy said, half accusing him, half teasing him, after Jennie walked away.

"More or less. But I thought it was a good idea, too."

"You—"

"Yeah," Buddy said. "Me. You remember. The one who's a coward. The one you never wanted to see again. Well, tough luck, sweetheart," he drawled in his best Bogart imitation. "Here I am, back again."

"Show time! Thirty minutes!" somebody shouted. And, all around them, lights began to come on and the girls in little yellow leotards started to jump up and down. "Come on! We've got to finish our dance or we won't remember how to do it at all!"

"I've got to go." She clutched the ball tighter and gave him a sad little smile. "Do a fine job, Buddy. Good luck."

But he touched her arm before she could turn away. "This has nothing to do with luck, you know. It took a lot of fighting. And, looking at you, I don't believe I'm finished. Fighting, I mean. For what I want."

Andy ignored the lights and the swelling music and the little girls still jumping around. "I hope not."

OUT IN THE AUDIENCE, at five minutes before seven, select members of the Dallas Symphony struck up a rousing rendition of a calypso song and the lights began to fade. "I've gotta go, Dad!" Cody told Michael. "They told me I had to go backstage when the music started."

"You'd better get back there then. I'll be watching you."

"I'm in the second song. I'll be the third one on the right." It would be his only appearance in the show. He just hadn't been ready to try some of the harder numbers. "Be sure you find me. In the first song, be sure to find Megan and Vanessa. Mom will point them out to you. They're on my swim team, too."

"I'll show him," Jennie promised. "Now get back there. Andy's going to kill me already. I don't want you to hold up the show."

Michael and Jennie watched as he wheeled his wheelchair up the front aisle away from them. He turned and waved once just before he started up the ramp to go backstage. "Don't forget to watch me, Dad!"

"I won't!" Michael called back. "I promise."

After Cody left, Jennie squeezed Michael's hand. "He's so proud and excited."

"I know," Michael said softly. "It's terrific to see him happy and enthusiastic about things the way he's been this week." He squeezed her hand back. "This show's a good thing."

"I know that." They sat together on the front row, not quite so afraid to be beside one another any longer. "He's done so well at the rehearsals because he knew we'd be here together."

Really, Jennie should have been backstage with Art and Andy and Buddy running the show. But everything had been practiced and polished what seemed like a hundred times over. Art was pleased with the newspaper's involvement and he was taking full advantage of it. He'd requested specifically that he be the one to introduce the mayor. It was easy for him to cue Buddy, too. So, despite all the work she'd done, there was really nothing more Jennie could do than sit beside Michael, two proud parents side by side in the front row, as the lights faded to total darkness, and Art Sanderson stepped out on stage.

"Ladies and gentlemen," Art said, the lights glinting on his gray hair. He spread his arms wide, looking spectacular in the black tuxedo and bright red cummerbund they'd rented for him. "The *Dallas Times-Sentinel* and the North Dallas Swim Dream Team want to welcome you to a spectacular evening, an evening of frolic and special guests...."

She leaned over and whispered to Michael. "The swim team's never had a name before. They had to come up with something so they could welcome everybody like this."

She was thrilled by the turnout. Several large corporations, one major downtown bank and several well-heeled individuals had supported the event. She'd seen Harv Siskell and Marshall Townsend take seats not ten minutes before.

Suddenly the spotlight wheeled around toward Jennie and, before she knew what was happening, the light was shining right in her face. Art was saying, "Ms. Jennie Stratton. A woman with foresight and guts, a woman with the know-how and the audacity to think a dream like this one could actually come true."

Strange, she didn't feel like a woman with foresight and guts, a woman who thought dreams could come true. Until she looked to her right and saw the one man who meant everything to her sitting beside her.

With Michael, she felt as if everything...everything...was possible.

"Jennie," Art said from the podium. "Stand up so we can show you our appreciation."

She did as told, waving at the crowd as the hall filled with thunderous applause. As she sat down, the music began to swell again and Art bid his farewell. It was time for the show to begin.

The curtain rose to Andy's seven dancers, all clad in sunny yellow leotards and grappling with the black-and-white leather balls, spinning them this way and that, behind a huge piece of green-blue cellophane that made it look as if they were dancing underwater.

"Buddy's coming out at the end of this one," she leaned over and whispered to Michael. "Then after Buddy talks a while, it'll be Cody's turn...."

"Shh," Michael said, leaning toward her and grinning, then unable to ignore the urge to kiss her on the nose. She was so enthusiastic, almost childlike. She reminded him of the way she'd been years ago when they first met. Yet, beneath it all, he knew there was something more, something different, something strong. She'd grown up during the past months and so had he. "Don't tell me any more. This is all supposed to be a surprise, remember?"

She covered her mouth with her hand and looked apologetic. "Sorry! I forgot. I really forgot. I'm just so excited about it all."

He draped one arm around her shoulder and snuggled close to enjoy the performance. And, at that precise moment, the beeper on his belt went off.

"Beeeep," it wailed out loud enough to make people around them notice. He turned to Jennie, knowing how upset she would be.

"I have to call the hospital," he told her. "There's a phone in the front foyer. Maybe I can get somebody to stand in for me."

"Oh, Michael. See if you can."

He rushed to the phone. When he came back moments later, his face was pale. "Jennie," he whispered frantically, "I have to go immediately. There isn't anything I can do. It's Bill Josephs. He's gone into cardiac arrest and they're bringing him in. I'm scared to death he's not going to make it."

On stage, Buddy Draper ran out amidst the girls' bouncing soccer balls and, around them, everyone was applauding again. Buddy was going to be the hit of the night.

"Ladies and gentlemen!" a voice from nowhere shouted out over the sound system. "Coach of the Dallas Sidekicks, Mr. Buddy Draper!"

Cody's number was the very next one.

Jennie clung to Michael for one long moment, fighting back tears as she closed her eyes. "Oh, Michael . . . Dear God, I wish you weren't going."

"So do I."

He knew it as well as she did. Here was the moment he had fought for, the opportunity to prove how faithful and trustworthy he could be, and he was betraying her. Betraying her and their son, too.

"Jennie," he said, taking both of her shoulders in his firm grip, praying that she would understand. "If I had any choice—any choice at all—I would stay with you. You are the most important thing in the world to me." Gently, ever so briefly, he touched her lips. "I love you, Jennie."

She nodded, not saying anything, tears streaming down her face, tears she never bothered to hide or wipe away.

CHAPTER TWENTY

WITH A CHILLED HEART, Michael raced toward the emergency room at Parkland Hospital where they'd brought Bill.

As he ran toward ER's cardiac room two, Michael saw Marge in the waiting room. With overflowing eyes and a streaming nose, she told him she'd asked for him immediately when the ambulance arrived to pick them up.

"Thanks for having them call me," he told her now as he squeezed her tightly and handed her a handkerchief. "Dr. Rosenstein's one of the best in Dallas. And I'm going to do my best for him now, too."

"You do that," she said, her voice still wavering as she released him.

Within seconds Michael was beside Bill and getting the rundown from Rosenstein. "What's been done, Mitch?"

"Patient found at home by spouse," Rosenstein told him. "Time of collapse unknown, approximately ten minutes. EMTs started resuscitation en route. First rhythm transmitted was V-fib. No blood pressure en route."

They'd gotten Bill in quickly but Marge had been on the telephone talking to their daughter when it happened. She hadn't heard him cry out. No one knew exactly how long he'd been unconscious before she found him. Add that to the time it took to get the ambulance out to their farm and back.

"Patient was defibbed times three," Rosenstein continued. "An amp of Epi was given. Patient then received into the ER, was defibbed again. Pushed Lidocaine, 85 milligrams. As you can see—" Mitch Rosenstein gestured toward the monitor and at the eight other people in the room working frantically"—still no response."

"Fine," Michael told him. "I'll take over, Mitch." He stood only feet away from his friend, a man he felt he had known forever. He knew he couldn't make emotional judgments now, yet he had to make the correct decisions and make them without feeling. "Defib with 360 joules."

"All clear," the paramedic announced sharply.

The jolt of electricity lifted Bill's body clear up off the table. Michael checked the monitor. Still no response. The steady hum of the machine continued mercilessly. Michael felt as if it were shouting at him.

"Come on, Bill," he whispered as nurses and paramedics and EMTs performed their duties in a frenzy around him. "Come on."

He had a decision to make. He gave the command loudly. "Administer Lidocaine, 43 milligrams."

A nurse ran to carry out his orders. He checked the clock on the wall. Time was of the essence. He looked at the monitor, waiting for a certain sign, anything, that he was getting somewhere.

The monitor hadn't changed. "Defib again," Michael commanded.

"All clear," the paramedic shouted.

Again the jolt. Again the lifting. Again no response on the monitor.

Bill. Come on. You've got a wife who loves you waiting out there.

And a friend who cares about you in here, too, he might have thought. Only he didn't dare. He couldn't equate the motionless man on the stretcher with the man who'd given him a tour of his barn and had constantly chided him about his bills. And, now, it had come to this.

Michael was getting desperate. "Give him Bertylium, 425 milligrams."

The line on the monitor continued. The evidence of any heart impulses was growing fainter.

"Defib."

"All clear."

No response.

"Let's go with more Epi."

No response.

"Defib again."

"All clear," the paramedic repeated.

No response.

"I want double the Bertylium. 850 milligrams this time."

The monitor continued to hum ominously. He didn't even have to look up and check it this time. He knew what it was going to tell him.

"Defib again." It seemed to go on forever, these electrical jolts and all of his choices of magic medicine. One of the nurses was keeping track for him or he'd have no idea now how many times they'd gone back and forth trying to save his patient. He did everything by the book, alternating between Atropine and Epinephrine, feeling as if hours had gone by while he sweated as though he were running a marathon.

"Bill," he said aloud. "Hang in there, Bill. You've got to."

"Michael," Mitch Rosenstein said from behind him. "You've got to think about calling the code."

"I know that, Mitch," he said calmly. "I'm not ready to do that yet." Louder. "Defib again."

"All clear," said the paramedic.

"Come—on—Bill," Michael whispered from between gritted teeth.

A jolt. Bill practically went flying off the table.

Another buzzer sounded. The line on the monitor had gone totally straight. "Doctor," the EMT said, "We have asystole." No heart response at all.

Dear, sweet heaven, Michael thought. *I've lost him.*

"Administer Epi," he ordered frantically. But in his heart of hearts, he knew it was over. He'd done the best he could do. And it hadn't been good enough. After everything, he still had no response.

"What's our pressure?" he asked futilely.

"We have no BP."

"I'm going to try one more time," he told them all. And after that, he knew he had to stop. He owed it to Bill to stop. "Defib again."

"All clear."

To Michael, the very last time seemed as if it happened in slow motion, the nurses clearing away, the

EMT climbing off the stool away from Bill's chest, the electrical jolt surging through the man on the table.

"Okay," he said almost beneath his breath. "Let's call it."

He hadn't said it loudly enough. "What did you say, Dr. Stratton?" someone asked him.

"I said—" This time his voice was clear and firm and loud "—let's call it."

THE FRENZY HAD ENDED. Nurses silently went about turning the machines off one by one.

"You did a good job, Doctor," Mitch Rosenstein said. "You did everything you could do and then some. I'll write that in my report."

"Thanks," Michael should have said. He should have thanked his colleague for this help. They both should have said, "Sorry, better luck next time—there's always a next time, you know—" But he couldn't do it. He'd just lost one of his dearest friends. He felt as though he'd lost a member of his family, as well.

He thought of Marge still in the waiting room, still pacing alone, still praying and hoping it might not be over. "I'll tell his wife," Michael said.

"Fine," Rosenstein agreed sadly.

But when Michael took his first step out of the cardiac room and saw the lovely, elderly woman waiting for him, it took everything he could muster to keep from breaking down.

"Doc? Michael?" she asked in a timid voice. But she didn't have to ask. She saw his face and the tears in his eyes.

"Marge." He reached for her, taking one of her wrinkled hands in his own and holding it there. "I did everything I could. And Bill was strong. But this was a massive heart attack. It was just too much for him."

Tears came to her eyes now, too. "He's gone, isn't he?"

Michael nodded.

He watched helplessly as her composure crumpled and she buried her face in his chest, her shoulders shaking.

Michael wrapped his arms around her, and held her as the nurses and all the assistants started coming out of the cardiac room to get out of their scrubs. They each cast knowing eyes in his direction.

They didn't know the half of it. As he gently held the old woman he'd known for what seemed like forever, as he watched her begin to come to grips with the fact she'd have to live her life now without her husband, he came to grips with the fact that he'd have to live his life without Jennie now, too.

He had betrayed her, left her alone to be there for Cody when she'd needed him most. It would be months, years, perhaps a lifetime, before he forgot the anguished acceptance he'd seen in her eyes.

And so, he thought, *it's over for us, too.*

No, you crazy fool, he reminded himself. *It was all over four years ago in a divorce court.*

Marge choked back the sobs against his chest and did her best to compose herself. "Michael. I'm so sorry."

"For God's sake, Marge," he said, gripping her tighter, his own eyes still bright with his pain. "Don't apologize, please. Go ahead and *cry* . . ."

"I know that you both did everything you knew to do. I thank you for that."

"I wouldn't have done less for him."

She was obviously in shock, and her mind was going in a thousand different directions at once. "Do you want the horses?" she asked. "I can't keep them by myself. He'd love for you to have Dan and Kimbo." She started to cry again, realizing she'd spoken of him as if he was still here. She gazed up at him with eyes so full of despair she looked as if a part of her own soul had died, too. And, really, Michael supposed it had. "I don't know—what—to—do now."

"Is there anyone I can call for you, Marge?"

She shook her head. "My daughter and her husband are on their way. They would have been here sooner but the kids were in bed and they had to find a sitter. And now they don't know he's *gone* . . ."

Michael lowered Marge Josephs to the sofa in the waiting room and held her there until her family came. After that, he finally slipped away to grieve alone. It had been a torturous night.

"EVERYBODY READY backstage for the second number!" Andy shouted.

"We're going to get a hot fudge sundae after the show," Cody told Andy. "My dad promised. You want to come with us?"

"Thanks for inviting me, little one," Andy told him. "I can't make it tonight. I'll tell your dad to get you an extra scoop so you can eat mine, too." She squeezed him. He'd been trying hard again lately and she was proud of him. "After how hard you've worked to get ready for this show the past two weeks, you deserve six hot fudge sundaes."

"Yum! You better tell my dad that. You can find him easy. He's sitting on the front row with Mom."

"You get onstage," she said, giving his chair a little shove. "You're on."

"See ya later, Andy."

"Do good."

Cody rolled out onstage and took his place beside five other kids from the swim team. The music began to play, and in the pit below them Cody could see the conductor leading it, his baton pointing crisply at each new group of instruments as they faded in.

Cody tried to see his mom and dad but he couldn't. The huge spotlight was shining right into his eyes. At least he knew they were there. He could feel them there.

The microphone stuck to his chest was bugging him but he knew he had to keep it right on his collar. They had already practiced this way all afternoon. He knew the little microphone would help everybody hear his lines.

"Down at the corner," he said as loudly as he could, "where the old well stood..."

He finished his poem and they all started singing. Cody puffed out his chest as far as he could. He sang so hard he knew he was red in the face. He stumbled on a couple of the words because he forgot to think when they came up. But that was okay because he knew his mom and dad would see that he was trying his best.

He even forgot to be scared. He just kept singing and smiling. Every so often he peered out through the blinding light, doing his best to find his parents. But he couldn't.

When the song ended, Cody felt as if he was just getting started. He wanted it to go on all night long. Everybody was clapping for them and, one by one, they each took the little bow they'd practiced with Mark.

"Way to go!" Andy shouted from the wings.

Buddy Draper stood right beside her. He was clapping, too. "Way to go!"

Just as Cody turned his wheelchair to start off stage, the curtain began to come down and the big spotlight flashed off. The audience became people again. He could see heads and hundreds of hands and faces.

"Mom!" he shouted. "Dad! Did you like it?" And then, his breath caught. The only thing beside his mom was an empty chair.

"WHERE DID HE GO, Mom?" he asked as they hugged in the aisle and Jennie told him what a good job he had done.

She knelt down beside his chair, and touched his hand. "He had to go to the hospital, pumpkin. One of his patients was very sick." She paused. "He didn't want to leave, sweetheart. I saw his face. He wanted to see you so badly."

"The whole time I was singing, I thought he was there."

"I know," she said, touching his little face. "I could tell by the way you were singing. I've never seen anybody sing quite so well." She kissed him. "Come on. Let's go get that hot fudge sundae."

When they got to the restaurant, they both ordered sundaes and, as the waitress brought them out, they giggled at how huge they were. The ice cream was jammed into icy fountain glasses and covered with huge knots of whipped cream. As Cody poured chocolate over his, Jennie spied a phone in the corner.

"I'm going to call your father," she told Cody. She waited on the line for almost ten minutes while they paged him. "He must still be in the cardiac room," the nurse told her.

Jennie and Cody finished their sundaes and headed home. Cody went to bed. Every half hour Jennie tried to reach him.

It was past midnight when Jennie found a nurse she knew. Someone told her that Sally Rogers was on the floor. Sally usually worked with Michael when he had patients at Parkland. "Let me talk to her. She'll tell me what I need to know."

"I don't know where he is, Jennie," Sally told her when she came to the phone. "We were all in cardiac room two but nobody's answering over there. Michael hasn't checked out yet. I know he's still in the building."

"What's going on with Bill Josephs? Will he be okay?"

Sally hesitated, but only for a moment. "They lost him, Jennie. Michael worked on him a long time but he couldn't save him."

Jennie hung up and sat down by the phone, thinking of Michael, remembering his words.

You're more important than anything, Jennie. I love you.

It was everything she'd needed to hear from him, years ago and now. She knew, from the expression in Michael's eyes when his pager had gone off, exactly where his heart was. It was with Cody. And it was with her.

Jennie bundled Cody up in blankets and carried him downstairs. She decided to drop him off at Andy's house. She knew she was imposing, but she had to find Michael.

He woke up when she put him in the car. "Where are we going?" he asked, rubbing his eyes.

"No need to wake up," she whispered. "I'm going to take you to Andy's for a while. I'm going to the hospital to be with your dad, okay?"

Even though he was half asleep, he smiled. "Yeah," he said, yawning. "That's real okay."

JENNIE FOUND MICHAEL in the hospital chapel. She guessed he might be there quietly grieving for his friend. And, as she silently closed the massive wooden door and stepped up behind him, she knew without a doubt that, because of the fine, caring doctor he was, there were going to be times in their lives that he couldn't put her first.

What mattered was what she'd seen in his eyes when he'd left the fund-raiser. What mattered were the words he'd shared, how he'd made her feel, how he'd made her trust him.

She wanted to be there for him, now, and for a life-time.

"Michael," she whispered. "I'm here."

He raised his eyes and looked at her almost as if he didn't recognize her. "Jen?"

"Hi." It was the only thing she could think of to say as she broke out into a crazy grin.

"What are you doing here?"

She reached out to him and stroked one strand of hair back from his face. She tucked it behind his ear. It was exactly the way she would have comforted Cody. "I heard about Bill. I'm so sorry."

Michael nodded his head, still too much in grief and shock to question her presence. "I can't believe we lost him, Jen. I tried everything. I don't remember it ever being so rough...."

"You probably have never done that for someone you cared so much about."

He met her eyes. "You're right."

"I figured things weren't going well when you didn't come back to the show."

"You thought I'd come back?" So he'd betrayed her once and disappointed her twice.

"Only if you could get away. Cody did fine. Very well, in fact."

"I wish I could have seen him." *I wish Bill could have lived. I wish we hadn't messed up so long ago.* His wish list was a mile long.

"Cody understands."

"He does?"

She nodded. "Yes." Her voice was so soft now he almost couldn't hear her. "Because he loves you very, very much."

He smiled at her, a sad smile but a smile just the same. "That helps me, you know."

"I'm so sorry, Michael." All of a sudden, she was babbling like a child. "I've had no right . . . I've done this to you all your life. I've been making you choose—or *say* you were choosing—when it really wasn't your choice at all. . . ."

With two hands, he cupped the top of her head and swept her long, straight hair away from her temples so he could read her eyes. "Are you saying that you're forgiving me?"

She shook her head. "I'm saying there isn't anything to forgive. Or there isn't now anyway. Once maybe there would have been. But not anymore. That's changed, hasn't it, Michael?"

"Yes," he said, his voice gentle. "It has." He gazed up at the window. "I can't believe Bill's gone. I had to come out of that cardiac room and tell Marge. Oh, Jen, that's the hardest thing I've ever done, telling her like that. And the only thing I kept thinking was that she'd lost Bill and that I'd lost you. I envied her even as I grieved with her. Because the two of them grew old together and we wouldn't have the chance."

"I'm so proud of you." She said. "Don't you see? It's exactly the same thing we've been telling Cody all these months. You didn't save Bill. But you gave him your best shot. You tried. Hasn't watching Cody all these months taught you the importance of that?" Then she gripped his arms with both hands. "You may have lost Bill Josephs, Michael," she told him, "but you haven't lost us. You haven't lost me and Cody."

He stared at her. "What are you saying? Are you saying you're willing to try again?"

As though the gesture were made by someone else, she felt herself nodding. The next thing she knew, he crushed her in his arms. "I'm saying I don't want to lose you," she said. "I'm saying that I want to save us." She pulled back just a bit from him so she could read his face. "I'm saying that I love you, Michael—very, very much." And she couldn't stop herself from laughing then because she'd finally said it. "All over again."

He held her shoulders, still astounded that the heartache of the past few hours was redeeming itself now with such promise. "I love you, Jennie. I don't think I ever stopped loving you—ever—but now it's more. More—and different."

"I know," she said as she nestled against him and felt safer, more complete, than she'd ever felt before. "I know."

ALL THREE OF THEM SAT on the couch the next night, munching popcorn Michael had made, talking about their lives together and planning the wedding.

"I knew it! I knew it!" Cody cried when they told him. "Are we going to live here? Or are we going to live at Dad's house?"

Michael glanced at Jennie. They hadn't had time to discuss this. But, really, things had happened so fast they hadn't had time to discuss anything. "I thought it might be more fun if we moved someplace new," he said.

Jennie raised her eyebrows at him. "Did you have something in mind?"

"I did." He didn't say anything else. He thought he'd just sit there and tantalize her for a moment. He loved teasing her.

"Are you going to tell us more about this?"

He crossed his arms proudly. "Maybe."

"Michael!"

"Daddy!"

They both hollered in unison and he grinned.

"Well," he said, drawing it out and taking a maddeningly long time. "I've found a place north of town, a small ranch close to Plano. I thought it might be nice to live there."

Jennie looked at him suspiciously, an idea dawning on her. "Have I seen this place by any chance?"

He raised his eyebrows and grinned again. "Maybe."

"Michael!"

Suddenly they were both punching and tickling him. Jennie was saying, "The place where we went riding! Michael, that place is beautiful! Michael!"

"I've—planned—it—for—a—while...." he said, gasping as he tried to fend them off. "I'd given up, though. I figured we weren't ever going to be all together to live there."

He waited until they'd calmed down to tell them that Marge had offered to let them have Bill's horses. "She'll be glad they've got a good home." When he said it, he had tears in his eyes.

"I can't believe this!" Cody kept saying. "I really can't *believe* this!"

"Believe it, son," Michael said, holding him close on the sofa and rumpling his hair. "Believe it. And know that most of it came about because of you. Your bravery has taught your mother and me some important lessons."

Cody grinned from ear to ear as he stuffed popcorn into his mouth. And it was after eleven o'clock before he went to bed. They each kissed him goodnight then they both sat by the fire, holding on to each other as the flaming logs turned into steady embers in the fireplace.

At long last, when they'd both checked on Cody and knew he was asleep, Michael scooped Jennie up from the sofa and gathered her against him on the floor, slowly unfastening the pearl buttons on her sweater as if he were opening a gift.

"I love you, Jen," he whispered. "Forever and always."

"Me, too," she said, touching his mouth with one finger and tracing the line of his lips in the firelight. "Me, too."

"May I?" He pulled away for just an instant before undoing the rest of the buttons. She nodded slowly as he bundled the sweater into his hands and pulled it off over her head. "Oh, darling," she whispered, "Oh, Michael, I love you. More than anything." She'd thought she loved him once but it was nothing compared to what she felt now, nothing compared to the steel-strong commitment she wanted to give him.

He explored her with his lips and with his hands and, minutes later, she lay before him, her body glistening in the red glow of the firelight, as he lowered himself to join with her. "My Jennie," he whispered. "My beautiful, beautiful Jennie."

Outside it was nearing midnight, the hour that marked a subtle, swift beginning to a new morning. And, inside, Michael made gentle love to the woman who had been, who would become, his wife, knowing that a new morning was dawning for the two of them, too.

EPILOGUE

THE SUN ROSE over the house in a watercolor wash of color, blues . . . lavenders . . . pinks. It would be hours still until the wavering heat of summertime hit the ranch in earnest.

A meadowlark sang out from the dew-covered Johnson grass where once, not so long ago, Jennie and Michael had ridden Dan and Kimbo.

The ranch north of Plano was theirs now. Michael had put the offer in with the realtor just as soon as Jennie had agreed to marry him. And it had been in Jennie's mind all along that the place would make a lovely backdrop for the wedding.

Upstairs, as the sun moved higher and cast an oblong shape of light on the floor, Cody rolled over and yawned. It was morning. Time to get up. And then he remembered what morning it was! The wedding day! The day his mom and his dad got married all over again.

He flipped back the covers and climbed out, reaching for his chair as his eyes grew even more accustomed to the growing light. Then he rolled across the room to the row of books on the shelf beside his desk. Right beside him, next to the wall, stood the crutches he'd never wanted to use.

Cody pushed his weight forward a bit in his chair and reached for them. They were wonderful things, new and shiny, like swords. As he held them in his lap, he thought about something. Just suppose he should give his mom and dad a wedding present. Just suppose he should try to stand up, right now. Just suppose he should do it. Just suppose.

Slowly, gingerly, he balanced the weight of the crutches in his hands. They felt cool and heavy. Strong. And just right.

He slipped one hand into each one and grabbed on to the handhold. He lowered their tips to the floor. Slowly, slowly, he pushed on them. They held firm. Instead his whole body felt like it wanted to rise up and stand with them. So, he tried it. He clenched his muscles tight just the way Andy had showed him. Then he pushed off.

His arms started shaking like an earthquake. He felt as if he were about to fall and break his head. But he kept at it.

Andy says if I can just do this, I can walk someday, he reminded himself. And, all of a sudden, he had it, he was standing there, straight up like a fence post, and his legs were supporting him.

"Hey!" he said out loud to no one. "Look at me! Look at this!" That's when he realized he had to show somebody. He started hollering as loud as he could. "Mom! Mom! Mom! *Quick!*"

She came running into his room, still in her nightgown, with her hair all loose and tangled around her shoulders and she looked scared. "Honey? Are you

okay?'' Then she saw him, and he thought her eyes
might pop out of her head. "Cody!"

"I'm doing it!" he shouted at her. "Happy Wedding Day present! I'm doing it!"

"Cody." She ran to him and bundled him up into
her arms and he had no idea why she had tears pouring down all over her face. "Oh, Cody!"

"It's your present for today. I'm going to show
Dad, too, when he gets here."

"You do that," she said, still crying. "He won't
believe it. He'll be just as proud of you as I am."

"I'm standing—I'm standing—I'm standing—" he
said over and over and over again.

"You'll tall," Jennie said. "I'll bet you've grown
three inches at least!" She hugged him. "You did it,
Cody," she kept saying. "You did it! You did it!"

"I did!" Cody hollered, throwing his head back and
letting it sink in at last. "I did! I did! I did!" He raised
one fist and waved it in the air for all of them, a little
fist that signaled an enormous victory.

And that was the way the day started.

Someone, one of their many friends who wanted to
make a big celebration out of this wedding, had
twisted miles and miles of pink crepe paper along the
white corral fences. Someone else had tied a huge satin
bow on the front door. Michael and Jennie both
wanted the service to be small and simple. But their
friends were elated. People brought so much food that
the tables were absolutely groaning.

It seemed two o'clock would never arrive. But, by
one-fifteen, guests started turning into the driveway.

"Hi, Mark!" Cody cried as Mark Kendall climbed out of his car. "Where's Andy?"

"She'll be along in a few minutes. She's coming with Buddy. He stopped by her place to pick her up."

"Buddy?" Cody asked. "Buddy Draper's coming? Wow!"

Marge Josephs came next, carrying a huge bouquet of rosebuds from her garden. They were the exact, delicate color of an eggshell. "These are for Jennie," she said after she'd hugged Michael. "Can I take them up?"

"Sure," he said, giving her one more squeeze. She looked good. Her eyes shone bright and her hair glowed like silver filigree in the sunlight. "They're beautiful."

"They're from Bill's garden." She smiled, a bittersweet smile full of love. "He planted them several years ago. They keep coming back."

"How are you feeling?"

She answered honestly. "I'm getting a little better every day. My grandkids are sure keeping me busy."

"Good." He squeezed her forearm. "Grandkids are just what the doctor orders." He glanced up at the window where he knew Jennie waited. "You be sure and tell her those are from Bill."

"I will."

Marge hurried off and the minister drove up. It was time for the service to begin. From just beneath the tree, a college girl they'd hired began to stroke the wedding march on a lovely old harp. As Michael bid a brief farewell to his friends, he looked around quickly for his best man.

There he was, sitting in his wheelchair beside the harp, dressed in a black tuxedo just his size, exactly the same as his father's. "You ready for this, kiddo?" He winked. "It's time to go stand by the minister."

"I'm ready," Cody said, rolling his wheelchair toward the makeshift altar, his crutches lying across his knees.

"You're sure?" Michael asked.

"I'm sure," Cody answered.

"If you get tired, we'll stop the ceremony and you can sit back down."

They'd planned it all today at lunch, when Cody had presented the wedding present to his father, too. He parked his wheelchair in the appointed spot and, with Michael gripping his elbow, he stood, proud and tall beside his father.

As the harpist strummed softly, out stepped Jennie.

Michael had never seen her look more beautiful than she did at that moment, standing in the sun, as she beamed and waved at Cody. She wore a beige satin dress that fell in a straight sheath to the floor, with miniature beige orchids woven into a circlet atop her head. She looked like an angel as she stepped forward, her dress trailing in the lush grass, and came to stand beside them.

"Dearly beloved," the minister began the vows. She took Michael's hand and squeezed it.

"Love you," she mouthed to both of them.

"Me, too," Michael mouthed back.

When the minister called for the rings, Cody held on to the tree trunk for support and handed his father the ring. "Here you go, Dad," he whispered proudly. "Put this on her."

And, as Michael slipped the wedding ring onto the finger of the woman he loved, the years seemed to sear together in his mind, how he'd wanted Jennie then, how he loved her now.

He met her eyes and repeated the age-old words, meaning, feeling, every one of them. "For better," which they'd had. "For worse," which they'd had, too.

"In sickness and in health." Perhaps, for now, it would be health. Dr. Phillips had recently confirmed Cody wouldn't need the surgery.

"For richer and for poorer."

"As long as we both shall live," the minister prompted.

Michael gazed down at the woman who stood before him now, at the mother of his son, and he felt as if he'd already loved her forever. Perhaps he had.

He could see the reflection of all he needed in her clear, gray eyes. "As long as we both shall live," he repeated.

ABOUT THE AUTHOR

Debbi Bedford was inspired to write *After the Promise* by the doctor who delivered her daughter, Avery, four years ago while his own mother was seriously ill. Debbi was struck by his agony—being in a position to heal strangers but unable to help someone he loved dearly. "For this story, I decided, if the hero couldn't help his son, I'd have him heal his marriage instead."

Debbi lives in Jackson Hole, Wyoming, with her husband, Jack, and her two children, Jeffrey, now eight, and Avery.

Books by Debbi Bedford

HARLEQUIN SUPERROMANCE

Don't miss any of our special offers. Write to us at the following address for information on our newest releases.

Harlequin Reader Service
P.O. Box 1397, Buffalo, NY 14240
Canadian address: P.O. Box 603,
Fort Erie, Ont. L2A 5X3

Fifty red-blooded, white-hot, true-blue hunks from every
State in the Union!

Beginning in May, look for MEN MADE IN AMERICA!
Written by some of our most popular authors, these
stories feature fifty of the strongest, sexiest men, each
from a different state in the union!

Two titles available every other month at your favorite
retail outlet.

In May, look for:

FULL HOUSE by Jackie Weger (Alabama)
BORROWED DREAMS by Debbie Macomber (Alaska)

In July, look for:

CALL IT DESTINY by Jayne Ann Krentz (Arizona)
ANOTHER KIND OF LOVE by Mary Lynn Baxter
(Arkansas)

You won't be able to resist MEN MADE IN AMERICA!

Relive the romance...
Harlequin and Silhouette
are proud to present

A program of collections of three complete novels by the most
requested authors with the most requested themes. Be sure to
look for one volume each month with three complete novels by
top name authors.

In June: **NINE MONTHS** Penny Jordan
Stella Cameron
Janice Kaiser

**Three women pregnant and alone. But a lot can
happen in nine months!**

In July: **DADDY'S
HOME**
Kristin James
Naomi Horton
Mary Lynn Baxter

**Daddy's Home...and his presence is long
overdue!**

In August: **FORGOTTEN
PAST**
Barbara Kaye
Pamela Browning
Nancy Martin

**Do you dare to create a future if you've forgotten
the past?**

Available at your favorite retail outlet.

HARLEQUIN Silhouette

THREE UNFORGETTABLE HEROINES
THREE AWARD-WINNING AUTHORS

MAVERICK HEARTS

A unique collection of historical short stories that capture the spirit of America's last frontier.

HEATHER GRAHAM POZZESSERE—over 10 million copies of her books in print worldwide
Lonesome Rider—The story of an Eastern widow and the renegade half-breed who becomes her protector.

PATRICIA POTTER—an author whose books are consistently Waldenbooks bestsellers
Against the Wind—Two people, battered by heartache, prove that love can heal all.

JOAN JOHNSTON—award-winning Western historical author with 17 books to her credit
One Simple Wish—A woman with a past discovers that dreams really do come true.

Join us for an exciting journey West with
UNTAMED
Available in July, wherever Harlequin books are sold.

MAV93

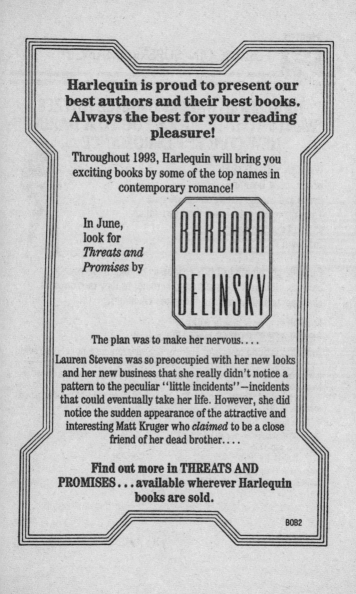

Harlequin is proud to present our best authors and their best books. Always the best for your reading pleasure!

Throughout 1993, Harlequin will bring you exciting books by some of the top names in contemporary romance!

In June, look for *Threats and Promises* by

BARBARA DELINSKY

The plan was to make her nervous....

Lauren Stevens was so preoccupied with her new looks and her new business that she really didn't notice a pattern to the peculiar "little incidents"—incidents that could eventually take her life. However, she did notice the sudden appearance of the attractive and interesting Matt Kruger who *claimed* to be a close friend of her dead brother....

Find out more in THREATS AND PROMISES . . . available wherever Harlequin books are sold.

BOB2